MURDER AT HENBIT MANOR

MICAH KAFKA

To Tim

I remember the first time your laughter at one of my stories woke up Mom and Dad. I remember the time you cried with rage when I killed a character you loved. And I'll always remember how I fell in love with storytelling from the look in your eyes as you listened. There is no exaggeration in saying that without you, this story would not exist.

PROLOGUE

Laundra Henbit died in the hallway. To be entirely accurate, her death began in the dining room, but the actual death happened right outside in the great hall. A case could be made that she began dying in Freiburg im Breisgau, Germany on a very snowy February morning sixty-two years earlier but that's more of a philosophical quandary and not relevant to the case at hand. For all intents and purposes, Laundra Henbit died in the Great Hallway of Henbit Manor in the Verlorland Islands. More specifically in the center of Alku Island, one of the southern islands in a chain of islands the locals described as somewhere between Iceland, England and Spain. It was a fact they clung to fervently despite the geographical impossibility of the claim.

CHAPTER 1

"Is it worse?" Laundra asked from her bed, her gold and white poshie, Dandy, sitting next to her. Over the years, Laundra's German accent had taken on a very singular quality. It was soft around the edges with a habit of rising in pitch near the end of the sentence. The past few decades in the Verlorland Islands were the main culprit, and in truth, she only kept the facade of her native accent for appearances.

"Not worse," Dr. Novak replied as she gathered her instruments into an overly trite black bag.

"Good. Good."

"I did not say good."

"Not worse is always good."

Dr. Novak frowned at Laundra forcefully. Amelia Novak's face was made for frowning. Even her best smile would be best described as a neutral expression. She had to put a great deal of effort into a frown if she wanted to make a point of it. Laundra met Dr. Novak's frown with a pleasant little grin only hinting at the bulwark of a willpower hiding underneath. Dr. Novak broke first, looking back at her bag.

"Laundra, 772 lbs isn't good."

"Two pounds less than last time."

"Still not good."

Laundra let her grin drop. She shifted her substantial bulk in her sturdy chair and patted Dandy on the head. At one time, Laundra had been an active, independent woman but that had been years ago. Now she rarely left Henbit Estate. Many days she didn't leave her rooms. She couldn't even leave her bed without the aid of her nurse.

"You should get out more," Dr. Novak said.

"Yes, I know. And I should eat less carbs."

"You should follow the diet I built specifically for you." Dr. Novak frowned again, but this time didn't attempt to point it at Laundra.

Laundra sighed. "It's not a good diet."

"It is if you want to live long enough to..." Dr. Novak searched for the right words. "Honestly, Laundra, if you want to see another Christmas, you need to take care of yourself."

"Not a big fan of Christmas."

"Laundra."

Laundra chuckled. "I know. I know. I'm sorry, Amelia. I don't mean to make light. You have worked very hard. After tonight, I will have Emma stick to your diet. Or I'll find a new cook."

"Thank you," Dr. Novak said, looking up to give Laundra an attempt at an encouraging smile. She almost managed to make the expression look pleasant.

Laundra sighed again and pointedly looked away from Dr. Novak.

"Where's Ari?" Laundra asked the room. "Ari!" Laundra attempted to push herself up.

"I'm here, ma'am. Don't strain yourself," a deep voice rumbled and a massive man stepped into the room.

There was an unusual cadence in the way Ari spoke, not quite like the natives of Alku but decidedly nordic. A hand, nearly the size of a catcher's mitt, came gently down on her shoulder. Laundra patted it softly. Laundra refused to have an elevator installed and spoil the Elizabethan ambiance of Henbit Manor, so leaving the bedroom on the third floor took time. Her nurse, Ari Björnssen, was a colossal man in his mid-twenties and was the only one who could single-handedly move her. He was merely two inches shy of seven feet with pythons for arms and tree trunks for legs. He was the type of man you'd hope had a very long fuse - which he did. Despite the definitively Scandinavian name, he was neither pale skinned nor blond haired. He was the type of man usually described as racially ambiguous.

"Let's not be late. How do I look?" Laundra asked.

"You look very good," he said.

"Nonsense," she said, smiling. "Amelia," Laundra called after the doctor. "If you can, fetch me Matilda on your way out. I want to look my best tonight."

Dr. Novak nodded and excused herself from the room.

"I used to be beautiful, you know?" Laundra said as Ari positioned himself to pull Laundra up from her chair.

"You are still beautiful, ma'am," Ari said.

The massive man's muscles bulged as he hefted her up and supported her with his body. Laundra waited until she was confident he had her, then took a tentative step forward.

"Thank you, dear," Laundra said, patting Ari with her free hand. "Are the guest here?"

"All except your sister," Ari replied.

"Of course. Well, we should hurry then."

There was a gentle knock at the door and a young blond woman in a simple black and white dress stepped inside. She moved with a natural poise of a dancer while somehow managing to not pull attention to herself. She waited patiently until Laundra waved her over.

"Good, Matilda. Let's see if you can take a few years off this face."

"Yes, Mrs. Henbit," she said softly.

"Tonight has to be perfect," Laundra said as her nurse moved her carefully to the vanity.

"It will be," Ari said.

Laundra gripped Ari tightly as he lowered her onto the sturdy bench.

"I hope," she said. "I do hope so. I have something very important to say. Very important."

Just outside the master bedroom, through the hall, down a flight of stairs, through another larger hall, and down the grand staircase, through the great hall and into the main dining room, Laundra's guests waited, semi-patiently. It was a big room, but then they almost all were in the manor. The walls were a vibrant red with a subtle striped pattern leading up to the ornate white and gold ceiling. It curved upward, and three gold chandeliers hung down, lit by candles. They looked like real candles and up until three years ago had been real candles. Laundra even still believed they were real candles, but Oas didn't see the practicality of using them when modern technology could give the effect without the hassle. He'd had them replaced discreetly and still instructed the other house help to "light the candles" whenever Laundra was within earshot.

A long hand carved table sat in the middle of the room, place settings ready but no food as of yet. Only one individual sat at the table, a chubby man somewhere between the age of eighteen and thirty-three. A case could perhaps be made for forty-two, but it would strain credibility. He didn't move much, content with staring down at his empty plate.

Another man watched him intently from across the room by a fireplace containing an incredibly realistic fire giving off a hint of heat. Like the candles, it only appeared authentic.

"Is that your aunt's husband?" the man asked the woman next to him. The two were a distinct pair. The woman, Sloan Okumu, had fair skin, straight blond hair and had been described most of her life as a sturdy girl. Her dress looked as uncomfortable with her as she was with it. The man, Regal Okumu, was elegantly tall and thin and no matter how he stood, he was poised. His black skin shone with an ebony radiance in the candlelight while his sharp eyes seemed to be watching everything at once while finding none of it worth seeing.

"Yes, that's him," Sloan answered.

"He's young?" It was mostly a question.

"I don't know."

"Where's he from?"

"I don't know."

"Weren't you at the wedding?"

"Yes," Sloan said, more than a bit agitated. "His name's Oscar. And I'm pretty sure he's husband number ten, although there were a few annulments in there so if you count them I think it's thirteen."

"And is he..." Regal said slowly. He always spoke slowly. Each word was thought thoroughly through until they were a bit charred at the edges. "Okay?" Just because he thought them through didn't guarantee he'd end up finding the best one.

"I don't know. He was when they got married. I think. Ask Lydia."

"Just curious. He's technically your uncle, right?"

"I stopped thinking of Aunt Laundra's husbands as anything a long time ago," Sloan said with a sigh and walked away. She searched for something interesting to divert her attention. A young gangly man with greasy hair and vacant eyes stood next to the dining room door. Sloan hadn't figured out what his job was, but he did a lot of standing by doors and opening of doors since they arrived two hours ago. There didn't seem to be any cause for interest there, so she moved on to the only other inhabitant of the room, an attractive young woman a few years shy of thirty. This one she knew well and liked well enough. Maybe not as well as someone should like her own sister but enough to get along when they needed to do so.

"Have you seen her yet?" Sloan asked as she sidled up to Lydia.

"Hmm?" Lydia asked back, bringing her attention into the room from wherever it had wandered.

"Have you seen Aunt Laundra yet?"

"Of course. I've been here for two weeks. What did you think I'd be doing?"

"She's a bit of a shut-in. I didn't know. Maybe she stays in her room all day. Counting her cats."

"We had tea together in the conservatory just before you arrived. And she doesn't have any cats."

"Well, I haven't seen her, and I've been here for hours now."

"Just two." There was just a hint of sass in Lydia's tone. Not thick, just peppered in for flavor. Sloan looked like she was about to retaliate but shrugged it off. Sloan had never had much in common with her younger sister. They didn't even look much alike. Lydia had bright brown eyes and a face that somehow always seemed to be happy even in the brief moments she wasn't smiling. When she was truly and fully happy her smile made the sun blush and wish for a set of dimples half as charming as Lydia's. Her auburn hair was cut into a classy bob. It was the one family resemblance she shared with her aunt, although Laundra's was mostly overrun with gray. Sloan and Lydia shared their South African accent, tendency to stand with arms crossed, and not much else.

"Has she said anything about why we're all here?" Sloan asked finally.

"I think she just wants to see us. We are her only family. Well, us and mother." Lydia pulled out her phone. "Has she texted you?"

"No, but she won't. She said her flight was delayed. I'm sure we'll know she's here when she's-"

The door flew open and a middle-aged woman in a black Chanel dress, stiletto heels, and inflated self-worth strode into the room with her head held high and arms raised out in a failed attempt at elegance. Her face was nearly wrinkle free which, like the candles and fireplace, wasn't authentic.

"Here," Sloan finished with a roll of her eyes.

"I am so sorry I'm late," Caprice Marigolds said with a flourish of her arms. "It couldn't be helped I just..." she stopped as she saw the mostly empty table. "You haven't started yet?"

A very average looking man with graying ginger hair and neatly pressed black suit bustled in behind her. He was the kind of man that you'd instantly forget was there. He took a few quick steps to catch up with Caprice while motioning for the greasy young man at the door to do something the poor boy didn't quite understand. "Lady Marigolds, if you'd-" he started.

"Caprice, dear, call me Caprice. Are you new?"

"No."

"Really?"

"Yes."

"I thought Laundra's butler was taller. Odd man. Named... uh... Bus."

"Oas."

"That was it!"

"That is me."

"Oh," she blinked a few times then shrugged. "And who's this... uh..." her tone shifted from interest to disappointment as she scrutinized the greasy young man at the door. She quickly shifted her attention to anything else and put her smile back in place. "I could murder for a drink. Who does that?"

"I'd be obligated to get you something," Oas said before Caprice found more words that hadn't yet been said.

"You mean obliged?"

"If you insist."

"Is it too early in the season for a gimlet? Do you think? Oh, what the hell. It's summer somewhere, isn't it?" Caprice laughed loudly.

"I don't believe it is. That is not a problem though," Oas lifted his wrist and tapped at the face of his watch. "Ah, Mrs. Henbit is on her way down now. If I could have you all take your seats..." he motioned to the table.

As they took their seats a door on the other side of the room opened, and Matilda crossed the room swiftly, setting a gimlet with a perfectly curled lime peel hanging over the edge in front of Caprice.

Caprice looked at the glass, then at Oas. "That was rather quick."

"Yes it was," he said with a nod.

By the time Lydia sat beside her, Caprice had already drained half the gimlet.

"Mother."

"Shush. You make me sound so old."

"It's a family dinner. No one cares how old-"

"Not so loud. You never know. Admittedly the footman is creepy, and the butler's a little old for my taste but that man that walked me to the house..." Caprice cocked her head to the side in thought. "Who was he again?"

"The chauffeur?"

"Yes. The chauffeur." Caprice made an inappropriate moaning groan. "And before you say it... yes, he is a little portly, but he has a nice face and a great backside. I can put up with a little extra around the waist for a good ass."

Caprice winked and in her moment of silence finally saw that the entire table was looking at her. No one winked back.

"Well," she said to fill awkwardness with more. "Oscar, I didn't even see you there. You're looking... well fed. Still riding horses?"

Oscar looked up from his plate, his eyes sort of focusing on Caprice. "I have a turtle."

"What?" Caprice said. It was less of a question and more just a reflex.

"He said he has a turtle," Lydia answered from the seat on her right.

"I know that. Why did he... er... what does that..." Caprice's mouth hung open, not exactly sure how to express her confusion verbally. She looked from Oscar over to Sloan and Regal. They offered no help. Lydia cleared her throat and slid her phone in front of Caprice. Caprice glanced down.

I'll explain later, it read.

"Explain what?" Caprice asked.

Lydia facepalmed but was saved from further embarrassment - for the moment - as the footman opened the dining room doors. Dandy ran through, yipping. Jingling bells accented every movement the dog made, emanating from a cluster of bells on the gold chain collar around the poshie's fluffy neck. Laundra followed, deftly supported by Ari. No bells followed her movements, only some grunts from the man supporting her.

"Oh!" Laundra said, looking at her guests. "This is lovely. Simply lovely." Regal began to stand, but Laundra held up a hand. "No need. Ari has me. He does very well. Very strong lad, aren't you?"

"Yes, ma'am," Ari answered as they reached the head of the table. In one well-practiced move, Ari had Laundra in her seat.

"If you need me-" Ari stated.

"I'd like you to dine with us tonight," Laundra cut in motioning to the last empty chair to the left of Caprice.

"Ma'am?" Ari said with a raised eyebrow. He stiffened as all eyes turned on him.

"I'm sure we're perfectly capable of taking care of you for one dinner," Caprice said loudly. Loudly for her. In lieu of a well-defined accent, Caprice just spoke in a loud choppy cadence of words. She'd been banned from over a dozen cinema's in six countries and at least one library. In her defense, she hadn't known it was a library.

"It is a family dinner," Ari said, in a low rumble, doing his best to keep his massive voice contained.

"Yes, it is. I would like you to be here though. For me. Yes?"

Ari nodded, checked to be sure Laundra was secure, then made his way to the last chair. Laundra waited for him to sit while keeping Dandy from jumping into her lap, then looked up until she found Oas.

"Oas," she said.

Oas nodded and discreetly hit the face of his watch. The doors at the far end of the dining room opened almost instantaneously. Laundra made a comment on the efficiency with which Oas ran the staff while Matilda and a short mousy woman in a white double-breasted jacket entered wheeling carts of food. The second woman sat a plate of meat colored mashed potatoes topped with a fried egg.

"Great," Sloan said, sarcasm leaking out of the corners of the word. "Mashed meat. I've missed that."

"Labskaus," the cook corrected. She had dull eyes and almost no chin.

"Well, pass it over here," Caprice said. "I have missed it. And Emma, is there any whitebait sushi? Oh, there it is," she said looking down the table to where Oscar poked at a glob of transparent white lumps flowing out of a ring of seaweed.

"I thought you'd enjoy it," Emma said as they finished setting the table. "Especially with Ari joining you." She gave Ari a dull smile.

"I don't think I've ever tried it," Ari said.

"Oh, pity." Emma said. "I always made it for your uncle when he used to join us for meals."

"Thank you, Ms. Fischer. That will be all," Oas broke in. He quickly cleared the staff from the room and after checking once more that Mrs. Henbit had everything she required, left the family (and one uncomfortable nurse) alone.

"I don't think I had time to get a drink order in," Caprice said looking after the departing butler.

"Oas will return in a few moments," Laundra said. "I wanted some time alone with all of you. It's so hard to get these days. Eat! Eat! Oscar, don't play with the fish."

Laundra's guests (and the nurse) began eating. Regal looked from dish to dish. It was mostly fish in different forms and sausages, lots of sausages. He leaned in close to Sloan, "Should I even ask if any of this is vegan?"

"Does it look like any of it would be vegan?"

"What's in that bread?"

"Other than ferns?"

"Wait, I see some asparagus over there. What's that around it?"

"Bacon. Just eat. It's not like you have to keep the weight off right now."

Regal frowned forcefully while Sloan did her best to avoid eye contact.

Little pockets of conversation sprouted and died quickly around the table. Laundra inquired about Sloan's summer plans (of which she had none) and job prospects (of which she also had none). Lydia asked Caprice about her flight delay which Caprice believed had something to do with poor scheduling. Laundra repeatedly asked Oscar to stop feeding Dandy. He stammered a few denials, but the jingling and yipping around his chair gave him away. The most successful exchange came from Ari asking Regal about his modeling.

"I'm actually moving into acting now," Regal answered.

"Yes! Your Dorothy movie!" Laundra said excitedly. "When does it hit cinemas?"

"It actually did. It's actually called OZ Corps, not really a Dorothy movie. Ensemble cast and all. It's actually a really great movie, uh, actually."

"Like Wizard of OZ?" Ari asked.

"Yes, actually, kind of," Regal said.

"What's with the actually's?" Sloan whispered.

"Right... uh," Regal fidgeted. "It's about the OZ characters. But we - I play Professor Scarecrow - come to Earth as a group of heroes. Superheroes really. And save the world. It's very epic."

"And then you get your own solo film too?" Lydia asked.

"That's all being worked out."

"You said it was going to be one of those big interconnected universe things, right?"

"Yes, actu-"

Sloan coughed.

"That is the thought."

"I don't think I saw it in theaters here," Ari said.

"No. That'd be right. It went right to video on demand."

"Is that normal?" Ari asked.

Regal poked at his bacon wrapped asparagus. The table fell quiet again.

"We should all watch it while you're here," Lydia spoke up. "I'm sure it will be very exciting. Could someone pass the salmon pie?"

Another long silence fell over the table. The only sound was chewing, the clinking of cutlery on china, a few yips and jingles from Dandy and a few more from Oscar - yips not jingles. Finally, Laundra cleared her throat.

"I suppose you'd all like to know why I invited you here."

"Not really," Caprice said quickly. "I just assumed it was a late Family Day."

"We don't have a Family Day here," Laundra said. "As I've gotten older-"

"Laundra dear, we are not that old," Caprice interrupted, punctuating with forced laughter.

"Caprice, please." Laundra held Caprice's gaze a moment before she continued. "I've begun looking back on my life, the things I'm proud of and the things I regret. To be blunt, I've started to wonder if the regrets outweigh the rest. I want to fix that before my time is up."

"Aunt Laundra," Sloan said. "I'm sure you still have plenty of time left. And you've accomplished so much. I'm jealous, really."

"It's not about what I've accomplished. It's about the things I let slip away. I've lived a selfish life." She raised her hand to stop the protests about to erupt around the table. "Please, let me finish. I have lived a selfish life and have kept far too many secrets from the people that should have been the most important. I've put it off for too long and almost to the point of it being too late. With my time so short-"

"This is just too much," Caprice interrupted again. "I for one am not going to just sit here while you talk like you're dying. It's nonsense. You're my little sister! You are happily married. You should be talking about having kids."

Regal choked on his bacon wrapped asparagus. Oscar dropped a blob of fish stuffed seaweed in front of Dandy who jingled happily.

Caprice seemed equally disturbed by her own words and quickly shifted directions. "We should be celebrating your life not talking about..." Caprice choked up. She grabbed a napkin and began fanning herself. Her emotions - again like the candles - almost looked genuine.

"Is it really that bad?" Lydia asked, not to Laundra but to Ari.

Ari sat up a little straighter and looked around at the family. "I don't think I'm allowed to share that."

"It's fine, Ari. It is not my health. That is not why I've brought you all here," Laundra said.

"Then what?" Lydia asked.

Laundra's expression became stern. She deliberately looked around the table, letting her eyes settle on each and every person at the table before turning to Lydia.

"I believe that someone is trying to mur..." Laundra shifted her weight. "I believe..." she shifted again. "I think the sausages have disagreed with me."

Laundra lurched forward. Ari was at her side before anyone else even had time to react. Laundra tried to stand up, nearly toppling over, but Ari managed to get her weight onto himself before the chair legs cracked under the strain. One of Laundra's feet fell on Dandy's tail. The dog yelped loudly and ran for cover under the table in a cacophony of jingles.

"What's wrong?" Lydia asked jumping to her feet.

Laundra gasped something in German as Ari steadied her.

"Should we do something?" Regal asked, pulling his phone from his pocket. "Who do you call here? 112? 999? 911?"

"9962833," Lydia said.

"That's just for small house fires. 9132298," Ari said.

"Seriously?" Regal asked.

The far doors swung open, and Oas rushed into the room carrying a bag.

"She wants air," Ari said to the butler.

"Oxygen?"

"No, air. Outside."

"She wants to go outside?" Oas didn't hide his surprise.

The creepy footman rushed into the room. "Dr. Novak is-"

"I'm fine," Laundra choked out then went back into German.

"Maybe we should just take her outside," Caprice said, getting up quickly. She looked at Laundra and said a few words in German. Laundra nodded. "She simply needs to cool off. I'm sure."

Laundra nodded again. Ari took her arm firmly and started walking toward the doors. Dandy pranced out from under the table, yipping, jingling and running circles around them. Oas rushed ahead, swooping the dog up and handing him off to the footman. He crossed the room ahead of Laundra and swung the double wooden doors open. A tall man with a dark mustache like a caterpillar stood on the other side. He was bulky. Not exactly fat and not exactly well built. He looked something like a brawny Pillsbury Doughboy with dark olive skin.

"Ramses?" Oas asked in a tone that indicated the man wasn't expected or needed.

"I heard a commotion," he said.

"Help Ari with Laundra. She needs some air." Oas motioned Ari past him, and Ramses took another arm. As they passed, Oas waved at Lydia adamantly. It took a moment, but once she saw, she strode over. "An ambulance should be here in ten or fifteen minutes," Oas whispered. "She won't want to go. I'll need help convincing her."

"Is it that serious? Maybe it's just heartburn."

"Take it slow there, Mrs. Henbit," Ari's voice came from the other room. The two turned in time to see Laundra stumble again. She jerked her arm toward her chest.

"Mord..." Laundra gasped then seized forward, pulling free of Ramses. Ari caught her in time to keep her from falling hard. She coughed violently, pink flecks spraying the air in front of her.

"Help her!" Lydia yelled. She tried to rush to Laundra's side, but Oas held out a hand, stopping her at the door of the dining room. He was saying something, but Lydia couldn't hear it. Laundra was on her back now. Ari pointed toward the grand staircase. Ramses bolted off in that direction.

Lydia's vision tunneled. She saw Laundra's hand waving weakly in the air then fall to the marble floor. She had pink around her lips. Ari leaned over her. He spoke quickly then tilted her head back. Lydia grabbed Oas' arm, trying to fight past him. The butler wrapped a surprisingly strong arm around her and held Lydia tight. Ari moved to Laundra's side and placed his hand together over her sternum. There was a cracking sound, and he pushed his weight down on her chest. Lydia didn't fight Oas as he pulled her back into the dining room. The doors swung shut. The room was quiet. It stayed that way until the sounds of approaching sirens intruded.

CHAPTER 2

The flight into the Verlorland Islands was turbulent. By Verlorland standards, it was unexceptional though. The islands existed in the middle of an anomalous weather pattern. It created fiercely unpredictable weather and made landings bring all but the most ardent atheist to pray for mercy. Jackson Ruck was the exception. He wasn't an atheist, but instead of white knuckling the armrests he contentedly gazed out on the extraordinarily green islands. He didn't seem to mind that the view jerked up, down, right, left and a dozen other unknown directions as the turbulence batted them around.

"You were saying?" he asked the obese man next to him. There was no response. "Mr. Perseval?" Jackson brought his attention back inside the jet. The obese man was staring directly ahead, sweat trickling down his broad face.

The two men had become well aquatinted on the long flight from JFK to Erfundenborg International Airport. While it was a fairly spacious airline, between Mr. Perseval's girthy midsection and Jackson's broad shoulders and large arms, they had been sharing each other's space for longer than either would have preferred.

"Yes," the man sort of gulped out.

A quick thought passed through Jackson's head without betraying itself externally as he took in the fat man's current state. Jackson pivoted the conversation in a new direction. "I've been a rafting guide most of my life. I tell you that?"

"Rafting guide?"

"Whitewater rafting. Mostly in Oregon. I grew up on the river. My dad owned a rafting company. Ruck River Rafting."

"I've never been white water rafting," Mr. Perseval said.

"I love it. Me and my little brother have been doing it as long as I can remember. We've expanded quite a bit since then, hang-gliding, bungee jumping. We're getting into wingsuits now. It's a rush."

"Sounds horrible."

"Honestly I don't get to do it much anymore. Been running the business side of it for a few years. I give lessons when possible but not as often as I'd like. We have a big sporting goods chain now, Ruck River Outfitters. Six countries and counting."

"Is that what you're here for?"

"No. no. Here to see my older brother. Henry. He never got into the family business. Hated all of it really. He didn't like that feeling of being out of control I think."

"I just like knowing that my feet are firmly on the ground."

"That sounds like something Henry would say."

"He lives here?"

"Yes, for about year now."

"I don't think I could live on an island. Tidal waves. They would just take out everything in a place like Verlorland."

"Maybe. I never really thought about that."

"How? It's all I'll think about the entire time I'm on these damn islands."

"Maybe that's why I like keeping my adrenaline going. Don't really have time to think about stuff like tidal waves. When you're on a river, it's just you, the raft and the water. Hopefully, your friends too if they haven't fallen out."

The man sort of laughed.

"Everything else just sort of doesn't matter."

"Except the drowning."

"I guess I don't really worry about that."

"Oh, I would. Like this flight. I hate flying. Landing is worse though. I'm dreading the landing. What if we don't stop quickly enough? We could roll right off the island. I nearly had a heart attack last time. This won't be good."

"You're fine."

"How do you know that?"

"We already landed."

"What?"

"Just a second ago." Jackson motioned to the window. The tarmac breezed by outside as the jet taxied toward Erfundenborg International Airport.

"I didn't even notice."

"It wasn't too bumpy." Deck crews sauntered about with an unhurried ease as the jet eased into place. "By the way, what language do they speak here?"

The answer was more complicated than Jackson had expected. The islands were united now but they'd once been divided between England, Norway, Iceland, Luxembourg and Egypt (how the later came to be was confusing and not worth getting into). Each island had spoken a combination of their mother countries native tongue as well as a local language called Verlorlandish that mostly sounded like well-rehearsed gibberish, but with a pleasant, nordic cadence.

The flight attendants all spoke English, but the messages playing throughout the airport were sometimes English, sometimes French, sometimes something Jackson could tell was Scandinavian and occasionally a strange melodic sound that was somehow both breathy and crunchy that he'd decided must be Verlorlandish. The signs weren't any more consistent. One near what ended up being a restroom read *break room* in English but the French word on it translated to *hallway*, and the Norwegian word translated closest to *shit* (the most accurate of all the words). Jackson gave up on flipping through his phrase books and instead just followed Mr. Perseval to the baggage claim (the sign read *álitamál*).

Jackson wasn't a tall man, more than a little on the stocky side. His back and shoulders were knots of well-used muscle, but he'd also developed a decent amount of beer-induced insulation. His dark hair was shaved close on the sides and covered in a ball cap. A scruffy beard, sandals, shorts hitting well above his knees and a Ruck River Rafting tank top rounded out his casual look.

As he waited for his own baggage, Jackson watched the people milling around him. The local staff drifted through the travelers. They never seemed to move in any particular hurry. The few that made eye contact returned Jackson's nod but not his smile. Despite that, they didn't seem exceptionally unfriendly. The passengers waiting with him were remarkably diverse. Jackson knew little about the Verlorland Islands and even less about what might bring other people to them. One by one they grabbed their bags and hurried off. Some looked to be on vacation. One small family wore oversized Hawaiian shirts. Jackson wondered if there were any good beaches on the islands or if they family merely liked flowery shirts.

The family rushed off leaving Jackson and Mr. Perseval alone. The baggage carousel came to a stop with only one bright red suitcase remaining. Jackson looked from it to Mr. Perseval.

"That yours?"

Mr. Perseval shook his head with an exhausted sigh. "Every time," he muttered. "Come on. I'll show you where to go."

Jackson tightened the straps on his carry on backpack and followed Mr. Perseval away from the carousel.

An hour later, a small blond woman sat a wad of clear plastic roughly the size of a suitcase in front of Mr. Perseval.

"What is this?" Mr. Perseval asked then switched to Verlorlandish.

The woman replied with a smile and a string of words Jackson couldn't extract any meaning from. Mr. Perseval poked at the bag meaningfully and ranted back at her. After a few more exchanges he pointed at Jackson and barked a few more words. The woman shrugged. Mr. Perseval sighed and turned to Jackson.

"It's lost?" Jackson said.

"Not exactly lost," Mr. Perseval said. "They do know where it is. It's just not here."

Jackson frowned. "And where is it?"

"It's on a train leaving Paddington sometime this afternoon."

Jackson raised an eyebrow. "Where's Paddington?"

"London."

"How'd my bag get to London?"

"How did they lose my suitcase but not everything in it? It's one of the many mysteries of these wretched islands. Fill this out," Mr. Perseval said, handing a card to Jackson. "They'll contact you once they've recovered your baggage. I hope you packed the important stuff in your carry on."

Jackson thought through all the things he wished he had put in his backpack as he filled out the card then followed Mr. Perseval outside.

"Taxis are down this way." Mr. Perseval pointed to his right. "I'll show you."

"My brother's picking me up," Jackson said looking at his phone. "I think. One second," he said pulling up his phone. "Call Henry," Jackson mumbled just audibly enough for the phone to pick up his voice. The phone announced that it would do just that and the screen filled with the dopey smiling face of his brother. Henry was in his late thirties, ten years older than Jackson, but Jackson had always been the older brother.

"You have reached Henry Pets Private Investigations, please-" Jackson ended the call. The first time he'd called he thought he had the wrong number. The voice had a distinctly British accent that his brother shouldn't have, and he was sure that Henry wasn't a pet detective. After he hung up though, he remembered the irritating British accent Henry used to use to impress - well no one really, but he thought it would. The accent on the message had been identical. For some reason his very American brother was using a British accent and had turned into a pet detective. Jackson had waited too long to find out what was going on. He should have intervened when Henry had suddenly left Cambridge for these islands. Now... he had no idea what to expect. And he didn't even have his damn suitcase.

"Not answering?" Mr. Perseval asked.

"No. He should be here."

"Just running late?"

"With my brother that could be anywhere from an hour to three weeks."

"He's in Erfundenborg?"

"Yeah," Jackson pulled up Harry's contact page. "48841F Bilun. I think it's near the coast."

"We're on an island. Everything's near the coast. Well, good luck. If you do end up getting a taxi, stay away from the Téméraire Taxis if you value your life. If you find yourself in a particularly bad way, give me a call."

Mr. Perseval handed Jackson a business card then said his goodbyes. He waddled away leaving Jackson alone, standing outside the terminal looking like a frat boy that had been given very poor directions to the beach party. He was still alone three hours and dozens of text messages later.

After discovering a complete lack of Uber availability, Jackson reluctantly made his way to the public transportation island and waved down a Tvítyngd Taxi. A few confusing words were exchanged with a driver that didn't speak any English, then he climbed in and finally departed the airport. As far as first impressions went, the Verlorland Islands weren't doing well.

That changed as the taxi moved off into the countryside. They headed out over rolling green hills, thick with a low hanging mist. Bright wildflowers stuck out of the vibrant greens, the smooth blanket of foliage broken with occasional clusters of low bushes or small rock faces where a stream had eroded away the soil. In only a few minutes it was as if they were miles from civilization. They crested a hill and the ocean stretched out below a green-capped bluff. Waves crashed against the rocks below. The lost baggage and missing ride faded from Jackson's thoughts as he took it all in. The outdoors had always pulled at Jackson. While other kids had played video games or watched cartoons, he'd built hideouts in bushes climbed anything he could get a handhold on. Miles of untouched nature surrounded him. It was an endless playground.

As they drove on, bright dots began to appear, nestled in the hills. Houses, each miles from their nearest neighbor. It was a good fifteen minutes before they passed the first house. He almost missed it. At first it appeared to be another pile of rocks stuck in the side of a mound. This mound had white window frames though. They gazed right out of the hillside. There was also an old woman sweeping in a door shaped opening.

"Are there a lot of houses like that?" Jackson asked, pointing at the house. The driver said something that sounded like ek-ee-ma-bee-a. Jackson couldn't find it in his phrase book. He wasn't sure if he should be looking through Norwegian, Icelandic or Verlorlandish.

The road bent south and soon they were passing brightly colored wooden houses that became more and more frequent. They sat in little clusters on the hillsides that gradually became denser. The colors were bolder than what Jackson was used to: nearly pink reds with mint green trim, yellow with pale blue, bright white and tangerine orange. Bright little boxes with a few sprawling green parks or ornate cathedrals mixed in to keep it interesting.

"Erfundenborg," the driver said forcefully as he thumped the windshield. "Good city." So maybe he knew two words in English.

"It looks..." the word that came to Jackson's mind was quaint but being a word he'd never said out loud before he went with, "good."

They began to level out, and houses gave way to big box warehouses, strip malls, and even a BP petrol station as the sun began to sink into the horizon. By the time they pulled off the main road, dusk was giving way to night. They drove on through winding narrow streets. Two and three story concrete buildings lined the road. Occasionally a pub, barbershop, or what might either be a brothel or a very strange restaurant popped up to break the monotony.

The taxi stopped in front of a particularly rundown two-story building sided with large pebbles. "Here," the driver said, tapping the window. So, three words of English.

"Are you sure?" Jackson asked. It was less out of doubt and more out of a need to protest the situation.

The number 48841 was marked in gold on a pink door, there was no debating that. The driver looked back at him, bored. Jackson paid the driver, hopefully, close to the right amount, and climbed out of the taxi. The Verlorland currency was a series of different sized bills. The smallest was a red-tinted square with the picture of a man in a strange hat on the front and a bluff on the back, and the longest was about four times the length with a mural of happy children on the front and a rock on the back. The confusion came in that the smallest was the largest in denomination and the longest was a midlevel bill. The six intermediate sized bills didn't seem to have any consistent incremental pattern, and then there were the coins.

One was actually a solid cube. He stuffed the money back into his pocket and turned to the pink door. The paint was chipped and covered what probably was once a very elegantly carved wooden door. Jackson knocked. After waiting a few minutes he tested the door. It opened.

Inside were two more doors and a staircase. The doors were marked "B," and "C." Jackson headed up the staircase. The second level was nearly identical except for the vaulted ceiling. It was a nice touch even if the wood was showing it's age. The doors up here were marked "F," and "G." Jackson crossed to "F" and knocked. He waited a few moments then raised his hand to knock again.

"He's not round 'ere," a heavily accented voice came from behind him. It was British-ish. Not the Queen's English. Something you'd associate with football fans and barroom brawls.

Jackson turned. The "G" door was open, and a short, sturdy built middle-aged man leaned in the doorway. He had a shaved head and unkept beard. Most notably, he wore only a pair of Union Jack briefs and a smattering of old-school tattoos including a sacred heart in the middle of his chest and an entire locomotive stretching from his armpit to his ankle.

"Hi," was all Jackson could come up with.

"The detective aint 'ere."

"Henry?"

"Ay," the man said, nodding. "Yous his client?"

"Client? No, he's my brother. Do you know where he is?"

"Brother," he said, eyebrow cocked. "You're American?"

"Yes," Jackson said. The conversation had gone on long enough that he was starting to feel weird about not giving the stranger his full attention.

"Agent Orange," the man said, sticking out his stubby hand. Reluctantly, Jackson turned around and took it.

"Jackson." They shook. "Is Agent your first name?"

"No. No. Secret agent. That's Agent Peaches," Agent Orange motioned behind him. What Jackson at first had thought was part of the furniture moved, and a person in a burka waved back. Jackson couldn't tell much of the occupant other than he or she had some intriguing brownish hazel eyes and dark skin. Jackson waved back.

"Code names, We's undercover."

"Right." Jackson tried to rationalize what he was seeing but there wasn't a logical answer, so instead, he just nodded in faux understanding.

"Wait 'ere," Orange said and stepped back inside. There was a clank of metal, and he returned with a knot of keys. "'He should be back quick sticks. I think he's on a case." Orange fitted a key in the door, and it swung open.

"Are you the landlord?"

"No. Jus' a good neighbor. Tell him hi, yeah?" Orange gave Jackson an unneeded pat on the back and headed back to G leaving Jackson in the hall alone. Jackson didn't move for a while as he let the moment sink in. Finally, he shook it off and went through the door.

"Henry," he said to the empty room as he shut the door. There wasn't a reply.

The room was a decent size with well-worn hardwood floors. Other than the door Jackson had entered through there was only one other door. It was on the same wall as the entrance but in the corner clear to the right, locked by a deadbolt. The room was sparsely furnished. One table sat in the middle of the room with only one chair, and there was a mattress stuck in the far corner under a window. To the left, there was a sink, microwave, refrigerator and two burner range top. The place was clean but cluttered. Stacks of newspapers and folders lined most of the far wall. The table was covered in piles of documents. One stack of folded newspapers let out a soft glow around them. Jackson picked them up, revealing an open laptop underneath. He hit the trackpad to kill the screen saver. The desktop was cluttered with icons. Jackson opened the calendar app. It was completely blank. Jackson set the newspapers back down and took another look around the room. He shook his head and sat down in the lone chair. The flight finally caught up with him, and Jackson drifted into sleep.

CHAPTER 3

Jackson wasn't sure how long he'd been out when he woke to the door swinging open. He jumped to his feet.

"Jackson," Henry said not with surprise, merely recognition. He did smile a little. Henry was taller than Jackson with dingy brown eyes as opposed to Jackson's nearly black brown. His eyes always seemed to be looking past anything in front of him, and his left eye had a squint that made his face look off balance. He had a very average build, not quite lean, a little soft but not at all fat. His face was clean shaven, and he wore a white shirt with a gray suit and tie, but everything was disheveled enough to keep him from looking well dressed. He held a bag of french bread and a cage with a very agitated bright yellow parrot. "You made it. Here take this." Henry handed the cage to Jackson and turned to the table. "You moved things. I need a flyer. I am almost certain this is the right bird. It does respond to Wallace."

"CHEESE!" the parrot squeaked.

"That's a response, right?" Henry asked.

"I waited for you."

"Waited for what? There was a newspaper here," Henry said, pointing to the stack of papers on the computer.

"At the airport. You were supposed to pick me up."

"Yes. I was. I don't actually have a car."

"Then why did you say you'd pick me up?"

"Did I?" Henry thought for one and a half seconds. "Yes, I suppose I did. I was probably thinking about something else. There it is." Henry snatched up a flyer and shoved the bread onto the table. A stack of documents on the other end of the table fell to the floor.

"You could have answered your phone."

"My phone. Yes." Henry spun back around and crossed to the refrigerator. He opened up the freezer, fished around for a moment and pulled out a phone. "Just as I thought. My suspicions were first aroused when I found a Cornetto in my pocket just over two hours ago."

Henry returned to the table and finally looked at his brother for the first time.

"You're fatter," Henry said.

"I'm not fat."

"Your stomach is larger than last time I saw you."

"I hurt my knee doing the Spartan Race. Had to lay off it for a few months. You did remember I was coming today, right?"

Henry looked up and bit his bottom lip. "Yes..." the word trailed off. "I do remember remembering it." He came back to attention. "I was actually going to borrow a car from Agent Orange-"

"You know him?"

"Yes, he's my neighbor."

"Did you know he has your key?"

"It's fine. He's an agent."

"Yeah, I don't think he really is."

"The snaps do suggest otherwise," Henry mused.

Jackson stared back blankly with no idea what that could mean.

"I changed my locks twice, and that didn't help," Henry continued. "Nothing's gone missing yet, and no one in the building's been murdered so I think it's probably fine. Unfortunately, they needed the car for *official business*, so I decided to take a bus, but on the way there I saw Wallace-"

"CHEESE!" said Wallace.

"Yes, cheese. I forgot to get cheese. Should birds eat cheese?" He glanced up. "No. That's why I got the bread." Henry looked at the bag of bread. "I might have gotten too much."

"Dude, why'm I holding a parrot?"

"It's a very important part of a case. And don't call me dude. You're a grown man." He looked Jackson up and down again. "Although you certainly don't dress like one."

"Is that evidence?" Jackson asked, ignoring the criticisms.

"Sort of. How's Dad?"

"He's doing well," Jackson said, a little surprised by Henry's interest. Jackson found a place on the table to balance the cage. He set it down carefully. "Still grumpy. Took up marathons, so he looks a lot like a skeleton now. New wife is about your age."

"I didn't know he was getting married."

"He did try to call you. A lot."

"I misplace my phone sometimes." Henry felt his pockets. "Where did I put it?"

"It's in the bread."

"I suppose that's a good place for it."

"Or your pocket."

"It's sticky. From the Cornetto."

"So what's with the accent?"

A buzzing started in the bread bag before Henry could answer. He quickly fished out his phone. "Henry Pets Private Investigations," He said in the poor impression of a British accent again. "Yes." He listened. "Yes." He listened again. "Yes, answers to Wallace."

"CHEESE!" said Wallace.

"One moment." Henry pulled the phone away from his face and looked at Jackson. "I'll be a minute. Are you hungry?"

"Not really."

"Good. I think I only have bread. Oh! And a few Cornettos. In the freezer."

"I'm just tired, and I need to piss. Should I be finding a hotel?"

"No. No! Use my bed for now. The washroom is through that door." He pointed to the door with the deadbolt. "If you need a shower there are towels in the... uh... cupboard by that window and I am out of soap, but dish soap works fine. We'll figure something out when I'm done here. Right?" Henry didn't wait for an answer; he put the phone back to his ear and continued in the fake accent. "By all means, good chap." Henry crossed to the door, giving Jackson a thumbs up before he exited the room.

Jackson chose to forgo a shower for now and crossed to the second door. It struck him as odd that the deadbolt was on the outside of the door. It seemed to be a fairly obvious design flaw until he went inside.

The room was just under half the size of Henry's main room, grimy green tiles covering the floor. There was a toilet, a short trough urinal and two sinks to his right and two shower heads sticking out of the wall to his left. For just a moment he wondered why there were so many fixtures, then he saw the other doors. There was one directly across from him and then two more in the two other corners. There were no deadbolts on this side of the doors.

"Seriously?" He said out loud. He slowly crossed to the door that he assumed led to the creepy "agents" apartment. He listened a moment but heard nothing. He waited a few seconds longer then, quickly went to the trough and relieved himself without intrusion, washed his hands and went back to Henry's room. He double checked the deadbolt. He would be getting a hotel, but for now, he decided to get a nap in until Henry was off the phone.

Jackson woke to the sun pouring light through the curtain-less windows. He felt around until he found his phone. It was dead. It felt early despite the surprisingly bright sun.

"Damn it."

He sat up on the mattress, stretching out the rest of the sleep hanging onto him. He was still alone. He went to scratch his chest and felt a note taped to it.

> *Had to pop out. Didn't want to wake you. There is a*
> *kettle if you want tea and I found some doughnuts at the*
> *shop. They are on the table. - Henry*
> *PS: You smell like socks and vodka.*

He sniffed at his shirt and winced. The nearly half day of flying and sleeping on a questionable mattress hadn't been kind to him. And he had drunk a few too many screwdrivers on the flight. Jackson snatched up the towel and stumbled to the washroom, trying to rub the sleep from his eyes.

He knocked. Waited. Knocked again. There was no reply. Carefully Jackson opened the door. The room was empty. That was a good start. Once again he looked for locks. There were none. Jackson considered his options. He didn't exactly want to have to inform the occupants of each room that he'd be using the shower. Finally, he convinced himself that any sane person would hear the water or at least knock. He'd be quick.

The water was warm, and for a moment everything felt very normal. Or at least normal enough. The green tiles had a strange gold pattern on them that was less a pattern and more a haphazard series of vaguely floral shapes. He tried not to think about how clean they might be. He knew he should hurry, but the water eased his aching muscles. He let it rush over his head and closed his eyes. At least Verlorland had decent water pressure.

"You're Jackson, right?"

Jackson's eyes shot open, and he spun around. No one was at the toilet or sink. The doors were shut. No. The voice came from much closer. Jackson glanced at the other shower.

A young woman stood under the water, pouring dish soap into her hand. She was the kind of woman Jackson would enjoy meeting under nearly any other circumstance: dark brown skin with a perfect amount of freckles, black hair hanging around her in thick curls and a soft but defined nose. Jackson had always found mixed-race women attractive but did wonder if that was some form of reverse racism. Or regular racism just nicer. She was shaped well in more areas than Jackson was comfortable looking at. He quickly moved his eyes back up. Her eyebrows arched seductively - or maybe he was reading that from his own feelings - long dark lashes and hazel eyes. He knew the eyes.

"You're the burka," he said, forgetting his situation for a moment.

"I was *in* a burka. I wouldn't say I *am* a burka," she smiled back. "Peaches. I'd shake your hand but..." she held up her soapy palms. Her voice was rich in tone with an accent that hit on the softer side of British but did dip a bit toward Orange's own.

Jackson raced through a dozen replies before opting to forgo any of them and instead turned off the shower and snatched up his towel.

"Don't hurry on my account," Peaches said.

"I uh... should get back..." Jackson pointed to the door, trying to avert his eyes.

"You're Henry's brother?"

"Yes," Jackson said.

"American?"

"Yes."

"I thought so. Henry's accent is... well..."

For a second, Jackson forgot how uncomfortable he was. "Horrible?"

"Singular. Anyway, welcome to Verlorland."

"Thanks," Jackson said.

Jackson headed for the door but stopped before turning the nob. He half turned back, enough to almost see her out of the corner of his eye. "You're not really an agent then, right?"

"Of course I am." Peaches gave a wry smile.

Jackson, unsure how to take her answer, headed back into Henry's apartment, bolting the door behind him. He dried quickly then crossed to the bed. His backpack sat by the bed but only then did he remember his missing suitcase.

"Damn it."

He looked around.

"Damn it," he said again. He'd left his only clothes in the washroom.

Jackson went to the door and listened. Water ran on the other side. He could wait. With nothing else to do, he found the doughnuts on the table. He noted the parrot was gone. He ate one of the doughnuts as he thumbed through one of the newspapers on the table. He wasn't sure what language it was in and gave up. He dropped it on the table, and a single sheet of paper fell to the floor. Jackson picked it up and was about to toss it onto the table, but a picture caught his eye. It was the Parrot. He couldn't read the word at the top, but as he skimmed the text, he did see the word Wallace and further down £1,000.

The front door swung open behind Jackson. Without turning around, Jackson said, "You find missing pets?"

"You're in a towel." It wasn't Henry's voice, but British-ish.

Jackson turned. Henry was standing in the doorway but just behind him was a graying ginger haired man in a black suit. He struck Jackson as the kind of man that wouldn't stand out in a one-man play.

"Please excuse my.... colleague, uh, Dr. Jackson," Henry said in his British accent. "One moment."

Henry grabbed Jackson's shoulder and pushed him toward the washroom.

"What are you doing?" he whispered sharply.

"Not going back in there," Jackson said.

Henry unbolted the door and tried to shove Jackson through. Jackson was relieved to see Peaches gone.

"Dude, I'm not-"

"He's a client," Henry pleaded.

Jackson sighed and allowed himself to be pushed inside, but he grabbed Henry before he could leave. "Why'd you tell him I'm a doctor?"

"It's half right."

"Not even close."

"I can't let him know I have an American brother. It throws off the entire vibe. And if I'm going to have a man in my room wearing only a towel, it would be better for him to be a doctor."

"How?"

"It just does."

"I don't follow that logic but more importantly, why are you pretending to be English?"

"Because nobody likes Americans, but they love British detectives. Now just stay here."

"You mean British Pet Detectives," Jackson said just before Henry got the door shut.

Henry stopped and looked back at Jackson, then to the man in the suit. "If you could give me a moment, Oas." Henry smiled then jumped back into the washroom and shut the door behind him. The washroom was thankfully empty. "It's Henry Pets. Not Pet Detective."

"Your message says Henry," Jackson pause briefly, "Pets Private Investigations."

"No, it's Henry Pets comma Private Investigations. It's all about the comma. I can't go using my American name."

"Well, you can't hear commas, so it sounds like Pet Private Investigations. And that parrot. He was a missing pet, wasn't he?"

Henry thought for a moment, realization crossed his face. "That would explain why I get so many calls for missing animals."

Jackson shook his head. "You left a perfectly good job in Cambridge to be a pet detective on an island no one cares about. This is exactly why dad sent me here."

"Sent you here? I thought you just were coming to visit."

"You forgot I was even coming."

"We have moved past that!"

Jackson shook his head. "Dad wants you to come home."

"Why would I do that?"

"Look at you. You're finding lost animals. You live in a one-room apartment with a mattress and table."

"I have a chair too."

"And you share a bathroom with three other apartments."

"They call them flats, at least when they speak English, and the elderly lady in "D" is only here every other weekend. I believe "A" is vacant."

"That doesn't make it less weird." Henry didn't have a quick response, so Jackson continued. "I have an empty house in Portland you can live in. We can get you a job with the company."

"I can't be a rafting guide."

"We're quite a bit more than that. It'd be in corporate. We'd find you a good fit. Something with remembering inane details."

"Inane?" Henry was offended.

"What color crayon did Chad shove into the toaster?"

"It wasn't a crayon. It was an oil pastel, and it was burnt umber - which is not ironic, it's a coincidence - and is not inane. I'm doing just fine here."

"Why here? Come do it in Portland."

"The Verlorland Islands are the place to be for private detectives. There are laws protecting the practice. If a family hires a private detective for a case, the police aren't allowed to shut them out. Also the crime rate is alarmingly high."

"How is that a good thing?"

"For a detective."

"Fine. Okay. But how many cases have you had in the last year?"

"So many. Let me think. Last month-"

"That didn't involve animals."

"Oh. Well, that would be, um... none, but-"

"It's time to come home, Henry. We can't keep paying for you to do... whatever this is."

"I'm just about to really break through. That man out there, that is my big break. If you didn't scare him off with your nakedness."

"If you didn't share a bathroom with-"

"Do not put that back on me."

"If anything was going to scare him off, I think it would be the building," Jackson said. "Which has shared bathrooms!"

"You're just fixating on one feature."

"Which is fairly common." The second voice wasn't Henry's. Jackson recognized it as Agent Orange's.

Jackson turned around. Agent Orange stood in the doorway dressed in a pink bathrobe and bunny slippers.

"Can I help you, ol' chap?" Henry asked, his false accent roaring back.

"Need da shitter," Orange said.

"I'll be but a moment," Henry said. He gave Jackson one last look then went back into his apartment.

"Wait-" the door shut on Jackson's words.

Jackson fumed a moment before plucking his clothes off a hook. He turned to see if the neighbor had left. He hand't.

"Would yous like some tea?" Agent Orange asked with a smile.

Henry bolted the door shut and smiled at Oas. "I apologize for that, my colleague had his water shut off."

"It's a bad time. I can return later," Oas said in a level tone.

"No, not at all. So, you said Miss Marigolds requested me specifically?"

"Yes," Oas said. "The Miss Marigolds was insistent that I find an English detective. She's under the impression that they're the best in the world. Too much television. It warps perspective." Oas shook his head in defeat. "You are the only British detective in the islands." Oas paused for a moment. "Allegedly." Henry was about to defend himself, but Oas produced a document. "She wrote this for you," he said, handing it over. "It's a note."

Henry took it, glanced at it, then placed it in his pocket.

"You should read it," Oas said.

"I did. She does not explain who might have wanted to kill her aunt."

"That's why it's a mystery."

"I see."

"The Miss Marigolds would like to meet you in person, to discuss the case."

"Of course."

"The address is on the letter. When might we expect you?"

"Actually, I don't have a car. I could ride with you now?"

Oas was silent a few seconds past comfort. "Yes. I'll give you a minute to get your doctor dressed. I can see myself out." Without waiting for a reply, Oas turned and left the room.

Henry let a huge smile break across his face. It was pure ecstasy. A knock came from behind him, and he snapped back to attention. "Yes?"

"Henry?" It was Jackson's voice.

"Oh, right." Henry ran to the washroom door, unbolted it and let Jackson back in. He was holding a cup of tea but was at least dressed, although they seemed to be the same clothes as the pervious day. They had the faint smell of vodka on them despite Jackson's shower.

"I'll just be gone for a few hours," Henry said. "I have a case."

"Like the last case?"

"Not at all. This could be my big break. And absolutely no animals involved. It's a murder," Henry let his smile out again.

"Don't smile when you say that."

"I'm sure I'll be back by this evening. If you need anything-"

"I'm not staying here by myself."

Henry thought a second. "I could see if Agent Orange could show you the sights?"

"I've seen enough of your neighbors."

"You could even say they've seen enough of you? Eh?"

"Never make jokes. It's weird," Jackson said. "I'm coming with you."

"I don't think that's a good idea."

"I'm not staying here."

"This is a legitimate case. I can't have my brother tagging along."

"I guess we're lucky I'm your doctor."

Henry frowned.

"Okay. So I think it's not going to be too much of a shock now for me to tell you Dad sent me here to see if you were actually making progress on the private investigator thing. If you are, great. If not, he's either bringing you home or cutting you off."

"I can make it on my own."

Jackson looked around the room.

"It's a very expensive city."

"Exactly. So, if this is a real case... I watch you work, I tell Dad you're doing good stuff, you don't have to come home and file papers."

Henry's thoughts spun a few different directions before a responded. He could think of a dozen ways this could go wrong but all were better than filing papers for his father. "Fine. But you have to dress nice. You're a doctor.

"My suitcase got lost," Jackson said.

"So what do you have?"

Jackson looked down. "This."

"Sleeveless shirts are for toddlers and Richard Simmons."

"Well it's this or your towel."

Henry wrinkled his face up. "That won't work at all. I have an extra suit."

"You think I could fit in your suit?"

Henry shook his head. "Perhaps Agent Orange-"

"No."

"You can't go like that."

"I'm open to suggestions."

A few arguments later, they exited the building. Henry fighting off a scowl and Jackson dressed in the same Ruck River Rafting tank top. Oas and a stout man with a well-trimmed beard, stood on the curb with the door open to a deep maroon Bentley Limousine.

"Alright, that does look legitimate," Jackson said.

"I can't believe you didn't bring any real pants," said in a stiff whisper.

"I can't help that they lost my suitcase."

"They better find it soon."

"I agree," Jackson said. "Although I don't know if I have any pants packed in there either."

"What?"

"It's summer."

"You look like a douche bag."

"What?"

"Douche bag. It's an insult."

"I know it's an insult. How do I look like a douche bag?"

"You're showing more skin than a prostitute."

"Would you rather I wear the towel?"

"Doctors don't go around with half their thighs hanging out."

"If you'd told me I'd be impersonating-"

Henry jabbed Jackson in the ribs to stop him as they approached the limousine.

"Mr. Pets. Watch your step."

"Thank you."

Oas' eyes turned to Jackson and he raised an eyebrow. Neither brother attempted an explanation as they climbed into the vehicle. The stout man shut the door behind them. Henry and Jackson settled into opposite seats as Oas and the driver climbed into the front seat.

"How much would you say you know about medicine?" Henry asked as the limousine pulled away.

"What?" Jackson retorted. "Nothing."

"You taught those classes."

"CPR. Not really medicine."

"I guess we could say you're a chiropractor," Henry said.

"Why would you have a chiropractor with you?"

"Good point," Henry fiddled with a panel next to him. It flipped open revealing a few bottles of hard liquor. "I suppose it's too late to say you're my bodyguard."

"Is that whiskey?" Jackson asked.

"Optometrist!" Henry nearly yelled.

"Again, why would you need-"

"Right right. What was it you were working on? Counseling?"

"Clinical psychology. How about we just don't say what kind of doctor I supposedly am and I just stand around looking smart."

Henry raised an eyebrow at the last few words.

"Shut up," Jackson said. "You look like you haven't changed your clothes in a week."

"You smell like-"

"Yes, I know."

"Merely pointing out-"

"I know."

Henry shrugged and leaned back into his seat. Jackson turned his attention out the window. They were on the road he'd taken from the airport but heading further south.

"Who's dead?"

"Yes! Sorry. Yes. That is where it gets interesting. Laundra Henbit."

"Who is..."

"She's the wealthiest woman in all the islands. She owns the entire island of Alku."

"We're going to another island?"

"It's the island just south of here. There's a bridge connecting it to Erfundeneyja. Her late husband bought the entire island and built a huge English country house in the middle of it. Very controversial. He left the entire thing to her when he died. She was originally from Germany, and he was from Hampshire. The only other thing on Alku is a small village also named Alku. There has been people living there for over a thousand years. None of the residents were very happy about the estate."

"So maybe one of the locals offed her?"

"Let's not jump to conclusions."

"How'd she die?"

"I don't have the information yet. Her niece is the one that requested my services. We'll be meeting with her."

Jackson nodded and milled it over in his mind. They were passing brightly colored houses again. He really wished Henry lived in one of those. "An entire island."

"What was that?"

"How do you go about buying an island?"

"Not really sure. Someone must have been selling it."

The houses thinned out until they were in open country, riding over bluffs that overlooked the ocean. The multilane main road dwindled into what might have been a highway then merely a poorly paved road that eventually led to a long suspension bridge. It stretched between two high bluffs, the ocean crashing beneath. Jackson - despite Henry's objections - rolled down the window and leaned out to get a better view. It looked like a perfect place for a bungee jump to Jackson. Although the water below was reasonably turbulent, waves crashing high above the waterline. It wouldn't take long to be within reach of the waves.

Before he could wonder about that any longer, they were on the other side of the bridge and driving onto the island of Alku. The village crowded the ledge right up to the bridge and stretched up the steep hillsides. Even steeper hills rose up behind the village. They were the kind of hills that were just large enough for locals to refer to as mountains while eliciting chuckles from anyone who'd actually been near a real mountain.

The road curved through what had to be a downtown of some kind. Little shops lined it, a decent sized stone church dominated the first of many roundabouts. Soon the road again transformed, this time paved in cobblestones. It curved through the stone houses and more shops. Every person they passed stopped to watch, eyes never turning away until they rounded the next corner. The buildings weren't nearly as brightly colored as they had been in Erfundenborg, most being made of dark stones or very old brick.

"Looks like we just went back in time," Jackson said. "Yup, there's someone riding a horse."

"It's an old village," Henry said, eyes glued to his phone. He flipped over the screen quickly.

"What are you doing?" Jackson asked.

"Research."

"On?"

"Laundra Henbit," he said, looking up.

"Anything interesting?"

"Quite a bit. She moved to Alku to marry Reginald Henbit, the last heir of the Henbit fortune. That was forty years ago. She was twenty-two, and he was seventy-two."

"There's an age gap."

"I think physical attraction wasn't the main motivation for the marriage."

"How long did it take you to deduct that?"

Henry gave Jackson a casual glare. Not threatening but meant to ward off any other sarcastic comments. "If you have more questions can you ask them now before I start again?"

CHAPTER 4

The village of Alku fell away as the limo headed further into the hills. The twists and curves became long switchbacks as they moved through the hills and on up a steep ridge. Henry wasn't sure how long it took until they crested the ridge. Jackson's gasp pulled his attention from his work.

Outside, the hills dropped into a soft rolling slope settling into a wide basin. The starkest contrast though was the sudden appearance of trees. Densely wooded areas covered the hills and stretched into the basin itself. That was surprising. Many of the Verlorland Islands had no trees at all. Erfundeneyja had few and nothing as dense as this. Beyond the trees sat one lone massive house. The Henbit Estate sat in the center of everything, in all its British grandeur.

The limo followed the road down into the trees, obscuring any view of the house until they passed through a tall stone wall. The ground smoothed out into a steady plane. The woods had been cut back, giving room for wild grasses that eventually gave way to a well-manicured lawn. As they drew nearer to the house, lavish gardens with sculpted shrubs and fields of brightly colored flowers surrounded them.

The house was beyond impressive. It dominated the landscape. The central section was three stories tall with rows of Gothic windows leading up to elaborate spires on every corner. The main entrance was a twin staircase, each arching out from the Roman-inspired pillars guarding the doors. Four wings fanned out from the main building with large halls each ending in buildings smaller in square footage and one less floor than the main building.

"Okay, I am feeling underdressed," Jackson said.

"You could stay in the car?"

Jackson declined Henry's offer and followed him out of the limo when the chauffeur opened the door. Oas invited - in a nearly polite manner - them to follow.

Henry did his best to absorb as much as possible. The chauffeur (white male, late thirties, 5'10", over average weight and smelled of cigarettes) stayed with the car. The only other person in sight was working in the gardens (male, race, age and height indeterminate at their distance, well-muscled arms, black mustache). They mounted the stairs, and the footman (white male, early twenties, just under 6', slight build, overly pink around eyes and overly greased hair) nodded and opened the tall white doors.

"Dude, you're staring," Jackson said.

"What?" Henry whipped his attention back to Jackson.

"You're staring at people."

"I'm observing. And again, don't say dude. You're a doctor."

"You need to try being more casual."

"I thought I was."

"No. You're staring. And your mouth moves like you're chanting or something."

Oas led them inside and the doors shut behind them. Henry looked out of the corner of his eyes at the young woman standing inside (white female, blond, early twenties, 5'9").

"That's worse," Jackson said.

"I am working."

Oas spoke quickly to the young woman, and she rushed to one of the twin sweeping staircases, heels clicking on the marble floor.

The room itself was just as Henry had expected. In his research, he'd found a Flickr page featuring architectural photography of the estate. It had been extensive, and despite the photos being seven years old, little had been changed with the notable exception of a discolored patch of marble near the set of doors to the left which Henry remembered led to the dining room.

"How large is the staff?"

"Six," Oas said. "And a nurse."

"So seven?"

"We won't retain a nurse now that Mrs. Henbit is dead."

"But the rest will keep their jobs?" Henry asked.

"That is yet to be determined."

"Then seven is the most accurate number."

"You are technically correct. This way." Oas pointed them under the twin staircases.

"Now who do we have here!" a loud shrill voice came from above.

A woman (white female, mid to late fifties, recent use of botox) sauntered down the stairs, her hand resting on the gold railing.

"You are a sight for sore eyes now aren't you?" The woman's green eyes were firmly set on Jackson. She looked him up and down then let her lips curl up into a sharply pointed smile. "Whatever you're doing to get those thighs, don't stop. It is working."

For the first time, Jackson felt that maybe his shorts were far too short.

The woman's heels clicked on the marble as she stepped off the stairs and crossed to Jackson. She made what could only be called a yummy sound. "Caprice," she said, holding out her hand like a limp white fish. "And you are?"

"Uncomfortable," Jackson said.

"I'm Henry Pets," Henry cut in. "And this is my associate, Dr. Jackson."

Henry took Caprice's hand and tried to shake the limp appendage. She slid it from his grip, keeping her attention on Jackson.

"A doctor?" Caprice asked in a voice between a purr and a bellow. She winked. "I wouldn't mind you giving me an examination."

Jackson took a step back.

"Mr. Pets is the private detective Miss Marigolds requested," Oas said.

All the stilted sultriness vanished from Caprice.

"Detective?" she squealed. "Why would we need a detective?"

"That is a question for Miss Marigolds," Oas said. "Excuse us."

Oas nodded for Henry to follow. Jackson quickly fell in after them, glancing back once at Caprice. Her green eyes followed them. There was nothing pleasant about her expression, but her eyes did linger on Jackson's backside.

The next room was again large but this time it was round. Oas called it the saloon. There they took a left into what obviously was a library. Without stopping, they exited the far side and passed down a long curved hallway. It ended in another large room. Jackson would have called it a greenhouse but Oas informed him it was a conservatory.

There, amongst the roses and greenery, a young woman stood watching the clouds drift by outside. Henry looked at her. She was beautiful.

"You're staring," Jackson whispered.

"I know."

* * *

A timid silence fell over the conservatory as Lydia Marigolds finished her version of the events surrounding her aunt's death. Her hands remained clasped neatly in her lap but her fingers fidgeted nervously with a fold of her dress. Jackson watched her discreetly from his place near some peach colored poppies. He pretended to be preoccupied with the flowers.

As she'd told her story, Miss Marigolds had seemed to forget that anyone existed apart from Henry, providing Jackson the liberty to explore the conservatory. But he'd kept an eye on the young woman seated with Henry. She told the story clearly and simply, but her apprehension was easy to see. Jackson guessed she was the sort of person not used to being in the spotlight. She hadn't cried but her voice had threatened to fail her as she reached the end. Murder or not, it was a traumatic way to see a loved one die. To see anyone die. Jackson felt for the poor young woman. Not that she was younger than him. Most likely she was a few years older. The vulnerability she emanated sitting in the ornately crafted Victorian wicker chair took a few years off.

Henry was quiet through the telling, not giving so much as a nod, even when the maid interrupted to serve them sandwiches. Henry's face held no indication of any emotion or really even a general interest. Jackson knew the expression well. It was impossible to tell what Henry was thinking from his face. Luckily - depending on the situation - Henry almost always felt the freedom to say exactly what was on his mind, so the guesswork only had to last so long.

"I should see the dining room," Henry stated in his faux accent, breaking the silence.

"Excuse me?" Miss Marigolds asked, taken off guard by the sudden break in Henry's silence.

"The dining room. I need to see it. That will help."

"Yes, of course." Miss Marigolds nodded. "I'll have Oas take you there. I can't..." she stopped and looked to her right, eyes searching out the floor to ceiling windows. "I haven't been back in there since it happened."

"She died in the hall," Henry stated.

"I was still in the dining room."

"Yes," Henry said, closing his eyes briefly. "Ari, the nurse, and Ramses, the gardener, were with her in the hallway."

"And Oas. Maybe the footman as well. I'm not sure."

"The food?"

"Footman. He's like an assistant to the butler."

"No, I understood that. I was moving to my next point. The food. I don't suppose I could see it?"

"I'm sure it's all thrown out by now, but I believe the police took samples."

"Good. I'd like the name of the chief inspector. Are they investigating this as murder?"

"No, that is why I asked for your services. The police are calling it natural causes."

Henry nodded. "But you believe it was murder?"

"Yes. That's what she was trying to tell us. Right before. Her last word was *mord*. That's murder. She knew someone was trying to kill her."

Henry kept eye contact with Miss Marigolds, not betraying any of his own inner thoughts. Miss Marigolds' eyes were pleading. Desperate. That's when Jackson understood the young woman's apprehension. She was afraid she wouldn't be believed.

"And would someone want to kill her?"

"I love my aunt. But there was so much I never knew about her. I do know she wasn't one to be scared of anything. She wasn't fanciful. If she thought someone wanted to harm her, someone was trying to harm her."

"Right," Henry said. "Did she say why someone was trying to kill her?"

"Not exactly. I think she was getting to it. She said something about how selfish she had been and that she had secrets."

"And someone wanted the secrets to remain secret?"

"I really don't know."

"Do you think that is why she invited all of your here, specifically to tell you that?"

"Maybe."

"What did she tell you was the reason?"

"She didn't. Aunt Laundra just bought us all tickets for when she wanted us to be here. That's sort of how she does things. Sorry, did things. She hadn't even called this time. The tickets showed up in the mail."

"And everyone just came?"

"Yes. We're used to it. Mother complained of course, but really none of us had anything too important to get away from."

"I see," Henry nodded. "I need a list of everyone that was in the house at the time of Mrs. Henbit's death and where exactly they were. Also, anyone that may have had access to the kitchen or larder. And the dining room. I'd like to see that as well." Henry cocked his head suddenly as if listening to a voice. "Right. Is there a will?"

"Yes," Miss Marigolds said. "Aunt Laundra's solicitor is bringing it around later today."

"Good. I would like to see that."

"I'll let her know."

Henry nodded. "Oas?"

"I'll call for him," Miss Marigolds took her phone out of her pocket and tapped it a few times. She put it back then looked up at Henry, lips pursed. "You will find out who killed her then?"

Henry frowned, surprised. "Suppose that depends on a great number of factors, many of which are outside my control."

It wasn't the answer Miss Marigolds had hoped for, but she nodded in acceptance. Jackson had never really decided if Henry's forceful honesty was a strength or a defect. He could imagine most detectives would have promised Miss Marigolds a swift solution but that wasn't Henry's way. It wouldn't have even crossed his mind to say anything other than the absolute truth.

Almost without pause, Henry continued. "Did your sister often speak German?"

"What? Uh... not often. Sometimes with Dr. Novak - she knew a little German - but only if she didn't want the rest of us to understand. Oddly never with the cook that I can remember. Emma. She's German too. Why do you ask?"

"Not sure." Henry shrugged. "Jackson. I'm going to the dining room. Are you joining me or should I give you more time with the poppies?"

CHAPTER 5

"You've cleaned," Henry said after surveying the dining room. Everything was in order, the table sat with the display place settings. Everything looked exactly like the photos. Except for the candles, Henry noted. While convincing, they were clearly LED. The ones in the photos had been real.

"It's not a crime scene," Oas replied without a note of emotion.

"That is to be determined."

"It was to be determined. Now it has been determined. Hence it not being a crime scene."

The Butler was a tough read. Jackson had watched him closely since he'd taken them to the library. On first meeting, Jackson had assumed Oas was merely annoyed that his time was being wasted. Even in the brief interaction in Henry's room, it was easy to tell the man was thoroughly unimpressed with Henry Pets. But there was more. There was something almost personal in his passive-aggressive disposition.

"Maybe. But there is doubt," Henry answered. "Which is why I am here."

"You are here, Mr. Pets because Miss Marigolds is grieving. She wants her aunt's death to have meaning beyond the inevitable result of years of poor lifestyle choices. It is my job to accommodate her fancies, so I have brought you here."

"Possibly."

"Excuse me?"

"It's possibly still your job. You did say you weren't sure how staffing would be affected by Mrs. Henbit's death, yes?"

Oas' frown deepened. "Yes."

"You have not seen the will then?"

"No."

"I feel it will be most informative. Now, I'd like to meet the staff."

"Of course," Oas said, expression unchanged.

Oas tapped one finger against his watch, and the door toward the kitchen opened. A man and a woman strode inside. One was the young blond woman from earlier. The other was the man from the garden. He was a brawny bullnecked man. Now closer, Henry had a full view of him and his most striking feature: a thick black mustache that coved over his lip and down to his chin. The two were followed by the poshie, running around them in circles, yipping. Oas gave it a lightning-quick glare then returned to his practiced neutral expression.

"Efficient," Henry said.

"Yes," Oas replied.

"How does it work?"

"It's an app. All of the house staff have a watch allowing messages to be efficiently sent to any or all staff members."

As the two took places near Oas, the other door opened and the gangly footman entered. He shut the door and quickly took his place next to the others. Henry looked them over.

"The others?" He asked.

Oas frowned and looked at his watch.

The greasy-haired young man cleared his throat and spoke with a staccato accent. "Laki is filling the car to make the trip back to Erfundenborg."

"Ari's helping Emma carry things up from the larder," the gardener added.

Both had accents. The footman's sounded Scandinavian-ish while the gardener's was unfamiliar.

"They should be here now," Oas said.

The woman blinked a few times, nervously. "We do still have to make the dinner." She had a soft voice with a hint of a French accent. "And you have made subtle hints that Ari would no longer be of service."

"Subtle?" The gardener laughed. "Subtle as a whomping willow in a nursery."

Oas gave him a dead stare. "That means nothing to me." He turned before giving him a chance to explain. "Matilda Desrosiers is the maid, Ramses Razek is the gardener, and Pip Skarsgård is the footman..." Oas glanced at them and stopped, another lightning expression crossing his face. This time disgust. The footman had bent down and was scratching Dandy behind the ears. "Mr. Skarsgård."

The footman jerked back up to attention.

"I have told you not to pet the dog while working."

"Yes, sr."

"Your hands," Oas said in a tone that indicated nothing else should need to be said.

The footman glanced at them then looked back up. "Excuse me." Quickly, he headed back through the door.

Oas breathed in carefully then continued. "The nurse, Ari Björnssen and the new cook, Emma Fischer will hopefully join us presently."

"New cook? What happened to the old cook?" Henry asked.

"He was let go."

"Of course," Henry said, waving off the unhelpfully obvious answer. He turned to the staff. "As you may or may not know, I-"

"They do know," Oas interrupted.

Henry cleared his throat, keeping his composure. "As I was saying. I am Detective Henry Pets-"

"Private detective," Oas added.

"Yes, thank you. I am a private detective. Miss Marigolds has employed me to look into the murder of Lau-"

"Alleged," Oas added.

Henry took in a sharp breath.

Jackson sighed and pulled himself off the wall he'd been leaning on. "Oas, would you help me find... uh... the others? Right? We still need them?"

Before Oas could respond, Jackson put one hefty arm around Oas' shoulder. The height difference forced Oas into a lopsided slouch. Jackson knew forcing a taller person to his height was a little overly aggressive but he had a feeling Oas was someone that needed taking down a peg or two occasionally. He quickly steered the butler toward the dining room door.

"The larder is not this direction," Oas started.

"I don't care," Jackson said. He looked back at Henry as he pushed the door open. "We'll be back." Then he shoved Oas out in front of him and kicked the door shut.

"I shouldn't leave Detective Pets alone," Oas said, straightening his jacket.

"He's not alone he's got the United Nations keeping him company. Now, I think we both see what's going on here so why don't we just let Henry have his fun, find out nothing's wrong, make your new boss happy and then we get out of here."

Oas narrowed his eyes at Jackson. "You are not a doctor."

"No."

"He is not British."

"Also no."

"Miss Marigolds won't be happy to hear that."

"No, but if she found out, what happens next?"

Oas thought for a moment. "She would have me send for a private detective from England."

"So what's your best option?"

Oas grimaced as he smoothed out his black suit. "I let Detective Pets finish his inquiries and make my probable next employer happy."

A light on Oas' watched flashed; he glanced down. "Excuse me."

Oas skirted Jackson and crossed to the front door. He waited precisely one second, then pulled the door open.

A red-haired woman, dressed in a form-fitting brilliantly blue pantsuit and black boots, stepped up the final stair and entered the hall. The boots reached well over her knees and a pair of long black gloves stretched clear up to her elbows. Behind her, the chauffeur entered carrying a large bag over one shoulder and stack of leather binders as well as one very blue purse.

"I left the Volvo running," the woman said to the chauffeur without looking at him. "Don't wait too long to garage it."

The chauffeur looked from her to his burdens then to Oas.

"I will take those," Oas said, holding his arms out to the stout man. As they made an awkward exchange, Oas continued. "Ms. Veratiri. We've been expecting you."

"Of course." She gave Oas a nod. "Gather the others. There is a lot to go over and..." her eyes fell on Jackson. "Who is this? Your..." she glanced between them. "Boy... boyfriend?"

"He is *Dr.* Jackson. Associate of the *preeminent detective* Henry Pets."

Jackson nearly rolled his eyes but managed to keep his composure.

"Detective?" Ms. Veratiri didn't sound pleased. She had a faint hint of the accent Jackson had begun to associate with the locals.

"Miss Marigolds employed him earlier today."

Ms. Veratiri shook her head and sighed. "This is not healthy. Not my job though. Reading this..." she indicted the chauffeur's burdens. "...is and I have other clients so pick a room and let's get this over with."

"Of course. Follow me."

"I think I'm still not clear on why you are here," the gardener said letting his elbows come to rest on the dining room table. He had a number of tattoos on his bare forearms. So far Henry had managed to pick out an Eye of Horus, a depiction of Anubis and scroll work reading *Expecto Patronum* near a stag.

"I'm investigating the death of your former employer," Henry answered again. Every member of the staff had asked a similar question.

"Laundra wasn't healthy."

"There are some facets of the case which require additional attention." That had worked on the footman and the maid.

"She was overweight and ate sausage three times a day."

Henry choked. There hadn't been any animosity in the gardener's voice, but the words were still shocking. "Her last words-"

"She was a paranoid recluse," the gardener cut in.

"I've been assured she was not a woman prone to fantasy."

Ramses made a sound somewhere between a chuckle and a sad sigh. "She was a practical woman. Kept a tight hold on her emotions. And yes, she lacked much imagination. Hated fantasy movies or science fiction. But that doesn't mean she didn't have her own little fantasies. This wouldn't have been the first time she thought someone was trying to kill her. It's just the only time her death came right after. Don't get me wrong here, she was a wonderful lady." He smiled slightly. "One of the best I've ever known. But she gave up on herself years ago. The first time she left this house in five years was when they wheeled her out with a sheet over her."

"How long have you been employed, Mr. Razek?"

"Call me Ramses. Twenty-six years as her gardener. But we'd known each other for a good while before that. I met her the summer before she went to university. Let's see... I would have been thirteen at the time."

"How did you meet?"

"Kitesurfing the Gulf of Suez."

Henry narrowed an eye at Ramses, trying to gauge if that was truth or jest. It was hard to tell. People were a jumble of idiosyncrasies that took time to unpack. Henry had spent years pouring over books on body language and psychology and had come to the conclusion none of it was helpful. What he liked were facts. Those you could know.

"I'd imagine it's not easy for someone of Mrs. Henbit's size."

"Laundra was a very athletic in her younger years. The weight came after the accident."

"Accident?"

"Broke her back. You'll have to ask Caprice about that though. They weren't on a dig."

"A dig?"

"Yes," Ramses said. "Archeological. You didn't know about that?"

"No."

"Ah, well, then you don't know Laundra. She was quite the budding archeologist before she married Reginald. Kept it up a bit after too but not in earnest. That's what brought her to Egypt in the first place. She'd spend entire summers on digs. My older brother was a kitesurfing instructor back then. I helped with rentals. We became reacquainted after Reginald died. She was back on a dig, I was living in Cairo with my sister, Rashidi. She had a little restaurant there. My sister, not Laundra. I recognized her instantly. She was quite the beautiful woman." Ramses let out a long sigh and sat back, crossing his arms. "We hit it off. I joined her on a few digs here and there. Met a few of her husbands when they'd join her. Then she had the accident and stopped coming to Cairo. But she needed a new cook and she always loved Rashidi's cooking so she hired us to come to the islands. Rashidi as a cook and I took over the gardens. I've been here ever since. Rashidi got married not long after and moved to Finland but I stayed on."

"I see. Where is Rashidi now?"

"She died. In Finland. Ari came to live here after that."

"Ari? That is Mrs. Henbit's nurse?"

"Yes. He's my sister's son. My... uh... nephew."

"I see." Henry gave him what he hoped looked like a sympathetic - but not too sympathetic smile. "Other than Caprice, I would think you've known Mrs. Henbit the longest of anyone here, correct?"

Ramses considered this. "Amelia Novak's been her doctor since she came to the islands so not exactly friends but they go back. But Oas, of course, has been working for Laundra ever since she married old Reginald. What would that have been?" Ramses leaned back in the chair and seemed to count at the ceiling. "Over forty years ago. Has to be. I may have met Laundra before then but I didn't really know her until Cairo. I'd say Oas is really the one that's known her the longest."

Henry frowned. "How old is Oas?"

"Fifty maybe?"

"That would have made him ten."

"Suppose it would have. Or less. Probably less. The Oas's are like house elves."

Henry blinked. It was the second Harry Potter reference from this unlikely source in a very short period of time, not to mention the tattoo. Henry had never actually read or seen anything Harry Potter related, but he had thoroughly studied the Wikipedia pages to have a passing knowledge of the subject. It was Henry's preferred way to keep up on popular culture.

"That doesn't seem legal." Henry mulled this over for a moment then finally filed it away. He'd come back to that, but for now, it was a distraction. "My point, being one of Mrs. Henbit's longest employees, do you know anyone that would have reason to want her dead?"

"I'm sure everyone has someone that would want them dead. Specifically though, no. Except maybe whoever gets all this." Ramses motioned around himself. "But seeing as no one knows who that is yet, it would have to be a crime of speculation."

"Speculation?"

"Yeah. Someone would have had to guess they'd be the one getting it all and kill her hoping they were right."

"She has family."

"And it's a safe bet it'll go to one of them. But who? The husband? The sister? The favorite niece? I've known Laundra a long time but I couldn't begin to guess what the answer is. She kept stuff like that close."

"Legal matters?"

"Family matters."

The study was full but not crowded. It was much larger than Jackson would have expected and seemed to double as a display room for the Henbit's long hunting tradition and a smattering of Egyptian artifacts. Jackson found a shadowy corner between a full-sized bear posed on two feet, mouth open in a silent roar and a statue of Egyptian god Set. It gave him a decent space to disappear in as the family and staff assembled on the assortment of chairs Oas and the footman had brought in. It would have been a simple task if they had been folding chairs but they weren't, and it wasn't. Oas's idea of finding a few more chairs meant lugging in ornately covered oak chairs with bright silk damask upholstery. He'd seen those chairs in the drawing room just outside the study. Why a house needed a drawing room and a study, was beyond Jackson except maybe to have something else to decorate. The drawing room had been cheery to the point of being oppressive. The study was manliness turned into a room.

The walls were painted dark green with flourishes of gold. The furniture meant for the room was of dark walnut and deep brown leather. The far wall displayed a portrait of an old man flanked on either side by zebra heads. Below that, Ms. Veratiri stood behind a massive oak desk carefully thumbing through pages with her gloved hand. Her vibrant blue dress stood out from the dark muted surroundings. Jackson had a feeling this was on purpose.

In front of the desk, in the four chairs meant to be in the room, sat the family. Caprice and Lydia, Jackson already knew. The young man and the sturdy woman, Jackson had not yet seen. Between Caprice and the young man, a small dog lay on a large silk pillow. It occasionally raised its head to yip at the young man until finally the young man turned and growled back at the dog.

The door opened, and Henry entered with the gardener. Ms. Veratiri flicked her eyes up. "Good. That is everyone. Ramses, if you'd find a seat, we will get started."

Henry stood awkwardly in the doorway a moment. Jackson hissed his name once then twice. Henry finally heard and saw his brother. He moved over to Jackson's secluded corner.

"You were supposed to bring the rest of the staff," Henry said.

"I was keeping the butler out of your way."

"Oh," Henry said with real surprise. "I suppose that was helpful. I learned a great deal." Henry's eyes darted everywhere at once but kept coming back to Jackson's bear companion. "There aren't bears in the islands."

"Probably no zebras either," Jackson added.

"Good point."

"Or pyramids," Jackson said, nodding toward the statue of Set.

"Yes, Mrs. Henbit was an amateur archaeologist."

"Of course she was," Jackson chuckled.

"If everyone is ready," Ms. Veratiri spoke out loudly, giving Jackson's corner a quick glare. "There is quite a bit of reading to do. Now, it is all written in German. So I will be reading it, then giving a translation in English. Is that acceptable to everyone?"

"Why is it in German?" Caprice asked.

"You are German," Ms. Veratiri answered.

"Well, Germanish. Neither of us has lived there for years. I hardly even remember the place let alone the language." She ended in a high pitched laugh that startled the dog and the young man next to it.

"That doesn't change the state of the will," Ms. Veratiri said.

"You could just do the translation," Lydia suggested. "I don't think many of us know much German, apart from Emma of course."

"I do need to read the original text out loud. That is expected."

"Fine, fine," Caprice waved. "Let's do this."

Ms. Veratiri gave Caprice a sardonic smile then dropped her eyes to the pages. While the solicitor started into the German legalese, Jackson watched the room. The staff sat and stood in small groups. The maid and the footman sat on either side of Oas just behind the family. The cook and the chauffeur sat off to the side both looking disinterested. Furtherest back, the gardener and the giant nurse leaned against the wall near the opposite corner from Jackson. The nurse seemed uncomfortable while the bulky gardener kept his eyes fixed on Ms. Veratiri.

"Did you meet the family?" Henry whispered, nodding to where they sat.

"Only the ones I met with you," Jackson answered.

"I would like to speak to her husband next," Henry said.

Jackson looked over the group. There were only two options, the chubby man fighting with the dog or the tall, slender man seated just behind Lydia and her sister.

"The cubby kid?" Jackson asked.

"Oscar Henbit, formerly Oscar Chu. He took Laundra's name. Well, technically Reginald Henbit's name." Henry motioned to the portrait. "Also, not a kid."

"How old is he?"

"Thirties, I think."

As if on cue, Oscar turned and let out one loud bark at the dog. Ms. Veratiri stopped. All eyes turned to Oscar. Unfazed he slumped back into his chair and began fidgeting with his jacket buttons. Ms. Veratiri began reading again.

"He seems..." Jackson began.

"Matilda said something about a head injury."

Jackson frowned. "That doesn't seem right."

"Jackson, do I need to remind you that you aren't a real doctor?" Henry said with a twinkle in his eyes. "I did make that up."

"Shut up."

Henry smiled with self-satisfaction and both settled back to listening again.

"Right," Ms. Veratiri said putting aside a folder. "Now we can get into some specifics."

"I do have to ask," Caprice spoke up. "Is it essential that everyone is here right now? I mean, couldn't you read the pertinent points for the staff, etcetera etcetera, then get into the more... I don't know... sensitive portions with maybe just the family. Or even me if the others would rather have gimlets and I don't know... croquet?"

"Croquet?" The sturdy woman asked.

"As previously indicated," Ms. Veratiri broke in sternly. "I was specifically instructed to have you all…" her eyes once again flicked up to Henry and Jackson. "Here."

"Even them?" The sturdy woman spoke up again, nodding back to Jackson's corner.

"I asked them to be here," Lydia said quietly.

"Who are they?" The woman asked.

"He's Henry-"

"Unimportant as of now," Ms. Veratiri said. "Unlike my time. So, if that is all out of your system. The specifics." Ms. Veratiri cleared her throat and started back into the German. She carried on monotonously for quite awhile until Caprice let out a gasp. Ms. Veratiri stopped.

"That can't be right," Caprice nearly shouted.

"What?" Lydia asked, eyes wide.

"I thought you said you didn't understand-" Ms. Veratiri started.

"Bugger off. Of course I still know German. Did you really just say that my sister's entire fortune is being left to the damn dog?"

The room fell silent.

"No," Ms. Veratiri finally said.

Lydia laughed. "That would have been absurd."

"I said that the Henbit Estate - including the island of Alku - and the bulk of Laundra Henbit's liquid assets are being left to a trust set up to care for Dandy. The dog."

At the sound of its name, Dandy sprung up from its place under Oscar's chair and yipped. A weak jingle of bells followed.

"Oh," Lydia said. No one else spoke for quite a while.

The tall, slender man raised his hand. Ms. Veratiri seemed annoyed at this but looked at him directly. "Yes, uh… Mr. Okumu?"

"Are you saying that this dog will own an entire island?"

"Through the trust, yes."

"That's legal?"

Ms. Veratiri nodded. "Yes."

"What about us?" The footman asked. Oas elbowed him subtly.

"The trust will continue to employ all current staff as long as they continue on and remain able to carry out their duties."

"What about the family?" Caprice nearly shouted. "She's leaving everything to the dog and just forgetting about-"

"If you would stop interrupting-"

"I will not stop," Caprice jumped to her feet. Lydia tried to pull her back, but Caprice shoved her away. "I am her only damned sister, and she's leaving everything to a dog I have never even seen in my life and giving me nothing? I don't believe it!"

"She isn't leaving everything to the dog," Ms. Veratiri said. "There are provisions for each family member, and we haven't gotten into the holdings outside the Islands. I do believe you will be receiving the house and property in Cape Town."

"You mean my house?"

"I do believe you live there but ownership-"

"Baaa!" Caprice threw up her arms. "This is nonsense. When did she make this will? It can't be right. You're not even the family solicitor."

"I do have the signatures of the witnesses if you would like to authenticate the document."

"I'd like to see those," Ramses spoke up, an edge to his voice.

"I'm sure it's all in order," Lydia said, coming to her feet. She put an arm around Caprice and did her best to seat her back to her chair.

"I'm not," Ramses muttered. Jackson hardly heard him above the murmurs coming from the rest of the staff.

"The shock... it is a shock," Lydia said, trying to smooth over the tension.

"I just don't believe she left everything to a dog," Caprice muttered.

"Oh," Ms. Veratiri said. "I may have said that slightly wrong. Excuse me. The liquid assets derived from the Henbit Estate will go to Dandy's trust. Laundra's liquid assets derived from her own sizable fortune are to be divided out in a scaled manner to all those present at the time of her death assuming they survive her by at least one month and remain on Henbit Estate until the time of her internment."

"Internment?" the sturdy woman asked.

"Burial," Ms. Veratiri clarified.

"I know what it means," she said. "But that says we can't leave the estate until she's buried?"

"That is correct."

Once more the room went dead silent. As one, they all went back over Ms. Veratiri's words trying to make sense of the statement. Caprice, of course, was the first to break the silence.

"That's shit."

CHAPTER 6

Orange and pink light bathed Alku through the window of the limousine as the sun sank below the horizon. It was much later than Jackson had expected. How long had they been at the manor? The village of Alku crowned the horizon, the lights growing steadily closer.

In the chaos that ensued after the reading of the will, Miss Marigolds had suggested Henry leave for the evening. She would send for him the next day. Henry had been keen on watching the events unfold particularly on a heated conversation between the gardener and Ms. Veratiri, but Jackson forced the issue. Henry eventually relented, agreeing he needed time for research.

"What do you think happens when the dog dies?" Jackson asked, watching the landscape slip into darkness outside.

"That's a great question we could have asked if we had stayed," Henry said.

Jackson rolled his eyes and turned back to his brother. "A family just found out that their relative preferred her dog to them. I think they needed some space."

"One of them did murder her."

"Maybe."

"In all of Europe, the Verlorland Islands statistically has the least amount of murders by persons unknown to the victim."

"What?"

"Most likely she was murdered by someone she knew."

"If she was murdered," Jackson said.

"Right now, we're assuming that."

"I guess that makes sense." Jackson let his attention drift back outside the limo. "That last part. The part with the money split between everyone there. That seemed a little messed up."

"How so? I did get a look at the scale. It did weigh family higher than the help."

"That's not what I mean. The whole part where they have to survive by at least a month. And they can't leave the estate? That seems..."

"Ominous?"

"Yes."

"I would agree with that."

"Why would she do that?"

"Eccentric wealthy woman? I don't know. I will have to find that out. It is all a distraction for now though."

"Distraction?"

"No one had knowledge of the will, so we must assume the contents of the will were not the motive for the murder. At least the actual contents. Maybe not the assumed contents."

"You can cut the accent with me you know," Jackson said.

Henry cleared his throat but continued in the faux accent. "It helps to stay in character."

The first buildings of Alku breezed passed, and the limo slowed. As they began the weaving route through the village, the window separating them from the driver slid open.

"You've been to Alku before?" The Chauffeur asked.

"Yes, once," Henry said.

The Chauffeur turned back, looking at Jackson, waiting.

"Oh, no. I've never been anywhere around here."

"That's no good. Alku is a very good place. My cousin's pub is the best in all the islands. I'll take you."

"That would be very kind but we-" Henry started.

"Good. Good."

Before either could object further, the window sprang back up.

Henry sighed. "I suppose it is past dinner time."

"Is it?" Jackson asked. He pulled out his phone. It was past eight if the time zone had adjusted correctly.

"One word of warning," Henry said. "Do not order anything someone recommends while grinning too much. It will probably have eyes."

Two dishes dropped on the table together. One held a juicy cut of beef, surrounded by diced potatoes, carrots and something green. The other was a mass of suction cup covered tentacles. One drooped low out of the bowl then slopped heavily in front of Henry.

The plump lady serving them smiled, clipped something pleasant sounding in Verlorlandish then strode away.

Jackson pulled his plate closer to him and cut into the meat. "Well, it doesn't have eyes," he said, glancing up at Henry's tentacle soup.

"In Erfundenborg this is usually cut much thinner and breaded," Henry said, poking at his tentacles.

"That so?" Jackson said with a chuckle. "I recommend the meat and potatoes. I'm not sure what the green bits are, but they taste like what I've always wished broccoli tasted like."

"The Verlorland Islands are known for their seafood. If you wanted beef, you could have stayed in America."

"But now I get to enjoy this heavenly broccoli and beef at the same time. And you get to chew on an octopus corpse." Jackson glanced around. "Where did the driver go?"

Henry prodded his food while glancing around the room. It was a small pub, warmly lit and furnished in dark oak. The place felt old and lived in but still well taken care of. The patrons were mostly older and looked as lived in as the pub itself.

"He could still be in the kitchen."

"If he leaves us here..." Jackson started but then wasn't sure how to end the thought. He wasn't exactly in a hurry to get back to Henry's flat. And of everywhere he'd been on the islands so far, this was easily the most comfortable he'd been. Jackson put the rest of the thought away and stuffed more of the green bits into his mouth. "I'm gonna get a beer," Jackson said as he swallowed. "Want one?"

"I'm sure our server..."

"Bar's right there. I'll get you something."

Without waiting, Jackson jumped up and crossed to the bar. He had a feeling that very soon he'd have to have another difficult conversation with his brother but not tonight. Tonight he was going to pretend this was a vacation.

Jackson leaned onto the solid oak bar and waited for the portly bartender. He wasn't a tall man but decidedly thickset. His red hair and beard exploded together into one large mane. The bartender smiled at him and asked him something in Verlorlandish.

"Sorry, I only speak English," Jackson replied.

"Of course," the man said in a disapproving tone. The smile dropped. "Don't often get Americans here."

"I heard this is the best pub on this island."

"In all the islands," the man corrected. "You came all this way for a pub?"

Jackson shook his head, "Following a dead end most likely."

The man cocked an eyebrow. "I don't get that one."

"Never mind." Jackson took in a breath to give himself time to think. He'd started off wrong, and he never wanted to be on the wrong foot with a bartender. He looked over the beer tap handles. They were simple. Jackson didn't recognize any of the names. There was a good chance they were from the islands. Maybe even local to Alku. "So what's your best beer?"

"Can there be a best beer?"

"I guess that's almost worse than asking who's your favorite child."

"That question I could answer for you," the man said with a small chuckle.

Jackson relaxed. That was a better start. "Fair enough. What should I start with?"

The man contemplated the question a moment and looked down the row. Finally, he answered. "Ledtrådssen Rauchbier. Named after Elias Ledtrådssen. And just like good ol' Elias it's got a strong kick and tastes like smoke."

"Elias tasted like smoke?"

"Ah, that might not translate. He burnt to death so..." the bartender shrugged. "It's something they say his wife, Vera, used to say."

"I do like rauchbier," Jackson said carefully not wanting to travel down that road any further.

"Really now?" The man asked. "I took you for an IPA type of fella."

"I can get overpriced Christmas tree swill back home."

The bartender let out a genuine, hearty laugh. "Use hops with restraint, and they won't steer you wrong. That's what my grandfather used to say."

"Sounds like a wise man. I'll take two of the rauchbiers."

The red-bearded man snatched up two steins and began filling them while Jackson looked over the liquors stacked behind him. His eyes kept on moving until they fell on a large wood panel hanging near the bar. Rectangular golden plaques hung at regular intervals from top to bottom. What looked like thin gold threads or wires connected the plaques together in a chaotic but purposeful manner.

"You like that?" The bartender said, dropping the first stein down and filling the second. "That there has ended more than one star-crossed romance."

"What is it?"

"That's Alku's family tree. Started by Elias himself. Starts with the founding families, at least as far back as Elias could find records, and traces down through all the generations. See, there's me down there by the three knots clustered together."

Jackson leaned forward to get a better view allowing him to see names etched on the plaque: *Otto Eliasssen*. "That's everyone in Alku?"

"Everyone ever born or died in the last two hundred years, give or take a decade or two. Not sure why Elias started it, but we keep it up to help avoid... well... when you live somewhere as small and old as Alku, you're related to more of the village than you're not. It's good to be safe."

Jackson wasn't sure if he was impressed or appalled. But then again, if it kept someone from marrying their cousin then perhaps it was worth it. Still, it only made him more sure he could never live somewhere like Alku.

Once he had both beers in hand, Jackson started back to the table. The chauffeur was back, he leaned over Henry, speaking to him quickly. He had Henry's full attention - no easy feat. As Jackson neared the table, the chauffeur stood and headed for the front doors. Henry pulled out his wallet and started counting out some of the strange bills.

"What's going on?" Jackson asked, sitting the beer in front of Henry.

"No time to drink," Henry said looking up. An excited grin filled his face. "There's been another murder."

Jackson frowned. "Okay, the smile. Stop it with the smiling."

"Yes, sorry."

"So we're going back to that house?"

"Yes."

Jackson gave a defeated nod then kicked back his glass. He didn't stop until the entire beer was gone.

"I'm not sure that's professional," Henry said.

"I'm on vacation," he replied.

Jackson set the empty glass down and picked up the second glass. He downed it too. It took longer this time. Henry eyed him disapprovingly. Once it was gone, Jackson took in a deep breath.

"Alright. Let's go."

Reluctantly, Jackson followed Henry toward the door. The bartender hadn't lied, the beer did have a strong kick. Jackson could already feel that. It was also damn good. Maybe they could stop in again on the way back through.

"He looks dead."

"That is why we're here."

"Should I fetch the ambulance?"

Chief Inspector Klar turned one eyebrow up at her generically good-looking constable.

"Is that a no then?" the constable asked.

"Sham, what do you think would happen to the scene if we drove an entire ambulance back here?"

"It'd be trod on a bit."

"A bit? More than a bit."

"Then how should we move him?"

"You think maybe we should investigate first?"

Sham studied her a moment before talking carefully. "He's sort of old. Maybe a heart attack. The other one was."

"Heart failure isn't a thing you catch." Chief Inspector Klar turned her grey eyes back on the matter at hand and brushed her ratty not quite blond hair aside. As Chief Inspector, her jurisdiction was the entire Verlorland Islands. The job took her out of Erfundenborg often but rarely to this little corner of the islands. Alku was a quiet place with very little crime compared to many of the other islands but two deaths on one estate in less than a week, that was something Klar needed to see for herself.

It was dark behind the main house. The body was only visible by the light Sham held, but it was enough. She recognized the man immediately. The thick black mustache and distinctive tattoos were dead giveaways.

"Gardener dead in the garden. What are the odds, right?" Sham said.

"I'd say seeing as how he worked in the gardens, very high."

"I suppose so," Sham admitted.

The body lay in the well-trimmed grass, partially concealed in a hedge. There were no visible signs of blood or any other wounds. It could have been a heart attack. Maybe a stroke.

Lights flickered behind them. Hopefully, it was Oas with a flood light or at least something higher powered than Sham's pocket torch.

"Sham, once they get here with more light go tell Vin to get a gurney over here. This shouldn't take too long."

As the men with the lights crossed the lawn, Klar crouched down by the body. She'd been settling in to watch Netflix with Thuert when the call had come in. Another death at the Henbit Estate. A dead gardener wasn't something that generally required the Chief Inspector, but the heir of the Henbit Estate would be the owner of an entire goddamn island. Inside the World's Toughest Prisons would have to wait.

More light illuminated the body. It wasn't as much as Klar would like, but it would do.

"Laki Ünwichtigbock is fetching some work lights," Oas' voice came from behind her. "I apologize for the delay. He was previously engaged."

"Thank you," Klar replied. "Tell me. Did.. uh... Mr...."

"Razek."

"Did Mr. Razek make a habit of walking the gardens at night?"

"Only when he was upset. Or annoyed. Or generally in a poor mood."

"How often was that?"

"Often."

"It does appear this is where he died." It was a new voice - possibly British - that Klar didn't recognize. Maybe one of the staff. One that thought they were helpful.

"It wouldn't be easy to move someone his size."

"Yes," the voice said. "But I meant because of the state of the shrubbery."

Klar cocked an eyebrow and turned enough to see those behind her. They were shrouded in darkness, and the lights blinded her further. Klar held up a hand to shade her eyes, getting a decent view of her new companions. Other than Oas and the greasy footman she'd seen before, there were two more men. The taller one wore a disheveled suit and had a strange squint in one eye. The shorter and heavier of the two looked to be dressed for the beach.

"State of the shrubbery?" Klar asked.

"Yes," the taller man said. He pointed at the bushes above the body. "Look at how the greater part of the shrub is sculpted meticulously but here," the man pointed to the part above the body. "The branches are exposed and of course the leaves and twigs around him there and there. He fell through the bush as opposed to being placed under it."

Klar looked at the man a moment longer before turning to Oas. "Who is this?"

"This, unfortunately, is Detective Henry Pets. He is a private detective."

Detective Pets stuck out one hand toward her. Klar frowned. More. She didn't take his hand.

"And he is here because...?"

"At the request of Ms. Lydia Marigolds."

Klar sighed and stood. Generally speaking, law enforcement on the Verlorland Islands was simple. There was one police force for all the islands. But Verlorland's liberal recognition of private detectives had a tendency to needlessly complicate matters.

Reluctantly Chief Inspector Klar took Mr. Pets hand and shook. "Pleased to meet you."

"And you. This is my colleague, Dr. Jackson." Mr. Pets indicated the young man in short pants and bare arms.

"What sort of doctor?" Klar asked.

"There does not seem to be any indication of blunt force trauma," Henry added quickly, stepping past Klar.

Klar quickly moved back to the body. "No."

Mr. Pets crouched down next to the body. He didn't make an immediate move to try and touch it, but Klar readied herself to knock him down if he did. His eyes darted around, seeming to take in everything at once. They settled on the man's left arm. Slowly he leaned forward, squinting. After a few seconds, he fished a pen from his pocket and pointed it at the sleeve near the crock of the arm.

"There. Blood spot. That wasn't there when I questioned him."

"Questioned him?" Klar said as she leaned in to see the indicated spot.

"Mr. Pets is investigating Ms. Laundra Henbit's death."

Klar turned on Mr. Pets, not sure if she was confused or angry. "Why would that need investigating?"

"There were lingering questions," Mr. Pets started.

For a moment, Klar thought about diving into that idiocy, but there was a body to deal with. She'd have to worry about the *lingering questions* later.

"Do you have another pair of gloves?" Mr. Pets asked.

Klar gave him a dead stare. "I can manage," she said. Carefully, she reached for the sleeve and pulled it above the crook of his arm. There was more blood there, seeping from a fresh puncture between a tattoo of a cobra and a circle encased in a triangle bisected by a single line. The scars around it were instantly recognizable.

"Ah," Mr. Pets sounded almost disappointed. "We should search his room."

"Should we?" Klar said in a stilted pitch.

Henry didn't seem to notice. "Yes. I don't see any paraphernalia around the body so I'd assume he injected elsewhere and then came into the garden."

"Mr. Pets, as helpful as your insights are," Klar layered the sarcasm on a bit heavier, hoping the detective would finally catch it. "I believe I know what to look for. Sham!"

Sham shouted back at her and Klar gave him a few quick instructions, this time speaking in Verlorlandish. It was merely instructions to photograph the body and move it to the ambulance, but she did not want to give Mr. Pets any more chance to have an opinion. He had seen the blood spot quickly - yes - but she would have found it soon enough.

As Sham got to work, Klar approached Oas. "Were you aware of Mr. Razek's-"

"Yes," Oas cut in. "For some time."

"We will do some tests to make sure, but I think it's safe to make a few assumptions here. I would like to see his rooms though."

"Ramses resided in the guest house," Oas said. He pointed out away from the main house. There was nothing but a thick grove of trees visible in the direction he indicated. "I have a key."

"Good," Klar held out a hand. "I can take that. I'm sure you need to be showing the good detective out."

"I would like to see-" Mr. Pets started.

"As far as I've been told," Klar started, turning to face Mr. Pets. "You've been hired to investigate the death of Laundra Henbit, not Ramses. So while I am legally obligated to let you do what you do in that case - for now - there is no reason to believe this death has any connection to the other. So until Miss Marigolds hires you to investigate Mr. Razek's death, I'd appreciate it if you would bugger off."

The second limousine ride home was quieter than the first. Henry was lost in thought, and Jackson was just dead tired. He wasn't even sure how long he'd been in the Verlorland Islands at this point. As the chauffeur let them out in front of Henry's flat, Jackson groaned.

"What?" Henry asked as the limousine screeched away down the dark street.

"I meant to find a hotel," Jackson said, pulling out his phone.

"You don't need a hotel," Henry said with a frown.

"Dude, you have one bed in one room," Jackson said. "And you share a bathroom."

"I think I've mentioned that isn't unusual-"

"I don't care if it's not unusual. I've already seen too much of your neighbors, and they have seen too much of me. I don't need to stay here another night."

"I see," Henry said. "There is a hostel-"

"No, not a hostel. I want my own room. I want my own bathroom."

"We can ask Agent Orange if he knows of any," Henry said, moving to the front door.

"No," Jackson said pulling out his phone. "I got it. We don't need to ask your neighbors." Jackson put his attention on his phone, hoping Google would find him something that wouldn't end up being a murder hostel.

"I suppose it's for the best," Henry said into the silence. "I do need to do some research."

"Research?" Jackson asked absently.

"For the case."

Jackson looked up. He searched for a trace of irony on Henry's face but came up empty. "You're not serious. Right?"

"I'd prefer to have the will first, but I can start looking into the family. Maybe there's an old relative of Reginald Henbit that's in play. Or an ex-lover. I doubt either, but it would be good to eliminate the possibility."

"Henry," Jackson shook his head. "There isn't a case. A morbidly obese woman had a heart attack and a struggling addict overdosed. Both are tragic, but neither one is a murder."

"That we know of."

"Dude-"

"Don't call me dude."

"What is your problem with Dude? It's something I say."

"You're not from California."

"What does that have to do with..." Jackson waved the argument off. It wasn't worth the fight. "You're leading that poor girl on."

"I am not!" Henry said defensively.

"You're feeding her delusion that her aunt was murdered."

"Oh, that. I thought you meant..." Henry let the thought hang. "If Laundra Henbit died of natural causes, then that is what I will find. Then Miss Marigolds can have complete peace of mind."

Jackson shook his head, he didn't agree, but when said that way, it didn't sound quite as shady. "Fine, do what you need to do." Jackson looked back at his phone. There was one hotel only three blocks from Henry's flat. "Hotel Skugga."

"Oh no. Not that one."

Jackson eyed Henry. He shook his head emphatically. Jackson scrolled on. "The Candlestick. That doesn't even sound like a hotel. It has four stars, but no one's bothered to write a review."

"I haven't heard of it."

"Is that good or bad?"

"Good."

"Fine, I'll get my backpack and head that way."

They didn't speak as they walked up the stairs. As Henry fumbled for his keys, the door to "G" swung open. Jackson forced himself not to turn around.

"Exciting day, yeah?" Agent Orange's voice boomed behind them.

Henry turned without unlocking the door. Jackson considered taking the key from him but decided that wouldn't go over well. He turned to the other apartment. Agent Orange leaned in his doorway wearing all but the head of what had to be an animal costume of some sort.

"Yes, a murder. I can't go into details but-"

"A murder? On Alku?"

Jackson raised an eyebrow. "I don't think we said where we went."

Agent Orange laughed the comment off as if it was meant to be a joke. "I think I'd of heard of a murder out there."

"It is very exciting," Henry said.

"Henry," Jackson nearly barked.

"Sorry, tragic."

"Can you open the door," Jackson said. "I just need my backpack."

"Leaving already? We haven't even had yous for dinner yet."

While Jackson weighed the strange syntax of the last comment, Henry told Agent Orange about the hotel and before Jackson knew what was happening he was being informed the secret agents would give him a ride. Despite a few emphatic protests, Jackson soon found himself in the back seat of a small orange car that looked something like worst parts of a Volkswagen Beetle and a Nissan Cube mixed together. He shared his seat with the dog head part of Agent Orange's costume. The agent himself drove with Peaches seated next to him dressed as a nun. Jackson didn't ask why. There was no way he wanted to know the answer. He did wonder if the color of the car had any connection to the man's chosen name. He wouldn't even consider the possibility that Orange was his real name.

"Your brother," Agent Orange said, breaking the silence. "The bloke tries hard."

"What?" Jackson asked reluctantly. He didn't want to encourage conversation, but the car was far too small to ignore it.

"He's giving it a good go 'ere. Done some good things for some people."

"For their pets?"

Orange shrugged. "Mostly pets. Yeah. But he's reunited some very happy owners with their fur babies. That might not of happened without him."

"He could have found missing pets in Portland."

"Yeah, and he'd be living under your shadow, right?"

"My shadow?" Jackson cocked an eyebrow. "You do know he's the older brother?"

"Huh," Orange gave Jackson a quick once over in the mirror. "Way he talked, always assumed he was the youngest. Here it is."

Orange slammed on the brakes, and the orange machine skidded to a stop. Jackson quickly thanked the agents for the ride, giving Peaches a quick uncomfortable smile then headed for the hotel. It looked surprisingly normal. Flat fronted white buildings lined both sides of the narrow street. One - slightly wider than the others - was trimmed in gold. An ornately gilded sign hung over the door reading *The Candlestick*. Jackson wondered why it had an English name.

A pleasantly plump woman greeted him inside and shortly after he was making his way down the second-floor hallway to his room. He checked the time. It was nearly ten. He tried to do the math, but the best he could come up with was it was sometime after lunch in Portland. He knew he should call his dad to check in, but after the day he'd had, Jackson couldn't muster up the energy. He let himself into his room. It was on the small side and only contained one wooden high backed chair and a bed that looked maybe large enough to be called a double. An oversized fur blanket draped the bed. At the moment, it was the most inviting thing Jackson could have laid eyes on. He kicked off his sandals and fell into the soft fur.

Tomorrow. Tomorrow he'd deal with his brother. After breakfast. No. He'd need to call their dad first. Tell him everything. Damn it. He looked at his phone again. 10:01. If he didn't call his dad now, he'd have to wait until afternoon. Finally, he accepted the conversation would have to be tonight. But first, he wanted a real shower.

Jackson looked around the room again. There was one closet and then another small door. He pulled himself up, crossed the short distance and opened the door. The room inside was painted all white. There was a toilet, sink and clawfoot bathtub. And on the far wall, another door. Jackson stared at the second door in disbelief.

"Where the hell am I?"

CHAPTER 7

Jackson's phone buzzed, jolting him from his sleep. He stuck his arm out from under the warm fur blanket and blindly flung his arm around until it found his phone.

He'd been up well into the night arguing with his father. Jackson had hung up once and his dad twice. His dad had a harsh voice and quick temper. Jackson usually managed to get along with him well enough but not when Henry was involved. Henry may have been his first son, but they'd never seen eye to eye on a single thought. It had only grown worse over time. The phone call started in an argument and ended in an argument. His dad hadn't even bothered to ask how Henry was doing before jumping right into the issue at hand.

"Is he making a fool of himself?"

"He's working."

"He thinks he's a PI. That's not work. What kind of clients does he get? If that's what they're called. Clients? Or... gigs?"

"They call them private detectives here."

"Stop splitting hairs. What does he actually do?"

Jackson had let the phone slip from his hand for a second and mouthed a few obscenities at the ceiling. His dad was asking the question again when he put the phone back to his ear.

"I still don't like this. I'm not Henry's handler."

"I don't even know what that means."

"Spy thing."

"You're not spying on Henry. You're looking out for him. It's what a big brother should do."

"He's the big brother."

His dad had laughed at this. One strong low "HA." That would serve as his defense of his statement. "It has to be you, Jackson. If I'd sent Chad, he'd already be up to his ears in hookers and opium."

"Opium?"

"It's what they do in Europe. You're evading, Jackson. What the hell is Henry doing out there?"

After that, Jackson finally gave in and told him about the pet problem and the dead-end case with the overweight woman's heart attack. One of the hang-ups happened in the middle of that story. In the end, Jackson finally agreed he'd give Henry the ultimatum. Somehow he was always the one to give bad news. On the upside, the argument had kept him awake long enough he forgot to worry about the shared bathroom. If there was an occupant in the adjacent room, he or she didn't bother Jackson, and he was finally able to wash the day off him and fall into a deep, dreamless sleep. A sleep that was ended by the buzzing phone far too quickly.

Jackson forced his eyes open and looked at his phone. It was Henry.

"Hello?"

"Good, you're awake. I'm outside."

"Outside? The hotel?"

"No, your room."

Jackson looked up at the door. He groaned a bit and pulled himself out of bed. He stumbled to the door. He opened it. Henry stood on the other side, phone in hand. He looked disheveled but was once again dressed in a suit.

"Why didn't you knock?" Jackson asked.

Henry blinked at Jackson then quickly pushed him into the room and shut the door behind them. "Good grief, Jackson. Put clothes on before you open the door. You're a grown man, not a teenager."

"My luggage is still missing," Jackson said, gritting his teeth to keep from saying more.

Henry looked around the room. "It's nice."

"It shares the bathroom with the next room over."

"I told you that was very normal here."

"That should be normal nowhere. Why are you here? What time is it?"

"9:53. We're late. Get dressed." Henry cast about until he saw Jackson's backpack. He opened it. "Where are you clothes?"

"In my suitcase," Jackson said, grabbing the bag from Henry.

"You don't have it yet?"

"I called them last night. Apparently it's in Sydney now."

"That's unfortunate."

Henry's own clothes were as wrinkled as ever and his shoes were two different shades of black. "Your shoes don't even match."

Henry blushed. "Yes, I seem to have misplaced the other shoe."

"Then wear both of the other shoe."

"Yes," Henry said slowly. "I see how that would have been better. But that's not important. Hurry up."

"What are we late for?"

"We're needed at Hell's Mouth as soon as possible."

Jackson grabbed his shorts from the floor by the bed and pulled them on. "Hell's Mouth? That better be a pub."

"No," Henry scoffed. "It's what we call the Erfundenborg police headquarters. It's a long story."

"Maybe you could have started with that. Are you in trouble?"

"No, now get dressed," Henry said snatching the Ruck River Rafting tank top from the floor. He sniffed it.

Jackson snatched it away from Henry. It stank of sweat and vodka. He needed new clothes.

"Chief Inspector Klar is unfortunately under the impression we work as a team, so we are both needed. I should have brought you different clothes."

"I'll buy something," Jackson said.

"Not enough time," Henry said. "We're late."

With no other options, Jackson donned the dirty tank top and found his sandals. He followed Henry outside and a brief cab ride later, they stood in front of a large looming dark gray building. The front doors were Gothic style and stretched two stories high. Panes of bright orange glass shone out with eerie light. Jackson could instantly see where Hell's Mouth got its name. It was both sinister and intriguing.

The young constable from the previous night greeted them and quickly led them through the labyrinth inside. Jackson was a bit surprised by the lack of basic security anywhere in the building. No metal detectors. All the doors hung open. Jackson was sure he could have wondered the halls himself without anyone stopping him.

Sham stopped at the first closed door Jackson had seen and knocked. A female voice clipped out a response, and Sham spoke loudly back to her. The only words Jackson could pick out were their names. The woman gave what sounded like an affirmative response, and the constable opened the door. He ushered the brothers in and shut the door behind them.

A bank of orange colored windows dominated the room. Jackson wondered who thought that was a good idea. The light it cast clashed with the overhead fluorescents, bathing the Chief Inspector in strange contrasting shades or orange and off-green. She sat on an overstuffed chair, feet up on an ottoman. There was no desk. Only a coffee table between her and a very comfortable looking floral couch. She motioned for the two to sit. Jackson quickly followed the request. He sunk awkwardly deep into the couch cushions. Henry sat beside him, and Jackson had to force himself not to tilt toward his brother as their weight bowed the couch.

Klar turned her attention to a tablet she held in her lap. She flicked her finger over the screen. "Your permit is up to date."

"As I said, everything should be in order."

"Apparently so. You can drop the accent."

"Accent?" Henry floundered.

"I have your permit right here. Do I need to read you your nationality?"

"No, that's not necessary." Henry let the stilted British-ish accent drop.

"I don't care how you present yourself but in here, don't try to pull anything over on me. Understood?"

"Yes."

"And you," she pointed at Jackson. "Are a doctor of...?"

"He's a rafting guide," Henry said.

"I'm a businessman. I'm just here visiting my brother."

Klar frowned at Jackson then at Henry then once more at Jackson. It wasn't an aggressively mean frown, more condescending. "You don't look alike."

"We're both allergic to pears," Henry offered.

Klar eyed Henry a moment with half a confused expression then dropped her attention back to her tablet. She tapped the screen a few times. "Do you understand the importance of the Henbit Estate?"

"I believe I do," Henry said.

"It's not just Alku," she said, moving her eyes up to him. "The Henbit Estate owns property on almost every one of the Verlorland Islands. Whoever has control of the Henbit Estate has a considerable grip on the entire country."

"That is why-"

"I'm not finished," Klar said firmly. She took her feet off the ottoman and leaned forward. "If there was foul play involved in Laundra Henbit's death, that puts me in a very precarious position. There will be considerable pressure to influence the outcome from too many sides to name."

"You can't cover up a murder because it's inconvenient."

"I'm not going to cover up a murder," Klar barked. Her eyes flashed. "Laundra Henbit's death was not unexpected, and it did appear to be natural causes at work."

Henry brightened. "Did?"

Klar sighed. She handed the tablet to Henry. "I'm ruling Ramses Razek's death suspicious. I still contend that Mrs. Henbit's death seems to be natural causes but Mr. Razek's death does cast a different light on Mrs. Henbit's passing."

Henry pulled himself up from the depth of the couch and squared his attention on the screen in his hands. His eyes darted over it then stopped. "Rat poison?"

"Yes. Not trace amounts either. It was mostly rat poison."

Jackson perked up. "Wait, you'd already done toxicology on him? Overnight? That seems a little too quick."

"Are rafting guides experts in toxicology?" Klar asked.

"I'm not a rafting guide."

Klar nodded dismissively. "It will be a few weeks before we can have those results but there was more heroin in his rooms. And that... well, it would have killed anyone who used it. It's enough to be concerned. Once the rest of the tests are in, we will know for sure. For now, it's enough to take a second look at Laundra Henbit's death as well. There's been a murder at the Henbit Estate. We can't risk overlooking a possible second murder."

"First," Henry corrected. "Mrs. Henbit's would be the first. Ramses' would be the second."

"Don't correct me," Klar scowled.

"Sorry."

"Lydia Marigolds has hired you as her own private detective on her aunt's death. I'm assuming she will expand that to include Mr. Razek's as well so I'm having this conversation with you preemptively. Once she officially expands your capacity I will be obligated to allow you to do your job."

"Thank you."

"Don't thank me. If it was up to me..." she shook her head. "It's not, so that doesn't matter. Just don't make a mess of this, okay? These islands are my home, and this case could make living here much more difficult for a lot of people. So, do you have a tablet or a notebook with you?"

Henry frowned. He pulled out a small pad of paper from his jacket. "Will this do?"

"No, it won't do. I can't put files on that."

"Oh, files. I could give you my email?"

"I can't email you sensitive files. Go get a tablet or something and bring it back. Kirahvissen will set you up with everything case related you're entitled to. Have a good day."

"Just one question," Henry said. "Regarding the legality of the dog inheriting the estate. Is it... well, legal?"

"Technically the trust will own it all. It will be the trust's responsibility to care for the dog."

"And who will run the trust?"

"They haven't figured that out yet."

"That seems important."

"It is. That is one of the reasons I would appreciate it if you left me to my work."

Henry walked briskly out of Hell's Mouth. Jackson could tell his mind was dancing through a few hundred thoughts at once. A few random words leaked out here and there but not enough to follow his runaway train of thought. As they hit the sidewalk, he turned on Jackson.

"I should buy a tablet. That would look good, right? Better than a laptop. Yes. Where should I get one?" The British had come back into his voice without warning.

"Slow down..."

"We should head to the manor as soon as possible. I'd like to see the guest house. Yes! There's a stationery store on Moro. We can walk there. I'm sure they'll have a good tablet."

"A stationary store?" Jackson balked, but Henry had already taken off. Jackson took a few quick steps to catch up. "Uh, there's one thing we should probably discuss before you make any large purchases."

"And that is?"

"Maybe don't."

"Jackson, the Chief Inspector is going to give me access to their records."

"You have a computer at home."

"It only works when it's plugged in and smells like grape jelly."

"Henry, just stop for a second."

"There is urgency at play in this. Murder and all. Who knows who's next? There is a killer on the loose!"

"Henry stop." Jackson's voice rung with a commanding force. Henry did stop. He turned to face his brother. The command leaked away as quickly as it had come. "The thing is, your card might not work."

Henry measured the comment and came up with nothing. "Excuse me?"

"Dad. He shut your account down."

"When?"

"Last night."

"Why?"

"I had to tell him what I'd seen. That's what I'm here for. I told you that."

"I am in the middle of the biggest case of my life and you-"

"At the time you were investigating a heart attack and a drug overdose. I didn't know it would actually be a murder!"

"Couldn't you have waited one day?"

"He called."

"You shouldn't have said anything."

"I wanted to get it out of the way."

Henry sighed and shook his head. "I'm not even mad. I'm just disappointed."

"Don't even use that on me," Jackson spat back. "Disappointed? Dad was going to just cut you off without warning. I had to convince him to let me come out here and try to make sense of what you're doing."

"If you're done," Henry said. "I need to get a cab since I have to go all the way home and get my mostly broken laptop." Henry turned to the red brick street and looked over the sparse traffic.

"If we go back to my hotel, I have an iPad there."

"This is serious casework. Confidential. I can't be putting things like that on my brother's electronic devices."

"Luckily I'm your doctor."

Henry didn't even look at Jackson. "No you aren't and how would that make any difference in this situation?"

"Come on. I'll give it to you."

"Would Dad-"

"Henry, damn it. Just take my damn iPad already and stop pouting. I'm sorry I told Dad you were a pet detective."

Henry waved down a cab as he did his best to hide a sniffle. "You didn't have to tell him that."

"Yeah, probably not. I'm sorry."

The bright pink cab stopped in front of them, and Henry climbed into the back. He looked back at Jackson. "Coming?"

"Do you want me to?" Jackson asked, leaning over the door.

"I can't very well get your tablet without you, can I? Besides, you could be useful if I need to punch or chase anyone."

Jackson nodded and climbed inside. Henry exchanged a few words with the driver, and the cab pulled out into traffic. They sat in silence so long Jackson couldn't bring himself to break it. He waited for Henry to make the first move.

"You smell like-" Henry started.

"I know."

"You told me you were coming out here to scout for a possible European headquarters for Ruck River Outfitters."

"That's what Dad told me to say. Thought you'd see through it."

"It didn't cross my mind to be suspicious of my own brother's intentions."

"Why would we put a European headquarters on an island?"

"It would be a shorter flight to Portland."

"And longer for everything else. No, that's going to be in Munich."

"Oh." The word rang with disappointment.

"What?"

"Nothing. I merely thought it would be nice having it here."

Jackson looked at Henry. His eyes were watching the road. There was genuine disappointment in them. "Yeah, I could see how it would be."

The dining room table had been sat with a late brunch. It was the least Oas could do. The atmosphere hanging over Henbit Estate was... Oas couldn't even think of the right word to describe it. Somber was a start but didn't hit half of the whole. There was palpable tension. Uncertainty. And a strange sense of dread.

Oas shook off the last thought and busied himself with refilling the maple syrup.

"You don't have to do that," Regal said from what was becoming his usual seat.

He shared the table with his mother-in-law, who sat as far from the chair Laundra had last occupied as possible. Oscar sat about midway between the two, slurping his cereal loudly and kicking at Dandy. The dog yipped back but no longer jingled. Someone had thankfully taken off the bells. Lydia had again declined to join them in the dinning room. Sloan had convinced her to join her for a round of badminton in the gardens instead. She'd balked at this as well, not wanting to be near where Mr. Razek had died. Laki and Pip, at Oas instruction, moved the net to the other side of the house and that eased Lydia's distress. Some exercise would be good for her. She'd hardly eaten a thing or left the house since Laundra's death. She'd even skipped her regular morning swims in the pool.

"He's doing his job," Caprice squawked from down the table. "Let him be."

"But with everything... is it still your job?" Regal asked probingly, eyeing Oas timidly.

"I have not been told it's not," Oas said.

"In that case, I'll have another mimosa," Caprice said raising an empty glass.

"That was orange juice."

"Was wondering why it tasted off. Well, fix that this time."

Oas nodded and lifted his wrist. He quickly tapped the change into his watch and sent it to the kitchen then waited. The confirmation didn't come immediately. Oas waited a long, painful five seconds. What was wrong?

"Excuse me."

Oas quickly exited toward the kitchen door.

Caprice chuckled to herself. "Service has suffered a bit, I'll say."

Regal fixed Caprice with a disapproving stare. Caprice rolled her eyes and picked at a particularly plump sausage.

Oas pushed through the kitchen door and entered the long curving hall to the kitchen. It was nearly identical in construction to the hallway leading to the conservatory wing as well as the ones leading to the staff apartments and the guest apartments. Windows lined both sides of the walls providing views of the gardens. There would have to be another gardener soon, or it would all fall apart, but Oas wasn't sure how that would work now that they ostensibly worked for a dog. Oas pushed on into the kitchen and looked around. Dishes and other sundries cluttered the counters and sink. The floors were strewn with food. But there was no cook in sight. Oas grunted and lifted his watch. He flipped to the employee badges and tapped, Cook.

"Miss Fischer."

He waited. Then waited slightly longer.

"Miss Fischer."

He waited one more time. Once again, he grunted with displeasure then tapped on Maid.

"Matilda."

There was a brief pause then the maid's voice squeaked back. It sounded hollow, as if distant. "Yes, Oas?"

"Where is Miss Fischer?"

"I believe she went for a walk."

"We are serving brunch."

"She said it was over."

"It is not over." Oas let a sharp breath out through his nostrils. "I'll be needing you presently then."

"I uh... I am in the shower."

"Finish that then come down."

"Does this mean we do still work here?"

"Of course we still work here. Good grief. Has everyone gone mad?"

Oas didn't wait for a response. He tapped the connection closed then hit Footman before remembering he'd sent Pip out to walk the dog. He hated to encourage the young man's affection for the creature but it was now their employer. It was in everyone's interest that it was healthy. Oas caught himself nearly tapping Gardener but stopped his hand. He felt a small pang somewhere near where maybe his heart was. He'd worked with Mr. Razek for a long time. A very long time. Oas pushed the feeling aside. Or tried. Before he could a shadow loomed over him. Oas spun around. The giant hulking form of Ari filled the space behind him.

"Are you wearing slippers? Make some noise. Shouldn't be hard for someone your size..." Oas trailed off. Ari's dark eyes were red and swollen. There was even still one tear hanging on near his chin. It was a strange sight. "You've been crying."

Ari wiped the tear from his face and cleared his throat. "I just thought I'd make some tea."

"There's tea in the dining room."

"That's for the family."

"No one seems to be concerned about decorum at the moment."

"I'd rather just be in here."

"Understood," Oas said with a nod. It was comforting to see someone else with a sense of decorum. "Carry on. I have a mimosa to-"

A quick trill from his watch stopped him mid-thought. He glanced down. It was a call. Not his personal line but the house. It was from Hell's Mouth.

"I must take this."

Oas moved past Ari's bulk and back into the hallway. He shut the door and tapped his watch. The conversation was short but informative. Oas hung up and found the nearest seat. It was a decorative bench beneath an ornate stained glass window. The bench wasn't really for sitting as much for looking nice, but Oas needed to sit. One word from Chief Inspector Klar hung over him heavier than the unmade mimosa... *murder.*

CHAPTER 8

Henbit Manor's guest house stood off from the main house in the middle of the orchard. The trees obscured the small cottage entirely until well into the orchard. Standing on the front step, it was easy to imagine there was no one else around for miles. It wasn't large, comfortable for one but cozy for two. To Jackson, it looked like something out of a Thomas Kinkade painting, minus the eerie orange glowing windows and lack of discernible light source.

Without using the lock, Oas opened the door and stepped aside.

"Is that always unlocked?" Henry asked.

"Ramses rarely locked the house, despite my insistence."

Henry thanked the butler and entered followed by Jackson and their new shadow, Constable Sham. The Chief Inspector had insisted on a police presence to ensure there was no contamination of the crime scene. As Sham was the only police presence on the entire island of Alku, the duty fell to him.

Henry scrutinized the living room while Jackson scrutinized Henry, Sham scrutinized them both and Oas stared blankly at nothing much. Henry was fascinating to watch. There was no discernible logic to how Henry took in his surroundings. There never had been. His eyes darted back and forth, and he turned often. He'd zero in on a small detail in the carpet then spin to look at the doorknob then take a few minutes to study the well-worn recliner. Much of the furniture seemed old, possibly antique. But Ramses had added his own touches. Along with the recliner, a TV hung on the wall and a few movie posters. Henry squinted at the TV closely. It was an LG at least fifty-five inches wide, possibly 4k, but Jackson couldn't think it was pertinent to the case. Next Henry turned to the movie posters. They were for movies Jackson had never seen before, possibly Egyptian films. He did recognize Stargate. There was also a small one of the Jungle Book and one from every Harry Potter film.

"He lived in here alone?" Henry asked, ducking into the next room. Sham quickly followed.

Oas gave a curt nod. "Ari Björnssen had a room he used when he wasn't needed in the house."

Henry stuck his head back into the living room. "How often was that?"

"In the last year, very seldom. Mrs. Henbit liked to keep her nurse nearby. She turned the adjoining nursery into the nurse's quarters. That room is quite small though, so he kept his room out here as well." Oas frowned harder than normal. "Although it is quite small too."

"And since Mrs. Henbit's death?"

"He was staying with his grandmother in Alku."

"Really?" Henry puzzled that over a moment. "Last night?"

"I convinced him to stay on the estate. Ms. Veratiri assured us any departure from the estate before the reading of the will would not count against us. Mr. Björnssen was insistent on leaving but I persuaded him to stay."

"In here or the main house?"

"He camped somewhere on the estate."

Henry raised an eyebrow.

"He enjoys the outdoors."

Henry nodded. "Where were the drugs found?"

"The bedroom," Sham said.

Sham led the brothers up a narrow staircase and out into an equally narrow hallway. He pushed the first door open. The room inside was not large but looked comfortable. Clothes and dishes were strewn around the room. Health and gardening magazines littered the floor. For furniture, there was only an unmade bed, one small chair, a bookshelf, a nightstand and a dresser. Every drawer hung open.

"It's trashed," Jackson said.

"Yes," Sham replied. "Wasn't us. It was like this."

"Do you think someone was looking for something?" Jackson asked.

"No," Henry said, eyes darting over every object strewn around them. "This mess grew over time. Look at the way the dust has settled and the depth of the creases in the clothing. I'd infer that Ramses was not a tidy man. The drugs?"

"There," Sham pointed to the bottom right dresser drawer. Like the others, it hung open.

"Was it open?" Henry asked picking his way to the dresser. The drawer above it was closed just enough to see the inside. It was empty. "Do you have a photo of this from before?"

"It was open, and yes we do. Should be with the rest."

"Jackson," Henry said, holding out a hand.

Jackson handed Henry his iPad. Henry snatched it without even looking at him. Whether that was because he was focused on the job or still upset about the tablet situation, Jackson wasn't sure. It was hard to tell with Henry. Somehow his brother was the hardest person for Jackson to read at times. Right now he could tell that Sham was both intimidated by Henry and annoyed he was stuck with this job. But Henry... whatever emotions he was feeling were obscured by his uncompromising focus.

"Why the guest house?" Henry asked suddenly.

"What?" Sham asked. "Why? I guess because he lived here. Where else would he have kept stuff?"

"No. Why did he live here?"

"Oh, I don't know."

"I was asking Oas."

"He's still downstairs," Sham replied.

"Right," Henry looked around. "Why?"

"I told him to stay in the living room. The Inspector only wanted the two of you to come upstairs."

Henry nodded and exited the room, stopping by the bookshelf for a moment. He made a knowing "hmm" then walked into the hall. Jackson looked over it himself as he followed. It mostly held gardening books but also had the full set of Harry Potter novels.

Henry took a quick glance into the two other rooms, one more bedroom and a bathroom, then went downstairs. The others followed.

"Why was the gardener given the guest house?" Henry asked once he was again in the same room as the butler.

"He has been with Mrs. Henbit for many years."

"So have you."

"It is necessary for me to be in the manor house itself."

"Wouldn't it be useful to have the guest house available for guests?"

"The guest apartment wing is ample space and offers better amenities."

"Who had a key?"

"Ramses. Mr. Björnssen. Myself. There is also a spare in storage. But as I said, the house is rarely locked."

"And if he did, anyone could get a key?"

"Yes."

"Then anyone could have been in here?"

"Yes."

Henry nodded. "His interest in Harry Potter. Know anything about that?"

"I assume he enjoys them."

"That's unhelpful. I'm done here. I'd like to speak with the family and staff."

"All of them?" Oas asked.

"Yes. All."

Oas locked the door, and the four men headed back into the orchard where they were greeted by Lydia Marigolds smiling face. It was a genuine smile, Jackson thought, but her eyes were red and swollen. She clutched a handkerchief in one hand.

"I'm so glad you're here," Miss Marigolds said. "This is so frightful. Did you find anything?"

"I'm afraid it would be inappropriate for me to tell you that," Henry said as they approached her.

Miss Marigolds blushed but quickly fell into step with Henry. "I couldn't sleep at all last night. First Aunt Laundra and now old Ramses." She whimpered. It was a soft sound but sudden enough to jerk Henry's attention back to her. "Who could do this?"

"That is what I intend to uncover."

"Thank you."

Henry gave Lydia a lopsided smile then realized the others were still there and let it drop. "I'd like to speak to all the members of the household."

"The staff?"

"And family. Everyone included in the will."

"Oas can gather them."

"Not together. One at a time."

"Of course," Miss Marigolds said. "You could use the study or drawing room. The conservatory is also available if you'd like a better view."

"The study would be fine."

As Miss Marigolds set to arranging that with Oas, Henry dropped back to Jackson and leaned close.

"I'd like to handle the questions one on one. It would be helpful if you can get me photos of everyone."

"You could take them with your phone when you talk to them."

Henry's brow wrinkled and his hands went to his pockets. He patted them then quickly searched his back pockets. Jackson chuckled and held a phone out in his hand.

"No, I need my phone."

"This is your phone. You left it in the cab."

"I see," he said, taking it from Jackson carefully. He mulled the idea over in his head for a few strides then shook it quickly. "No. I don't see that fitting."

"Your phone?"

"Taking photos. It would ruin the mood. It should be you taking them. See if you can get a copy of the will as well."

Before Jackson could ask how he was supposed to do that, Henry took three quick steps and fell back in stride with Miss Marigolds.

There was a buzzing in Jackson's pocket. He fished out his phone to see a photo of a square-headed man with gray hair and Henry's dingy brown eyes. The name read Randy Ruck. Jackson stuck the phone back in his pocket. His dad could wait. He needed to see if this case was really going somewhere before he talked to him again.

They entered by way of the saloon. Oas ushered Henry into a door on the right, leaving Jackson and Constable Sham with Miss Marigolds. She smiled at them weakly. She looked to be on the verge of tears again.

"Would you like some tea?" she asked.

"I could use tea," Sham said. Jackson agreed, mostly because he thought the young woman would burst into tears if she didn't stay busy. She again smiled weakly and excused herself to locate the maid. Jackson was left alone with the constable.

Sham turned around in circles in the room, looking over the expansive white curved wall, gold trimmed in ornate designs verging on gaudy. A few murals hung high above the four exits. Purple velvet upholstered chairs lined the walls. Sham headed for one and sat, eyes still examining the room. They now traveled up to the domed ceiling.

"What is this room for?" Sham asked.

"What?" Jackson asked. It was more reflexive than a request for an explanation. "I've never been in anything like this." Jackson hadn't. He'd been in large houses. They had large houses. But this was... something else. "I'd guess it's for walking through."

"A room just for walking through."

"Maybe cocktail parties. Or wine tastings. You could stand a lot of people in here. And there's art..." he looked up at the murals. They were vaguely pastoral but nothing memorable. They were dressing. "I don't know, dude. It's the backdoor. Maybe there's a coat closet."

Sham shook his head. "Mom always said this place was a waste of perfectly good farmland. She's not too happy that I'm spending time out here."

Jackson let a laugh slip. "It's not like you want to be here."

"This place isn't well liked in Alku. You've probably noticed they don't employ any locals, right? No one from Alku would ever work for the Henbits."

"The chauffeur?"

Sham made a sound something like a growl. "Erfundenborg is not Alku."

"He did say his cousin owned the pub."

"Laki's mother might have been born here but Laki was not. Erfundenborg is not Alku."

Jackson was about to dig deeper into that quagmire when voices echoed into the room. A moment later, Miss Marigolds returned followed by the maid. She held a tea tray which she brought over to them. With more grace than Jackson would have thought possible, she handed each of them a small china teacup.

"Is there somewhere less... uh..." Jackson looked around. "White... we could wait?"

As Oas led the chauffeur from the study, Henry leaned back in the brown leather chair and wondered one more time if this was the right way to proceed. Four interviews down and he had nothing of use. Not much at least. He had begun to piece together the events around each death - where people were, what they were doing, what they remembered and didn't remember or maybe chose to forget - but not much more. Perhaps it was the room. It was dark and smelled musky. He'd pulled two of the chairs around to face one another after trying to interview Oas from behind the desk. That had been worse.

The only useful information Henry pulled from Oas was a surprisingly specific description of the location of the staff during both incidents. Although that did little to narrow down the suspect list. This was poison. Both murders were the result of poison. The murderer didn't need to be near the victim.

The cook, Emma Fischer, knew very little of use. She was sure no one could have poisoned her food while it was in the kitchen. She tested every dish herself. Having only been on staff for four months, she knew less about either victim than anyone else. Although the maid, Matilda

Desrosiers, came close. She consistently deferred to Oas, who wasn't even in the room.

"Where were you when they discovered Ramses?"

"I'm not sure. 1 would need to check with Oas."

"Do you know who might wish Ramses harm?"

"I'm sure Oas would know. He is very observant."

After a few dozen answers along those lines, Henry dismissed the maid, and she was replaced by the footman, Pip.

"You discovered Mr. Razek's body, correct?"

"Yeah. Thought he was sleeping."

"In the bushes?"

"Yeah."

"Did he do that often?"

"No."

"Then why did you think he was sleeping?"

Pip shrugged. "Maybe he was sleepy."

Henry frowned. He couldn't tell if Pip was intentionally acting difficult or if he was merely dense. It could also be a language barrier. His accent was thick.

"What were you doing in the gardens?"

"Walking."

"For what purpose?"

"The dog. 1 walk the dog."

"1 see," Henry said. That was slightly more useful.

"Do you know why anyone might wish Ramses harm?"

"Someone that didn't like wogs."

Henry blinked once. Twice. "What?"

"Wogs. Like him. You know. Squints. Coconuts. Orientals. Not everyone likes them."

"Mr. Razek was Egyptian."

Pip shrugged. "Not everyone likes them either."

"Right. Yes. 1 think that would be all," Henry said quickly. "Oas," He called out loudly. "Next please."

Aside from that last interaction, so far everyone had been cooperative, but Henry wasn't even sure what he was pressing them for. He knew he'd know when he knew but didn't know how to ask for what he needed to know but didn't know yet. Henry shook his head. That wasn't right.

He had managed to glean from the staff that some members of the household knew of Ramses Razek's drug use, and some seemed to be ignorant. Other than that all he could say for sure was the footman was probably racist and the chauffeur didn't seem to know much of anything at all including half his coworkers' names. The latter chain smoked cloves, and the former had poor personal hygiene, but that wasn't helpful.

The door opened again, and Oas ushered the tall, ebony-skinned man in. Regal Okumu, Henry reminded himself. This was the first member of the family he'd interviewed. The thin man smiled politely and seated himself across from Henry. He was the most graceful man Henry had ever seen.

"Are you sure you do not want Sloan here as well?" Regal asked.

"Hm? Yes. I'm interviewing everyone individually."

"There is not much I can tell you, I would think. This was my first visit to the islands. I had never even met Mrs. Henbit."

"Or Ramses?"

"I had heard him spoken of. Caprice likes to reminisce. They've known each other for a long time."

Henry spun through his mind for his next question. What could this man possibly know that he needed to know? He was less informed than the chauffeur. What Henry needed to know was why Ramses had died that night. If Mrs. Henbit had been murdered, why wait that long to kill Ramses? Was it the will? If so who could have known about it ahead of time?

"The night Ramses died. Did you notice him interacting with anyone?"

"It was a strange night. Caprice was very upset which was upsetting Sloan."

"So your wife wasn't angry about the will?"

"Not particularly. We never expected to get anything from Mrs. Henbit. She wasn't close with her aunt like Lydia was. I don't think she had even seen her since she was a girl outside the yearly visit."

'Yearly visit?"

"Yes. Once a year her aunt would call Sloan telling her she'd bought her a ticket to come see her. She wouldn't ask. Just bought it. Sloan would go. She likes the islands well enough, and it was never more than a few days."

"That seems odd."

"It was."

"And you were never invited until this time?"

"Sometimes she would, but usually my work prohibited accepting the invitation. She was insistent we all be here this time though."

"And you had no work to get in the way?"

Regal grimaced at the question. "True."

"Why do you think that was?"

"Maybe the marketing. I think the director never had a good handle on the script either. It was a brilliant script. Garry is a genius. I think maybe we pushed too hard into the shared universe part. If we'd taken more time and let it grow organically..." he sighed. "I think it would have worked."

"I meant the insistence on you all coming this time."

"Right," Regal cleared his throat. "I guess she wanted to see everyone."

Henry nodded but kept his face neutral. That was interesting. He didn't know if it was pertinent yet, but it was not normal. However, he wanted to go back to the matter at hand.

"Regarding the will. What was Miss Marigold's reaction?"

Regal shrugged. "She has been in a state since Mrs. Henbit died. I cannot say the will effected her more than that."

Henry nodded. "And the staff?"

"I did not pay much mind to them. My concern was my wife." Regal shook his head apologetically. "That is all..." Regal cocked his head slightly. "Except maybe one thing. Ramses. I honestly never saw him much outside the gardens, but he seemed to be generally laid back. Friendly. He always gave a smile and nod when I'd pass him, often greeted me by name. He didn't that night. Didn't even seem to notice me. And he had some terse words with the solicitor. I couldn't hear, but that was unusual. I had never seen him so much as raise his voice other than that."

"How long did the argument last?" Henry asked, perking up.

"Not long. His nephew pulled him away. He took Ramses outside. Maybe to the guest house."

Henry thanked Regal and called for Oas. His mind spun. That had been surprisingly informative. The gardener had fought with the solicitor. Over what? And the nurse possibly had been the last one to see Ramses alive, if he had taken him to the guest house.

As the door shut, Henry realized he'd forgotten to ask Regal anything regarding the night of Mrs. Henbit's death. He'd have to return to that though because his next interviewee had arrived. The bulk of the nurse loomed over him. He wasn't a man you could easily miss, and Henry felt more than a little vulnerable alone with him. Ari took a position behind the chairs, leaning against the wall. Henry half expected the wall to break. It didn't, fortunately and he turned to gauging the man's expression, but there was no obvious emotion in it. The man had lost an uncle; it could be grief but it could also be guilt.

"Have a seat," Henry said, pointing to the chair.

"I'd rather stand," Ari said crossing his thick arms. "I break chairs, sometimes."

Henry nodded quickly. He doubted these chairs would break under the man's weight. They looked sturdy enough to hold an elephant but he felt an urge to not upset this man. That wouldn't do. There was a good chance much of what Henry needed to ask would upset him. Henry shook the feeling off.

"Ramses was your uncle, correct?"

"He is my uncle. Death doesn't change that."

Henry nodded again, giving himself a little time to examine the man. He was in a text book defensive position. If he were grieving, it would have to be in the state of denial. Yes. That made sense. He eyed Ari a moment longer. It annoyed him when people didn't show what they were feeling. What good was memorizing the psychology behind body language when people did their best to show anything other than what they were really feeling?

"You were the last one to see him alive, correct?"

"That I know of. He was upset after hearing the will. I took him back to his house and tried to calm him down."

"What exactly had upset him?"

"I don't know. Something about the will. It is messed up. Almost cruel. Not that I think Mrs. Henbit wanted it to be cruel. That wasn't her way. But she could be unintentionally cruel. She had a complicated relationship with emotions. So, yeah, the will upset my uncle. He just kept saying it wasn't right. We didn't talk long."

"But you calmed him down?"

"No. I eventually just left. He wasn't..." Ari trailed off. "Yeah. I was the last one to see him."

"Did your uncle have anyone that might wish him harm?"

"Yes."

"Oh," Henry sat up. He hadn't expected that. "Who?"

"My father. Most of his relatives. The florist in Alku. And I don't think Mrs. Marigolds liked him much."

"Caprice?"

"Yes. She wouldn't even look at him most of the time."

"That is informative but I meant someone who would wish him dead."

"People wish people dead all the time."

"But they don't act on it."

"Until they do."

That was less than helpful. Henry readjusted. "Were you aware of your uncle's drug use?"

Something flickered in Ari's dark eyes. He took in a sharp breath. "Six months ago I helped Uncle Ramses flush everything he had. As far as I knew he was still sober up to the night he died. I should have stayed with him. Shouldn't have left him like that." Ari took in another breath, slower and deeper than the first. Tears. There were tears in Ari's eyes. He quickly scratched them away with his thumb. "Raudur Sildsson. That's who you'll want to talk to."

"Who is he?"

"He lives on Erfundeneyja. That's who would have sold Uncle Ramses the stuff." Ari said the last word with disdain. He couldn't even bring himself to call it by name. "If my Uncle bought the shit, it came from Raudur. I think I can find an address."

Henry hastily took out the iPad. Part of him hoped this would be a dead end. It would be disappointing if this led back to a drug dealer. Then he'd be nowhere with Laundra Henbit. But Ari Björnssen had given him a way forward. And more than that, he was getting somewhere with the will. Ramses knew something about it. Things were looking up.

"One more thing," Henry asked suddenly on a whim. "Why did your uncle like Harry Potter so much?"

"What does that have to do with anything?"

"I don't know. That's why I'm asking."

Ari shook his head and muttered something Henry couldn't make out. "We'd watch them when I'd visit. Mom and Dad let me come see him a few days every year. We watched the first one together in the theater, and after that I'd always visit when the next one was coming out. Just something we did."

"You were close with your uncle?"

"He's the best man I know."

There was emotion there. Henry could see it for a brief moment before the colossal man tucked it away. The memories Ramses had with his nephew had to have been important to him. He decorated his house with reminders, even after his nephew had come to live with him. He'd inked them into his very skin. Henry decided to push a little further.

"Even after all these years, he still has the posters up."

"They're good movies."

"The tattoos-"

"He liked the movies."

"Yes, but he seems an unlikely man to be so..." Henry looked for the right word, didn't find it so went ahead with the wrong one. "Obsessed."

"You shouldn't make assumptions from appearances."

"True. Still, could you make a guess as to what about Harry Potter specifically appealed to him?"

"I have no idea," Ari said. "And yes, he talked about them way too often. Ever since I can remember. He loved them mostly but..." Ari laughed. "It always bugged him that the old wizard left Harry with his Aunt and Uncle. Said it wasn't fair. Maybe that's..." the smile left Ari's face. All joy of the memory vanished replaced by a deep sorrow. "Can I go?" Ari choked.

"Yes. I think that's all."

The large man left the room, Henry thought he could hear him sobbing outside.

Jackson looked back at the list of names he'd been given. Last one. Emma Fischer. He turned back to his phone and tapped in the name into Facebook. He was pretty sure this wasn't what Henry had meant for him to do but it seemed more efficient than waiting outside the study and snapping photos of everyone. And he was getting a fascinating look into the lives of the staff and family. Not always helpful. Sometimes disturbing, such as the footman, Pip. It was mostly memes which seemed to be vaguely racist. He'd had little luck translating them from Swedish though.

Caprice Marigolds and Regal Okumu had been the most interesting. Caprice had little on facebook but her Instagram more than made up for it. It was a barrage of of high angle selfies and photos of cocktails, often backed up by pristine beaches. Regal's facebook featured heavy promotion of his film, OZ Corps. Jackson thought he'd heard of the movie before. Maybe he'd seen it on a Red Box. From what he'd heard, it was horrible in almost every possible way. The press images did nothing to persuade him otherwise.

There were far too many Emma Fischers listed. Jackson settled back into the overstuffed chair and flipped through.

Miss Marigolds had taken Jackson and Sham to the billiard room. It filled the space between the dining room and the library. The entire room was arranged around the billiard table, but for once the seating was designed for comfort, and there was even a seventy-two inch TV hanging over the hearth. While Jackson went to work cyber stalking the family and staff, Sham had settled into watching a strange sport that looked like basketball without dribbling and goals instead of baskets.

No profile image looked like the cook, so he started clicking on the profiles that had a cat or inspirational messages for the picture. Finally, he had it narrowed to two. Both lacked any identifying images or information.

He had no better luck with any other social media. He'd have to get a photo of her himself.

Sham suddenly shot up and yelled something in Verlorlandish at the TV. Jackson turned to the screen. The man pointed his finger and yelled a bit more. Jackson waited for him to fall back into his chair before speaking.

"What is that?" The game or match or whatever it was called took place on a large outdoor field. It was smaller than a football field and slightly rounded. Somewhere between thirty and forty players ran around bumping into one another dressed in what looked like wrestling singlets and mittens. Sometimes there was a tackle and occasionally a fist fight or wrestling match. There was a ball as well. The action seemed to mostly converge around it as people kicked, tossed and head-butted it up and down the field.

"This?" He pointed at the screen, dumbfounded. "The Land Sharks and Gillies."

"No, I mean the sport."

"Oh." Now Sham was completely taken off guard. "Slasspallo."

"What?"

"Slasspallo. It's our national sport, although water polo is, of course, popular here as well as I'm sure you know."

Jackson had no idea why that was something he should know, but he nodded anyway.

"This is a very important game. If the Gillies win then they..."

The door opened, and the blond maid entered meekly. "We are making some sandwiches for the family for late lunch. Would you like me to bring some in here?"

"How much longer is Detective Pets going to be?" Sham asked not exactly directing the question at the maid or Jackson. The maid only smiled apologetically. Jackson shrugged. "Yes then. I'll take sandwiches."

Jackson looked down at his phone. There wasn't much more to keep him busy here, and he didn't really feel like learning the intricacies of slasspallo. He jumped up. "I'll help you get them."

"I can-"

"It's no trouble," Jackson cut in before she could object. He quickly moved to the door and gently nudged her back through. Sham was already yelling at the TV by the time they were in the dining room.

The maid almost made another objection but blushed and instead headed for the door toward the kitchen wing. Jackson followed. They didn't meet anyone until they'd arrived in the kitchen itself.

They both heard Emma Fischer before they'd even exited the curved hallway.

"Tea and cold sandwiches are ready, but you'll have to come back for the paninis."

The maid pushed through the door with Jackson one step behind. The cook darted around back and forth over the black and white tiles from the stove range to the prepping station. Dandy followed her closely, occasionally jumping to his back feet, begging for food. Once or twice the cook obliged the dog and tossed him scraps of lunch meat. Near her, two large silver trays lay on the prepping station. One was set for tea, the other stacked high with the smallest sandwiches Jackson had ever seen.

"We need a small tray made for the guests."

"Guests?" The cook finally looked up and saw Jackson. "What's he doing here?"

"I can take the food for us," Jackson offered.

The maid pursed her lip, but a chime from her watch set her to moving again. She tapped the watch and made for the trays. "Thank you. I'll be back for the paninis." With that she snatched up both trays elegantly, spun and slipped out the door, they'd just come through.

Jackson turned from the flapping door and came face to face with Emma Fischer. She scowled at him.

"Matilda is an impressionable young thing. You remember that."

"What?" It was the only thing Jackson could think to say. He glanced back over his shoulder. "I wasn't-"

"Here," the cook said snatching up a plate and putting it in his hands. She turned back to the counter and in a few minutes had a decent stack of miniature sandwiches ready for him. "I'll send someone with tea."

"Thank you," Jackson said slowly.

The cook didn't respond, merely turned back to the range and flipped a few paninis.

Jackson milled over asking her to let him take a photo, but he had a distinct impression she was a woman that avoided having her picture taken. Instead, he brought up his phone and pointed it toward the cook. "Ms. Fischer. One more thing."

"Yes?" She turned, exasperated.

The phone clicked. "Thank you again," he said. Before she could protest or even react, Jackson was through the door. There was a yipping behind him, and for a moment he wondered if she was going to come after him. Jackson glanced back. It was only the dog. It bounded up and begged for more food. Jackson ignored it.

Jackson had all the photos Henry needed. That was done. He hoped he wouldn't have further need to interact with the cook. Voices ahead let him know there were people in the next room.

Dandy reached the far door before him and scratched furtively at it. Jackson pushed the door open, letting the dog through then followed into the dining room. Four people sat at the table: Oscar, Caprice, Sloan, and Regal. Only Regal looked up. He seemed a little surprised to see Jackson but said nothing. Jackson had to stifle a chuckle. Now that he had seen Regal as Professor Scarecrow, the image stuck. Dandy raced right for Oscar and sat down directly in front of him, mouth open, ears perked up. Oscar kicked weakly at him but didn't connect.

Caprice - whose back was to Jackson - was the one speaking.

"I don't see why they need to ask us anything. I'm sure there's a reasonable explanation for all this."

"For murder?" Sloan asked, dryly.

"They say it's murder," Caprice waved the thought off.

"Yes. The police say it's murder."

"Police of what? A few little islands?" Caprice broke into laughter. "And that god awful private detective."

"Mother," Sloan hissed, eyeing Jackson.

"He's quite the piece of work, isn't he? Looks like he just crawled out of a hamper, too. Oh, Lydia. Lydia. So..." Caprice trailed off and stared into her drink. "What's the word that means easily caught up in... oh, I don't know. She's that. Whatever that is. Now that doctor though..."

"Mother," Sloan hissed again.

"I could find a good use for him." Caprice made a yummy sound. "Just want to pinch him. Admittedly he could use a shower but there's something about a man with a powerful musk to him."

"Mother!"

Jackson quickly took the last few steps toward the billiard room and pushed his way inside. His final look into the room landed on Oscar. The man was looking at him, amused. And... not at all vacant. The door slammed behind him, cutting off the image. Sham looked up from the TV.

"We're in overtime!" Sham said excitedly.

"Great. Sandwich?"

CHAPTER 9

"Am I taking you to Hell's Mouth or somewhere else?" Sham asked as Henry and Jackson made their way down the front steps.

Henry hardly heard the question. He was lost in thought in the back seat. Jackson gave the constable instructions as they climbed in, and the car began moving away from Henbit Manor. Miss Marigolds waved goodbye from the front entry. Henry nodded and gave her what he thought was a polite but professional wave in return.

The final interviews had not been as helpful as Ari Björnssen and Regal Okumu's had been. Sloan Okumu had less to say than anyone else. She'd spent the evening after the reading of the will working out in the gymnasium. It was located in the basement. That was new information to Henry. Henry hadn't even been aware there was a basement. It hadn't been in any of the Flickr photos. She also had little useful information about the night of Mrs. Henbit's death. Still, all said and done he felt he had a good handle on everyone's movements for the time around both deaths.

Caprice Marigolds hadn't stopped talking. It had been a task to get in any questions. Most of her babble revolved around assurances that no one would ever want to harm her sister or the poor gardener. She did provide a few "colorful" anecdotes about Ramses' time on digs with them in Egypt "years and years ago." She didn't clam up until he asked about the will. She showed textbook signs of agitation which Henry felt very proud of noticing despite the fact she tried to hide them quickly. All she would say was it seemed like a cruel joke and not at all what she'd expected.

The least helpful had been the husband, Oscar. He loped in with the dog yipping after him and flopped down in the wrong chair, forcing Henry to move his. The interview mostly consisted of Oscar giving him blank stares while kicking at the yipping dog. Fortunately, someone had replaced Dandy's jingling gold chain with a none-noise making black collar studded with silver points. An odd choice but Henry guessed it might keep the dog safe from larger animals. Possibly.

Even without the jingling bells, the interview floundered consistently. Oscar mentioned being hungry a few times and claimed his head hurt. The only thing he had to say about his late wife was, "She was very nice to me."

Henry saved Miss Marigolds' interview for last. He started by broaching the subject of Oscar's mental health.

"Mr. Henbit, what happened to him?"

"Old age I think. It's not something Aunt Laundra spoke of much. Anytime someone said anything about Mr. Henbit mother would go on and on about how smart it was of Aunt Laundra to marry a nearly dead man as wealthy as Mr. Henbit. She always made it sound so... I don't know... calculated."

"I see," Henry said. That was not the direction he'd meant to go, but it was possibly even more informative. Still, his original question needed addressing. "I was actually meaning Oscar Henbit."

"Oh, yes. I think I'd forgotten he'd be Mr. Henbit. So strange that he took her name."

"I was told he had a head injury."

"Yes. I think about a year after the wedding. He was very into horseback riding. No one knows for sure how it happened, but somehow he fell off and got kicked in the head. It was hours before anyone found him. He's been different ever since."

"Really?" Henry thought about that. Oscar was definitely different, but it was such a peculiar different. "How did he meet Mrs. Henbit?"

"Online. None of us even knew about him until they were going to be married. But that was how it usually happened with Aunt Laundra. Mother always said he was merely trying to do to Aunt Laundra what Aunt Laundra had done to Mr. Henbit. I'd like to disagree but... uh... the site was... well... it was a sight for wealthy women to find younger men."

"I see."

"Aunt Laundra was always... well, Aunt Laundra. I think Oscar was exactly what she wanted right now. Well, until the head injury."

"Does he have a family?"

Miss Marigolds puzzled over that for a moment. "You know, I don't know. None came to the wedding. It was a small wedding, here in the house."

"I see. Do you have any idea who might have wanted Ramses dead?"

"I've been thinking about that. I thought you might ask. Normally I'd say no one. He was very sweet. He's been here as long as I can remember. As I was thinking about that though, I had an idea. Maybe he saw something. Maybe he knew who wanted to kill Aunt Laundra. That would be a reason to kill someone, right? Especially if that person knew he knew." Miss Marigolds smiled as if she'd thought of something never thought before.

Henry gave her a pleasant smile. She could be right, but that wasn't a new idea. Still, it was something to give more thought. He continued to think that over as Sham drove them into Alku. The passing buildings pulled Henry back out of his head. He looked up at Constable Sham. "Excuse me, is there any chance we could stop by and see if Ms. Veratiri has a copy of the will ready for me?"

"Check your inbox," Sham said. "Should be there."

Henry patted his pockets. Nothing. Where had he put that?

"I got it," Jackson said from the front seat. He pulled out the iPad and tapped it to life.

"Could I..." Henry said, holding out a hand.

Jackson ignored it. He tapped the iPad a few times. "Yeah, it's here."

"Could I..." Henry said again.

Jackson glanced back. "Could you...?"

Henry turned away. He knew Jackson knew what he wanted. He knew Jackson knew he knew. But that wouldn't change anything. Jackson wanted him to ask for it. "Give me the tablet."

Jackson gave a half smile and handed it back. Henry snatched it up and looked at the document Jackson had pulled up. "It's in German."

"Yup," Sham said.

"There's not a translation?"

"Nope."

"That's unhelpful." Henry continued to look over it. A thought hit him, and he flipped to the end. There was a scan of the signatures there. Laundra Henbit's signature was there. So were the witnesses. That was what interested Henry. "Amelia Novak and Aleksandar Novak."

"Who are they?" Jackson asked.

"They witnessed the will. I believe she was Mrs. Henbit's doctor."

"That's right," Sham said. "She has a private practice in Erfundenborg. They were from Eastern Europe, her and her husband. Been living on the islands for quite a while though. Longer than Mrs. Henbit, I believe."

"I'd like to speak with her."

"I'm sure her number is in there somewhere."

Henry nodded. "Good good."

For the remainder of the drive, Henry busied himself going over the profiles the police had pulled together on all the recipients of the will. He noted that not a single one was a native to the Verlorland Islands. No. One was. The chauffeur. His birthplace was Erfundenborg.

Only one had a criminal record: Ari Björnssen. Both Pip Skarsgård and Emma Fischer had lived in the Verlorland Islands less than a year. Other than Ramses and his nephew Ari Björnssen, the chauffeur was the only one to have any relatives on the island. One other thing took him by surprise, Mr. Björnssen, the nurse, was a citizen of the Verlorland Islands. Not only that, but of Alku. That was unexpected. Although Henry acknowledged maybe that was because of Ari's obvious Egyptian heritage. But he'd also been under the impression none of the house staff was native to the Island. Henry looked up. They were passing through rolling countryside again. He hadn't even noticed they'd passed over to Erfundeneyja.

Henry's thoughts drifted back to the manor. It was its own little world outside the rest of the islands. Foreigners artificially grafted into Alku. It didn't belong. Did that help? Henry didn't see how right away. He brushed the thought aside and scanned through the files until he found what he needed: Doctor Novak.

"Yes, thank you. I completely understand. It's just-" Henry dropped the sentence and waited.

The conversation had gone on like this for a few minutes now. Jackson tried to imagine what the other side sounded like. But as he'd never even met Doctor Novak, it was a challenge. Instead, he fidgeted in his uncomfortable seat on Henry's mattress. The chairs were all stacked with papers that Henry had been unable to commit to moving. There was little else in the room to distract Jackson. It was the dullest room Jackson had ever occupied. The only interruptions in the tedium were Henry's occasional attempts to edge into the conversation Doctor Novak was having at him. That wasn't entirely true. There was also a deep operatic voice emanating from the bathroom. The sound of running water accompanied the singing however, so Jackson had no desire to investigate the source of the music.

"Yes. Of course. I see. Oh yes? I see. Yes. Yes, but-" Henry tried to continue.

Jackson sighed and stood, crossing to the window. The view wasn't much more than the street and a few more dull square buildings. He found himself wishing Henry lived in one of the Hobbit holes he'd seen in the countryside which led directly to him wondering if thinking of them as Hobbit holes was offensive.

"If I could read-" Henry swallowed the rest of the thought. "Yes. I appreciate your time. Enjoy your hike." Henry hung up the phone and frowned.

"Helpful?"

"Not entirely," Henry said. "She said she would call me back in a few weeks when her schedule opened up."

"So not helpful at all."

"Well, she did say she and her husband were witnesses to the will. She also said she wasn't surprised it had upset the family."

"But she didn't know why Laundra Henbit did it?"

"I didn't get a chance to ask that. I'll have to do that when she calls back. You'd think this would rate as higher importance than a weekly hike."

"What?"

"Hike. She had to go because she and Mr. Novak were going on a hike. Although I suppose if they'd waited they could have ended up losing daylight. It's dangerous to hike around here at night."

"Vampires?"

"No," Henry scoffed. "Cliffs. Did you get the photos?"

"Yup," Jackson held up his phone.

Henry frowned. "I was hoping for pictures. Printed ones."

"What for?"

"To hang on the wall."

Jackson looked from Henry to the wall then back. "You are not making a crazy person string wall."

"Why not?"

"Look at this place. It already looks like a serial killer lives here."

"It does not," Henry said looking around the room. He frowned. "Maybe a little. I don't have any heads in the fridge though."

Jackson stared at Henry a moment. "Were you trying to make a joke?"

"Yes."

"Don't. I'm banning you from any further jokes."

Henry rolled his eyes. "I haven't had much time to decorate."

"Or buy a bed frame?"

Henry waved the last comment off dismissively. "If I don't put it all on the wall, how else can I organize all of this?"

"I don't know," Jackson said sarcastically. "Maybe the iPad?"

Henry's mouth hung half open with an argument. None came and he snapped it shut. "I suppose that could work." He scanned the table. "I'm not quite sure-"

"Paper bag under the chair with the broken arm," Jackson cut in.

Giving Jackson a skeptical glance, Henry bent down and peered in the brown bag. A fleeting look of surprise passed over his face. He fetched out the iPad and stood. Absently, he moved a stack of papers from his chair and sat the tablet down in its place. "Exactly how would I do that?"

New technology had never interested Henry all that much but he was intelligent, Jackson had to give him that. He picked things up quickly. This being the case, Jackson only needed to give Henry a ten minute tutorial on iPad basics and his brother took it from there.

Jackson watched Henry work for a few minutes. Time stretched out in the silence. Jackson found his mind wondering how long it had been since Henry had cleaned his flat. It smelled of mildew and stale food and body odor. Although the last one was mostly Jackson. He needed clothes. Maybe he could convince Henry to work at his hotel room. They could stop by somewhere to buy clothes on the way. Henry was focused however so Jackson held the thought to himself. The room again settled into near silence. The opera in the bathroom had reached an epic crescendo.

"Is someone singing in there?" Jackson asked.

"Hmm?"

"The opera."

"Yes. That would be Agent Orange. He is quite good. Could we focus on the job though?"

"Sure. Where exactly do you start with something like this?" Jackson asked. He wasn't sure if he was actually interested or merely bored.

"Hmm?" Henry said again.

"What's your next step?"

"Oh, well in any murder you have to determine three things-"

"Means, motive and opportunity."

"No. Who did it. Why they did it. How they did it."

"Are those the same thing?" Jackson tried to play both back to see if they lined up.

"You could start with the victim and move out. Why would someone want them dead? Find answers that way. Or you could start with suspects. Especially if there's a small pool of people that could have done it. I like to do both."

"So, why would someone want the gardener dead?"

"Yes. But also Laundra Henbit. If the deaths are in fact linked, then Mr. Razek's death is probably tied closely to the why of Mrs. Henbit's death. In this case, the possibilities are... vast. So instead, let's look at our suspects."

"The family and staff."

"Yes. We're dealing with poison in both cases, so alibis aren't useful. Each person could have found a way to poison either of them. Which by the way... the pictures."

"Should be synced up. Check notes."

Henry tapped the iPad. He wrinkled his brow. "These are links."

"Social media. Better than pictures."

Henry nodded slowly at first then brightened up. "Yes, I suppose it is." His face fell. "I don't exactly have any accounts. Is that a problem?"

"I'm logged into mine."

"Good, good." Henry clicked on the first link. It opened Caprice's Instagram. "Caprice Marigolds. Sister of deceased. Well aquatinted with second deceased. Mother of two. Widow."

"And loves selfies, appletinis, and Ibiza."

"Ibiza?" Henry asked.

"She goes at least twice a year. Scroll through all the photos."

"I'll take your word for it." Henry did scroll through the first few though until he reached one that made him blush.

"I wasn't able to find much else about her."

"She's a widow. Married a wealthy South African businessman and has mostly lived there since. He died in a plane crash fifteen years ago."

"Plane crash?"

"Yes. He was the pilot. He and one other passenger crashed into the ocean." Henry bit his lower lip. "Doesn't seem important. Not yet at least. Anyway..." He jerked his attention back to Jackson. "Caprice was upset about the will. And also argued with her sister at dinner when she tried to bring up her possible imminent demise."

"She's still insisting that these aren't murders."

"Really?"

"I overheard her talking to Sloan."

"Yes. Sloan." Henry scrolled until he found her name in the links. He clicked on it and her facebook page opened. "Not much here."

"No. Some old rugby photos. She played professionally in South Africa until about two years ago. Had to stop because of... what was it? I think a knee injury."

"I don't see any of that here."

"Wikipedia. She and Regal both have one."

"Here's a wedding picture. If this date is right, they've been married ten years. Is that Charlize Theron?"

"She is South African."

"True."

"Are we going to do this with every single person?"

"Yes."

"Feels like that could get boring."

"It's murder. It's not supposed to be entertaining." The grin on Henry's face disagreed with his words.

"Alright! Alright! By the way, Emma Fischer doesn't seem to have any social media, so I just took a picture of her. It's in photos."

"Ah yes, the cook. According to the police documents, she immigrated four months ago."

"From Germany?"

"No - well yes she is German - but no. She had been living in South Africa for the last five years."

Jackson cocked an eyebrow. "Where the Marigolds live?"

"Yes. I'll earmark that for follow up. None of the other staff had much to say about her. She wasn't in the room when Mrs. Henbit died and was asleep when Ramses died."

"You know, if Laundra Henbit wasn't poisoned, then in a way the cook would be the killer." Henry gave Jackson a frown. "Because of the cooking." Henry continued frowning. "Her weight..."

"If you're not going to take this seriously..." Henry started.

"Sorry! Just trying to keep this light."

Henry sighed and clicked on the next link. "What is this?" Henry wrinkled up his face.

Jackson looked over at the iPad. "That's LinkedIn. It's all Oas has. And he only has one contact."

"Mary Oas. I believe that is his mother."

"We know anything else about him?"

"First name, Abraham. Son of Gerald and Mary Oas. Gerald was the Haas family butler."

"Haas?"

"Laundra and Caprice's maiden names. Abraham Oas was born in Germany actually, moved here with his father and mother when he was ten. Gerald Oas was the head butler until his death twelve years ago. Oddly enough, I don't believe Abraham Oas ever lived in England."

"He sounds British," Jackson said.

"He is a British citizen. His mother and father were from Scotland and England respectively. Both worked for the Haas family then Gerald and Abraham came with Mrs. Henbit when she was married. Abraham started working as a footman at sixteen."

"So this is literally all he has ever known?"

"In a hyperbolic sense, yes. He is a tough man to read. I will say that. I do get a strange feeling from him though. Not sure I trust him."

"He doesn't like you, so that could be it."

"Doesn't like me? I hardly know him."

"He winces every time you speak."

"Does not."

"Yes, he does. Just like Mr. Brattsworth. Remember him? Your old golf coach?"

"Of course I remember him," Henry said flatly.

"You just rub some people the wrong way. Oh, also Oas knows you aren't British. That might be why he winces when you talk now that I think about it."

"What?" Henry nearly jumped out of his chair.

"Dude, don't worry. He isn't going to say anything. He just knows your accent is fake."

"That doesn't matter. But..." Henry took in a deep breath and sat down. "This does complicate things."

"How?"

"How am I supposed to investigate him if I have to worry about him telling people I'm not British?"

"Maybe by not pretending to be British for no reason?"

"I've told you the reason. Matilda Desrosiers," Henry said loudly with no preamble. "She's been employed for three years. Before that-"

Jackson blinked back the dizzying change in conversation. "What order are you doing these in?"

"Hmm? No order. Just clicking through."

"Couldn't we do the most likely suspects first? I'm pretty sure it wasn't the maid."

"No one is beyond suspicion."

"But some have to be more suspicious."

"Not a reason to be distracted."

"Okay but if you had to make a guess right now, who is your top suspect?"

"I don't-"

"Just for my curiosity. This isn't an accusation. You won't lose the game if you're wrong. Just make a guess."

Henry sighed and leaned back. Jackson could almost hear his brain kicking into high gear.

"Ramses and Caprice Marigolds were the most upset about the will. That reminds me, I'd like to know what Ramses and the solicitor argued about after the reading."

"So since Ramses is dead, you're going with Caprice?"

"I didn't say that," Henry cut in quickly. "That isn't my guess."

Jackson smiled at his brother's bluster.

"Ari Björnssen."

"The nurse?" Jackson balked.

"He is the only member of the household with a criminal record. He knew his uncle had a drug problem. He was in the guest house a few hours, possibly minutes before Ramses injected the rat poison. He was the last one to see his uncle alive. And also as Mrs. Henbit's nurse, he had easy access to her at any time. He was sitting next to her when she died. He would have extensive information on her medical conditions."

Jackson nodded. "That is convincing."

"It's speculation. But it is something."

"He does seem pretty broken up about the dude's death though."

"Maybe he regrets killing him? Did it out of necessity not desire? Also, there is the fact that he knew Mrs. Henbit's health was failing. Why not wait?"

"To stop Mrs. Henbit from doing or saying something? Are you trying to talk yourself out of your own guess?"

"I'm keeping all lines of thought open."

"Okay. Mine is Oscar."

"The husband?" Henry said, eyes bulging in surprise.

"Yeah. I don't think he has a brain injury."

"He was kicked by a horse."

"Okay, maybe he has a bit of one but not what he's letting on. I looked him in the eyes. He is not as far gone as he pretends to be."

"You can diagnose brain damage from eye contact? Did you learn that in your incomplete clinical psychology degree?" Henry gave Jackson a smug grin.

"I know what I saw. Look into it."

"What possible reason could he have to fake a brain... oh..." Henry trailed off. "I do see how that would benefit him. Marry a wealthy woman of poor health. Fake a traumatic brain injury to avoid real intimacy." Henry ignored Jackson's groan of disgust. "Maybe it wasn't the plan, but when he did have a horse kick him he took advantage of the escape it would allow. But then she keeps living. You have to keep pretending. So... yes. That is a decent second."

"Do the police have much on him?"

"He's a citizen of Taiwan. Immigrated to the Islands three years ago when he married Mrs. Henbit."

"And he took her name. That's odd, right?"

"Maybe. It is the name of the estate." Henry scrolled through the tablet and clicked on Oscar's name. The page pulled up. "There's not much here. Not in the last few years."

"If you scroll back there's a bunch of polo photos. Some general horse riding. The wedding. Then not much more. Nothing really from before he came to the islands."

"That is interesting."

"So," Jackson asked. "How would we go about finding out if he really has brain damage?"

"That is a good question. But I'd like to dig into the rest of our suspects first. Who's next..." Henry clicked on a link. "Pip Skarsgård. The footman. Very fond of the dog." Henry said this last part as a statement of obvious fact.

Jackson raised an eyebrow. "How do you know that?"

"He had a considerable amount of dog hair on his pant legs and sleeves."

Jackson shook his head and smiled. "Didn't notice that."

"Of course not." Henry looked at the Facebook profile. Any smugness he'd displayed from the previous exchanged dropped. "Is he dressed as Hitler?"

"I think it's a Halloween costume."

Henry sighed. "I had a feeling he was slightly racist."

"Slightly?"

Henry nodded in deference. "I know this is entirely unprofessional, but I think I wouldn't be unhappy if he were the murderer."

"Just wait until you see his YouTube channel."

Jackson waited until Henry had exhausted the list of staff and family before deciding to head for his hotel. Once again, Henry insisted that Agent Orange drive him. The man was possibly in costume again. Either that or his normal wardrobe looked like a homeless leprechaun. Peaches was absent for this drive. While Agent Orange recounted an adventure he'd shared with Henry while tracking an escaped Maltese, Jackson decided he was going to get a rental car no matter what Henry had to say about it. After a few minutes spent trying to decipher the confusing search results he got from searching car rentals he decided to wait until morning and focused on finding a place to buy more clothes instead.

"What kind of clothes?" Orange asked when Jackson failed to find something by searching.

"Normal clothes." Looking at Agent Orange made Jackson decide he should add some clarification. "Where would an average guy go for clothes here?"

Agent Orange thought for a long time before coming to a decision. He gave Jackson a few options that meant little to him and they narrowed in on the least out of the way.

From the outside, it looked promising. It was a narrow building squeezed between more narrow buildings. The exterior was painted a bright blue with white trim. Inside he was greeted in Verlorlandish by a slouched old man in thick glasses. He was dressed in a strange ensemble involving a thick wool garment that was something between a coat and a kilt. It was brilliantly blue with red embroidery and green banding. A belt made of white puffy balls hung loosely mid waist. The leggings were bright green and looked to be right out of a poor stage production of Robin Hood. Somehow all of that was overshadowed by his towering hat, also made of blue wool. It was cylindrical and stuck up about a foot. It was embroidered in green, red and white and depicted some sort of scene involving a fish and two frogs. It didn't take long to realize the clothes on sale were simply more variations of the shopkeepers' own ensemble.

"I said normal clothes," Jackson whispered to Agent Orange. The shopkeep had given away no hint of knowing any English but Jackson still felt the need to whisper.

"A lot of local men shop here," the agent insisted.

"I haven't seen a single person wearing something like this."

"He is." Agent Orange pointed to the shopkeeper who had wandered off into the confused rainbow of clothing.

"He's selling it," Jackson said.

Agent Orange shrugged. "I get my clothes from Amazon."

A quick detour to a second shop proved equally as unproductive. It only sold clothes for small children and rain boots. Jackson gave up and Agent Orange took him back to his hotel. A new woman greeted him inside. She spoke very little English and while unhelpful with helping him find a decent place to buy clothes, he did find out they had a laundry room. If he couldn't get new clothes, he could at least get clean clothes. He was forced to spend the next two hours dressed in a fuzzy white robe waiting for his few items of clothing to get clean but he wouldn't smell like sweat and old alcohol anymore. It was worth a few hours of lost sleep.

Jackson regretted those lost hours the next morning when he woke to Henry's insistent knocking. He had the presence of mind to dress before letting his brother in this time.

"You're still wearing that?" Henry asked.

"I tried to find clothes but everything in this town is confusing," Jackson said. "They're clean."

Henry sniffed. "That is an improvement but I feel like a doctor should have a larger wardrobe than a cartoon character."

"You dress in a suit every day."

"Clean suit."

"They're practically identical."

"What time is it anyway?"

"Time to get moving. Hurry."

He was still too groggy to understand much of what Henry said after that. Eventually Henry gave up explaining and pulled Jackson outside. He wasn't surprised to see the bright orange beast out front, but this time it was Peaches in the driver's seat without Agent Orange. She seemed to be dressed normally for once, jeans and a black blouse. She gave him a coy smile, and he felt himself blush. The awkwardness hadn't waned. He gave her a weak smile and climbed into the rear of the vehicle.

"It seems really bright for this early," Jackson said as he took his seat.

"Sunrise is just about 4:30 this time of year," Peaches said.

"We're that far north?" Jackson asked.

"I suppose," Peaches said noncommittally.

The conversation died from there as Peaches took them through the city.

"We have a very full day ahead," Henry started in as they drove out of Erfundenborg. "I have an appointment with the solicitor then I hope to catch Ari Björnssen for some follow up questions. I'd like to know how he came to be a citizen of the Verlorland Islands."

"I thought I could rent us a car for-"

"I don't mind the drive," Peaches said. "It's a fascinating case, and I do have the day off."

"What exactly do you do?" Jackson asked, hoping he'd managed a casual tone.

"That's classified," Peaches said once again giving him a coy smile.

Jackson wanted to insist, but he could tell Henry had already dismissed the thought and wouldn't hear any more on the subject. As groggy and out of sorts as he felt, he knew he should be grateful Henry had even remembered he was here. Not only that, he'd gone out of his way to pick him up before jumping into his case. That wasn't something either of them had ever been particularly good at.

"You know," Jackson said to Henry. "I think I know where we can find out if Ari was born here."

CHAPTER 10

"What is this?" Henry asked, looking over the web of names hanging in front of him.

Jackson had been worried the pub would be closed but the smell of sausage wafting over them as they climbed out of the orange car alleviated the concern. It also reminded him he hadn't had breakfast.

"I already told you," Jackson said.

"Yes, but when you said there was a genealogy in the pub, I was expecting a book."

"I definitely told you it was on a big piece of wood."

"He did," Peaches agreed, munching on some kind of sausage pie. Jackson had one for himself as well. It was surprisingly good considering he'd never associated the words sausage and pie together before. He'd feared it would be sweet but instead, it was more like eating his second step mother's biscuits and gravy with the biscuit on the outside holding the rest in.

Henry hunched over. "There's a Björnssen," he said, placing a finger on the wood. Slowly he traced it down fingers spreading out in every direction. "This gets very tangled."

"Yes, it does," Jackson agreed.

Henry took a step back and let his eyes dart over the wood. "Question... uh... wait, what was your name?"

"Are you serious?" Jackson asked.

"No, not you." Henry looked around, the expression of interest on his face gave way surprise as he realized the bartender was no longer behind him. "The bartender."

"Oh. That's Otto."

"Otto!" Henry called out not looking to even see where the bartender was.

"Yes?" The man hollered back as he exited the kitchen.

"First, I feel slightly embarrassed not knowing this already, but I honestly haven't had the need to understand the construction of surnames in the Verlorland Islands up to this point."

The red-bearded man waited. Henry seemed to be done speaking. "Was that a question?"

"Question? No. A statement. My observation though is that some surnames seem to pass from one generation to the next but others seem to be derived from the father or mother's given name appended with a *ssen* or *tiri*."

"That sounds right."

"Is there a reason for the discrepancy?"

"The what?"

"Why the two different types of names?" Jackson offered.

"Oh, different islands, different names. As the people mix between them, it gets messy. The old families tend to still use patronyms."

"I see. So with that in mind, our Björnssen is merely the son of a Björn," Henry said then drifted back into thought, his eyes darting over the board again. He seemed to take in the entire wall at once. "Ah there." Henry crouched down and pointed to a plaque a few levels from the bottom and clear on the right-hand side. Ari Björnssen was etched into it. Henry followed the connecting golden wire up a level. "Björn Thorssen and Jackie Razek. Our nurse was born here in the islands."

"Ramses' sister lived in the Verlorland Islands?" Jackson asked.

"Yes, Ramses had mentioned that," Henry said. "She used to be the cook. He told me she moved to Finland after she married. He didn't tell me that Ari had been born before that." He turned back to the bartender. "Otto, did you know Björn Thorssen?"

"Ah, I remember the name. Hafthor's brother I believe. He was an odd man. Worked up at the Manor. Not many locals have worked up there."

"What happened to him?"

Otto shrugged. "Left. Hafthor doesn't speak much about him. Of course, that's because he lost his tongue."

Henry nodded appreciatively then turned back to the wall. "Right. That's sorted then. I think that does it for here. Let's go talk to the solicitor."

"Can I finish my pie first?" Jackson asked.

Henry sighed. "Fine. Pie and then the solicitor."

* * *

If Jackson had tried to imagine what the office of a village solicitor would look like, Ms. Veratiri's office was not what he'd have thought up. It was austere. All four walls were white and almost entirely absent adornment. One wall supported a tidy bookshelf and one painting hung behind the desk. It was a rural landscape full of trees and wildflowers and a lone house. Wooded hills gave way to a steep slope behind the house. To Jackson it looked like the hills surrounding Henbit Manor.

The desk had a small amount of personality. It looked old, possibly hand carved. Not overly ornate but well made. It was bare save for one desk lamp and a laptop. Ms. Veratiri herself sat behind the desk dressed in a well fitted bright yellow pantsuit. She folded her hands on the desk in front of her.

"I really can't speculate on Mrs. Henbit's intentions. It isn't my job to know the why of their last wills and testaments, only to make sure they're legally sound and properly implemented."

"But Mrs. Henbit wasn't just any client," Henry said shifting in the simple wooden chair under him. It creaked in a very disquieting way.

"Every client thinks they're special."

"She owned the island."

For a moment, Jackson thought Ms. Veratiri was going to explode on them, but whatever emotion he'd seen, it faded in the same heartbeat.

"That was no reason for me to question her intentions."

"It was an unusual will, you would agree with that, yes?"

"I try not to make judgments on my client's wishes."

It was Henry's turn to fume. His mouth opened and closed a few times as he tried to find another direction to take the questions. This was deteriorating quickly. Jackson decided to step in.

"That's a beautiful painting," Jackson said indicating the only painting in the room. Henry gave Jackson a small kick, but Jackson ignored it. "Is that of Alku? It looks very familiar."

Ms. Veratiri eyed Jackson a moment as if she were trying to will her way into his head. Finally, she sighed and gave dismissive motion behind her. "Yes. It is of the island."

"It's very well done," Jackson added. "Who painted it?"

"Vera Ansatiri. Would you like to know how much I paid for it?" Her tone had no note of invitation.

Jackson settled back into his chair. He didn't see any use in trying to soften the solicitor any longer. She was stone cold.

"How long have you been Mrs. Henbit's solicitor?" Henry asked, giving

Jackson one quick look of annoyance.

"She approached me a month ago to draw up her new will. Most of her affairs have been conducted with a firm in Germany, but she was in a hurry to get her new will in order, so she wanted someone in Alku."

"So before this, you hadn't worked with Mrs. Henbit?"

"No."

"She gave no explanation for why she needed this so quickly?"

"Again, I did not-"

"Yes. Yes. I know. Did she say anything about believing someone would try to kill her?"

"No."

Henry breathed in slowly and shook his head. He gave Jackson a defeated look.

"Is that all?" Ms. Veratiri asked.

"I uh..." Henry stammered. He patted his pocket then glanced around his chair. Without a word, Jackson handed Henry the iPad. Henry took it without question, glancing over a few notes. "If something happened to all the members of the family and staff... what would become of the estate?"

"It would remain in the care of Dandy."

"The dog?"

"That is the heir."

"And when he dies?"

"I would have to look into the legalities of that eventuality."

"And if I'm correct, it's the trust that is the owner of the estate, not actually the dog?"

Ms. Veratiri sighed. "Yes."

"And who will run that trust?"

"A committee of Alku community members."

"And who chose the committee?"

"Mrs. Henbit. The names are in the will."

"What if something happened to the committee members?"

"Then their next of kin would take their place. It's all spelled out in the will."

"In German."

"Then find a translator and let me do my work."

"One last thing."

"I have other clients."

"And are they the subject of a double murder investigation?"

Ms. Veratiri fumed but said nothing, so Henry pressed on.

"You were seen speaking with Ramses Radek after the reading of the will. He was described as agitated. What was the conversation about?"

"He was agitated. I believed he expected the will to be more personal."

"Personal?"

"Yes. Messages to the family and friends. He wanted the will to make him feel better, and it didn't. That's all. And that is all."

Ms. Veratiri turned her attention to her laptop and fell into silence. She made no sign to show them out so, awkwardly, Henry and Jackson stood, excused themselves, and exited the office. They didn't speak again until they were out on the street where Peaches waited by the garishly orange car.

"Strange lady," Jackson finally spoke up.

"Yes. I don't understand why Mrs. Henbit went to her for a new will. And only a month ago."

"She needed it quickly. Did you notice how dead her eyes look? Unsettling."

"Don't be dramatic. And I don't know why needing a will quickly would equal needing a new solicitor. I don't think a woman of Mrs. Henbit's wealth would have had any trouble getting her own personal solicitor here. No. There has to be a reason she wanted someone else."

Henry nodded in agreement with himself and quickly entered the backseat of the car. As Jackson opened the passenger side door, Peaches gave him a half smile.

"Pleasant woman, isn't she?" Peaches asked.

"You've met her?" Jackson asked.

"You meet a lot of people in my line of work." Peaches gave him another half smile and climbed into the driver's seat.

Jackson eyed her a moment before getting in himself. He still didn't believe she was a secret agent. Far from it. But she was interesting.

When they arrived at Henbit Manor, Miss Marigolds stood on the steps, smiling softly at them. She gave a little wave as Henry exited Peaches' car.

"It's more garish than I'd imagined," Peaches said quietly to Jackson before they too climbed out.

"You've never seen it?" Jackson asked.

"My work doesn't take me to Alku often."

Jackson fought off the urge to question what kind of work she was referring too. Henry, not waiting for the others, crossed the driveway and greeted Miss Marigolds.

"I have no idea how long we'll be here," Jackson said.

"Well, a place like this has to have some good drinks at least, right?"

Peaches winked at Jackson and took off after Henry.

Miss Marigolds eyed Peaches warily, glancing from her to Henry as she introduced herself. Thankful Peaches left off the agent part this time. When Henry referred to Peaches as their driver, Miss Marigolds visibly relaxed. She even managed a smile at the other woman.

"Where is Oas?" Henry asked.

"He's on the phone. Since he can't leave the estate for his usual weekly trip, he's having to find someone that will deliver out here."

"I see. Is Ari Björnssen in? I would very much like to speak with him."

"Yes. He's in the gardens. I could take you around."

"Is there somewhere I can wait while Mr. Pets works?" Peaches asked.

"Oh of course," Miss Marigolds said. "I could have Matilda bring you tea in the conservatory."

With that, Miss Marigolds headed for the entry. Jackson took a few quick steps to catch up with Henry.

"How long do you plan on being here?" Jackson asked.

"I have no idea where this questioning will lead. Could be a few hours."

"And Peaches is good with this?" Jackson motioned to the woman.

"She seemed to be very interested in seeing the Manor."

"How much do you know about her?"

"They've been my neighbors since I moved here."

"That doesn't answer my question."

"True," Henry admitted. "They are very nice. And have driven me many places."

Jackson shook his head. They needed a rental car soon. Sure, she did seem pleasant, and she wasn't terrible company so far, but it did seem strange that she was so willing to give up an entire day to drive them around.

"I could hang back. Keep an eye on her."

Henry eyed Jackson a moment. "What for?"

"In case she's... I don't know... up to something?"

"Sure. Keep an eye on her. Also, keep your eye out for anything unusual."

"Everything here is unusual."

"Well, then something unusualer."

"I was thinking," Miss Marigolds spoke softly as she led Henry through the saloon. They'd left Jackson and Peaches with Matilda. Henry declined any tea for himself. It was time to work. "If you're going to be traveling out here so often, you could stay in one of our guest rooms. We still have a few open."

Henry felt his ears turn red. He hoped Miss Marigolds didn't notice. "That... uh... I don't think that would be appropriate."

"I suppose not," Miss Marigolds said, a little disappointed.

"It might be useful for me to find a room in Alku though. Yes. I could see that being convenient."

"There is an Inn. We can put you up there," Miss Marigolds said cheerfully. "It's very nice. I'll make the arrangements."

"No need to trouble yourself. Are the rates reasonable?"

"Don't worry about the rates. It's Alku. The estate technically owns it, so I'm sure it'll be fine."

"The estate owns the Inn?"

"Yes. The estate owns all the businesses in Alku."

"Not just the land?"

"The land and the businesses too."

"Really?"

Miss Marigolds pushed open the far door and led Henry out into the gardens. The green grass stretched out ahead of them.

"Yes," Miss Marigolds frowned. "I suppose that is a bit odd. I hadn't really thought about it. It's always been that way. Ever since I was a girl. Everywhere we'd go, Aunt Laundra owned it. That was back when she still left the house."

"Why did she stop going out?"

"I don't know for sure. Her weight, I've always thought. Of course, she's been overweight since before I was born. I think the accident was thirty-five years ago. She was doing some climbing out on Heilaguryja. It's north of here. Beautiful island. Even less developed the Alku. She fell and broke her back. Aunt Laundra gained quite a bit very quickly after that, but there were a few years when I was about nine or ten that she did try to get healthier. One summer she even started hiking with me."

"You stayed here often?"

"Almost every school break when I was a kid. Sloan always had sports camps, and I'd visit Aunt Laundra." Miss Marigolds' smile dropped. Her head dropped too. "Honestly, I think it might have been when I stopped visiting as much that her health turned. I was going to drama camps or seeing other countries. Italy. Japan. I spent two weeks in London once. And of course Egypt. My mother still loves to go there. She spent entire summers there with Aunt Laundra when they were young. I always wished I could see it with Aunt Laundra someday." She looked up at Henry, wiping back a tear. "Sometimes I wonder if I was her only friend."

They continued walking toward a line of curved hedges. Henry recognized it as the maze he'd seen in the photos of the manor. It was at least eight feet tall and stretched off into two large arcs.

"I was born here, you know?"

"What?"

"Yes. My mother was very sick when she was pregnant with me. Aunt Laundra insisted she come here so Dr. Novak could take care of her. So I was born here, in the guest wing."

"I wasn't aware of that." They fell back into silence as Henry filed the new information away. That could explain why Laundra Henbit cared so much for her niece. She'd seen her birth. "The cook," Henry finally continued. "Miss Fischer. I saw she spent a few years in South Africa. Did you know her there?"

"Yes, we did. She was the chef at my mother's favorite restaurant. It was quite good."

"How did she end up here?"

"I don't know the details, but the restaurant ran into financial difficulties. Eventually, it closed. Mother took it on herself to help Emma find a new job and convinced Aunt Laundra to fire her cook and hire Emma. It was a bit of a fight but I will say Aunt Laundra was very pleased with Emma in the end. She makes wonderful German food."

Henry nodded, stalling a bit to place this in line with all his other thoughts. He could see Ari Björnssen now, standing on a ladder that strained under his bulk.

"Has he taken over the gardening?"

"He's been doing some but..." Lydia considered her next words for a moment. "He had an argument with my mother earlier. I think this helps him blow off steam."

"Argument over what?"

"I couldn't say. She can be infuriating."

They stopped a few strides from the ladder. Ari wielded large hedge clippers, attacking stray branches furiously.

"Ari," Miss Marigolds called up to him. "Detective Pets has a few more questions for you."

Ari half turned, eyeing Henry. "Mind if I keep working?"

"Not at all," Henry said.

"You really don't need to do that," Miss Marigolds said.

"If I don't, who will?"

"I don't know. Oas or the footman."

Ari let out one stern laugh. "I should keep working then." He gave an errant twig a quick chop. It sprung out over him and would have hit Henry if he hadn't stepped out of the way. Ari didn't notice. He was already busy hacking at the next offender. He worked sporadically, in bursts of aggression. Henry was glad he was not on the clipping side of those shears.

"This will be fine," Henry assured Miss Marigolds. He thanked her for escorting him, and she excused herself politely with a warm smile at Henry and an apprehensive glance at Ari. Once she was out of earshot, Henry continued. "I was under the impression that Henbit Manor did not employ any natives of Alku, but it seems you were in fact born on this island."

Ari laughed again. He stopped hacking and turned to him as well as possible on the ladder. "Do I look Verlorlandish?"

"I don't know about that," Henry said. "But you were born on Alku to a man that was Verlorlandish."

Ari made a somewhat confirming grunt and turned back to his work. "I was born here, but we didn't stay long. We moved to Finland, not that that was much better. My mother didn't like it there."

"Why did your parents leave the islands?"

"You'd have to ask them but not sure you'll have much luck. My mother's been dead for nine years, and my father doesn't like talking about that stuff."

"Stuff?"

"The past. Leaving here. They hadn't exactly planned on having me."

"Why not raise you here?"

"I don't know. Money? Maybe. My dad made good money in Finland. We were comfortable at least. Mom didn't even have to work anymore. What does this have anything to do with the case? Have you talked to Raudur Sildsson?"

"The dealer?"

"Yes."

"Not yet."

"He's the one you want."

"We are looking into all angles. Did Mr. Sildsson have any connection to Mrs. Henbit?"

"Of course not." Ari snapped off a rather stubborn branch with far more force than needed. It sprang out, striking him right about the eye. He shouldered the clippers and pressed his hand to his head.

Henry backpedaled as he felt a warm spray of liquid. He looked down at his shirt, bright spots of blood speckled the white fabric.

"Are you bleeding?" Henry asked. He knew the answer, but he wasn't sure how else to react. He wiped his face with his hand, and it came away with streaks of red.

"Damn it. You're distracting me," Ari said.

"You could take a break."

Ari glared down at him a moment, one hand still pressed to the wound. Finally, without a word, he climbed down the ladder and stood in front of Henry. He looked at the detective's shirt.

"How'd you get blood on you?"

"It sprayed."

"I'm sure Oas would be happy to clean it for you."

"That's not necessary. I just have a few more questions."

"Let me help you out here. Speed things up a bit. Mrs. Henbit died because she didn't take care of herself. And my uncle died because an idiot gave him shitty dope."

"I appreciate your insight, but I am not ready to narrow my investigation that far."

"Fair enough. So what else do you need to know? Who could have poisoned Mrs. Henbit? That would have been difficult. She ate the same food as everyone else. She was never alone all day. Either her doctor or I was with her at least and since she got here, Lydia as well. If Mrs. Henbit were poisoned, it could only have been medication or something she drank. Not the tea at lunch though. That was shared. It would have to have been her drink at dinner. A rose I think. Would have been served by Matilda. Probably prepared by her as well. As for the medicine, can't think that anyone but me or Dr. Novak could have messed with that. Maybe Oas but I kept it in my room and it was always locked."

"I see."

"Anything else?"

"I saw that you do have a few arrests on your record."

Ari sighed. "Yes."

"Most seem to have happened in Finland when you were a minor."

"I had some bad years."

Henry waited. Ari stared him down, hardly blinking. The two stood in silence for much longer than Henry was comfortable with. But he waited. If Ari wanted to be stubborn, Henry could be stubborn too. Finally, Ari grunted again and climbed back up the ladder. The wound had stopped bleeding.

"I got into fights," he said. "At school."

"Over what?"

"I didn't exactly fit in if you can imagine that." He sighed and let the clippers sag. He leaned against the ladder, turning back toward Henry. "I'm a big guy. I've always been big. If an average thirteen-year-old shoves someone, they'll move a bit maybe, but nothing happens. When I shoved someone, there was a good chance they could end up on the ground." Ari stopped a moment but then added, "or out a window. And I'm not exactly white."

"I see."

"You say that a lot."

"I've only said it twice."

"Seems like a lot."

"Here in Alku, you were also arrested for assault. That was only a few months ago."

"Yes. And when you talk with Raudur, he can tell you exactly why that happened."

"I..." Henry stopped before adding see. "What about uh..." Henry pulled up his iPad. "Fiskpisking?"

Ari groaned. "That shouldn't even be illegal."

"What is it? The arrest report doesn't explain."

"Hitting someone with a fish."

"That would also be assault."

"But this is for the fish."

"I don't understand."

"They charged me for being mean to a fish. A dead fish."

"Oh."

"They have odd laws about dead fish in Alku. You should learn them. It's an easy way to get on the wrong side of the law."

"Who did you hit?"

"A distant relative. He was being an ass."

Henry nodded thoughtfully. Ari was being more forthcoming than he'd expected. He wanted to keep pushing before the large man shut up again. "Your mother. How did she come to live on Alku?"

"She came with Uncle Ramses. Mrs. Henbit hired them. My mother was their cook, and of course Uncle Ramses was in the gardens. He always said she did it because she missed visiting Egypt. She'd stopped traveling much by then. She was already obese. Find her wedding pictures if you want to confirm that."

"Why did they take the jobs? It's very far from family."

"Uncle Ramses liked Laundra. They were old friends. And of course mother used to follow Uncle Ramses anywhere."

Henry forced himself not to say *I see* but took note that for once Ari had called Mrs. Henbit, Laundra. That seemed important.

"Did you have any idea you would be receiving anything from Mrs. Henbit's will?"

"No," Ari said without hesitation. "I was just her nurse."

"But your families have known Mrs. Henbit's family for a long time. And your Uncle and Mrs. Henbit were close, yes?"

Something crossed Ari's face. It was emotion but too subtle for Henry to read. "Not close."

"He moved from Egypt to be near her."

"To work for her. It was a good job."

"Of all the people in the world that could have been Mrs. Henbit's gardener-"

"Locals won't work for Mrs. Henbit. Not good ones. Not even many from the other islands. Take Laki. Most of his family won't even speak to him anymore. They hate the Henbits. She has to hire from outside the country, why not Egypt? She knew them both. My mother was an amazing chef and Mrs. Henbit loved her food. If you were as rich as Mrs. Henbit, why not hire the chef from your favorite restaurant. Bring Egypt to the islands. Now, I think I want to get back to work, and you have a drug dealer to find."

Henry didn't press his luck any further. He'd hit a nerve. What had done it? There had to be something more to why the Razeks had come to Alku. Henry was sure of that.

"One last thing," Henry said. "You were seen arguing with Caprice Marigolds earlier today. What was it about?"

Ari stared down at him long enough Henry wasn't sure he would answer. "She doesn't like me."

Henry nodded. He suspected that wasn't the truth but felt he'd gotten everything he could from the man. Ari was hiding something. Or at least part of something. But at the same time... he had again referred to a dead person in the present tense. He wasn't letting them go yet. Would a murderer do that? One thing Henry knew for sure though, he needed a new shirt.

CHAPTER 11

Jackson wiped sweat from his brow as he sipped his tea. Hot tea. Why did he have hot tea in a hot room with the sun beating through the glass walls? The conservatory had turned into a sauna. He was going to have to wash his clothes again.

"You look upset," Peaches said cooly from her seat near a rosebush. They'd taken up chairs in different parts of the room to Matilda's confusion. She'd had to bustle back and forth between them, getting the tea and cakes served. But that had been a good hour ago. She'd left them alone since then, and the two had fallen into polite silence.

"I'm hot."

Peaches smiled coyly. Jackson blushed.

"You're not very talkative. I thought you'd be more outgoing when I first saw you."

"I was taking a shower when you first saw me."

"No. That was the second time."

"Right," Jackson agreed. He'd forgotten about her being the woman in the burka. "I am outgoing. You're just... well, you insist on being a secret agent - which is crazy - and I don't even know your real name. And don't say it's Peaches."

"Okay. If I'm not a secret agent, what am I?"

Jackson frowned. There was something about Peaches that made him uncomfortable, and only half of it was because he always felt she was imagining him naked. It was her eyes. They were intense. And now they were intensely focused on him. Jackson turned away, unable to stand up to the gaze. Movement outside caught his eye. He sat up and moved to get a better view. It was Oscar and the dog. The dog had something in his mouth, and Oscar was trying to get it back. He was yelling something, but Jackson couldn't make it out.

"Who's that?"

"Mrs. Henbit's widower."

"That's interesting."

"They say he has brain damage."

"It does look that way."

Suddenly, Oscar kicked, taking Dandy right in the ribs. The dog spun up and over, the object flying free. Jackson choked. The poor dog flopped on the ground a moment before bolting away from the man.

"Did you see that?"

"A grown man punt a dog? Yes. I saw that."

Oscar bent down and picked up the object. It looked to be a smartphone. He yelled something at the dog, but it wasn't English. That wasn't what had Jackson's attention. Everything about Oscar changed for that moment he was yelling at the dog. He looked like a normal angry man, not the vacant man-child.

"Inbred mongrel."

"What?" Jackson turned back to Peaches.

"That's what he yelled. In Mandarin."

"You know Mandarin?"

"I'm a secret agent. Of course I know Mandarin. So, are we going to follow him or just sit here and sweat."

Jackson turned back to Oscar. The man was heading away from the house toward... well... nothing that Jackson could see. There were trees in the distance, but so far he'd seen nothing of importance in that direction.

"Yeah. Let's do it."

Caprice watched the young doctor strike out across the lawn below her second-story view with a young woman she'd never seen before. She narrowed her eyes at the offensive presence. It was a nuisance having the detective and his doctor poking around, but they could at least have the restraint to not bring attractive young women with them. It ruined the only enjoyment she could get from their intrusion.

"Excuse me," a voice said softly behind her.

Caprice nearly jumped but contained herself. She casually turned from the window. Matilda stood in the doorway with a polite if confused smile on her face.

"Yes?" Caprice asked as if she belonged in the room. Laundra Henbit's bedroom to be exact.

"Oas has instructed us to keep this room locked."

"Yes, I found the key."

"I believe it's to be locked so no one enters."

"Oh is it?" Caprice said in what she intended as an innocent tone but came nowhere close. "I do apologize. I just wanted to..." she looked around as if the room could finish her thought for her. "Feel close to my sister."

Matilda held her polite smile and made no move. None at all.

"Is there anything else?" Caprice asked.

"I do need you to leave so I can lock the room again."

Caprice let her own friendly expression drop. It had taken her a good bit of work to get into this room, and she hadn't finished searching it yet. She shouldn't have let herself watch the doctor cross the entire lawn. But it was such a pleasant view. How could she have done anything else?

"I do miss my sister," Caprice said, letting her hand come to rest on the bed frame next to her. "There's no way you could give me another minute to... uh... grieve?" Matilda didn't immediately object, so Caprice pressed further. "I could compensate you for the inconvenience?"

"Please, Mrs. Marigolds," Matilda said, motioning toward the exit.

Caprice sighed and crossed the soft carpet. She'd find her way back in eventually. Oas couldn't keep the room under guard forever. "It's Ms. Marigolds," Caprice said, giving Matilda one last smile - without her eyes. Matilda kept her pleasant smile in place. Caprice dropped hers and slipped past the maid and out of the room. She glanced back. Matilda was locking the door already. At least now Caprice knew where the maid's loyalties lay.

She turned back to the hall only to collide with the hulking bulk of Ari. She stumbled back. The giant man was exiting the old nursery. He held a duffle in one large hand.

"What are you doing?" Caprice spat as Matilda skirted the two with a polite nod.

"Getting the rest of my things. I don't think I'll be using this room anymore."

"You were in the nursery?"

"Mrs. Henbit wanted me close."

Caprice rolled her eyes. "That did her a lot of good in the end."

"If I'd been further away she could have died months ago."

Caprice waved it off. "Oh, I know why she liked to keep you close." She made a disgruntled laugh then pushed her way past Ari.

"I know exactly why she wanted me close," Ari said. "I know more than you think."

Caprice stopped and looked back warily.

"I know what she was going to tell us at that dinner," he said.

For a moment it looked as if Caprice would jump out of her own skin, then she settled and scoffed. "What? That someone wanted to murder her? HA. She was dying. All anyone needed to do was wait."

With that, Caprice left Ari in the hallway. She didn't stop sweating until she'd made her way down the grand staircase. She was shaking with rage.

Past the well-manicured gardens of the manor, the foliage fell into the islands natural state. Soft, mossy grasses blanketed the equally gentile rolling hills. Small white sprays of wildflowers peppered the landscape. Jackson and Peaches kept their distance from Oscar as they made their way through the hills. He rarely looked back, but if he did, Jackson didn't want to be seen.

Peaches proved to have a knack for following, quickly finding the most concealed paths in the valleys between the hills. Soon the hills dropped into a small valley, dense with thin evergreens. Oscar darted into the thicket.

"We can pick up our pace," Peaches said motioning for Jackson to follow.

She eyed the trees a moment then darted across the last stretch of open grassland with Jackson close behind. Carefully, they pressed on into the trees. A small trail seemed the most likely path Oscar would have chosen, and Peaches started down it. Only a few yards in, Jackson saw something else in the trees: a stone wall. Part of a stone wall at least. As they moved closer he realized it wasn't just a wall, it was the ruins of a small stone house. It felt somehow familiar. Jackson pushed the feeling aside for now though. Voices came from the other side of the wall. No, not voices. Just one voice. Oscar. He wasn't speaking English.

Peaches pressed one finger against her lips and carefully stepped toward a small open window in the wall. Jackson followed. They pressed against the stone on either side, and Jackson carefully leaned in. Oscar stood inside, pacing back a forth, a phone pressed to his ear. He spoke quickly and animated in what had to be Mandarin. Jackson looked to Peaches. She was listening intently.

The conversation lasted only another thirty seconds then cut off abruptly. Jackson's instinct was to get away from the house, but Peaches grabbed him by the shirt and pulled him back. A moment later Oscar jumped through a ruined portion of the wall and darted back down the path. Jackson didn't even take a breath until the little man had disappeared into the trees.

"He could have seen us," Jackson said.

"If we'd moved he would have," Peaches replied.

Jackson let out a long breath then looked at the enigmatic woman next to him. "Could you tell who he was talking to?" Jackson asked.

"Not exactly, but I caught quite a bit of what he said. It was something about it all being over soon. Three more weeks. He said that a few times. Also, there was a confession of love and a lot about not knowing how much money he would have."

"And it was all coherent? He wasn't... uh..."

Peaches laughed. "Did he sound brain damaged?"

"Right."

"No. That man's brain is fully functioning."

"I knew it."

"But how do you prove it?"

Jackson mulled that over for a moment but then shook off the line of thought. What was he doing following a strange man off into the middle of nowhere with a woman he barely even knew? This wasn't what he did. This was what Henry did. He was letting himself get caught up in Henry's delusions. "I think I'll leave that to Henry," he said, moving away from the stone wall. He glanced through the ruined portion of the wall Oscar had used to enter the building. It was a small house, nothing save the stone walls left. Most of it was overgrown with vines. A small tree grew inside what might have been the living room. "What was this?"

"An old farmhouse?" Peaches guessed.

"Think it burnt down?"

"Maybe. It's been abandoned for about forty years."

"How can you tell?" Jackson looked at their surroundings. He couldn't even make a guess as to how long it had been vacant.

"That tree isn't more than forty years old. I doubt the family let it grow there."

"Then it could be less than forty."

"Reginald Henbit forced the last of the farmers off his land right before his wedding to Laundra. That was forty years ago. Most of this island was used for sheep and crops before he bought it all up. Although quite a bit had already gone under, hence the island being able to be bought. Mr. Henbit preferred to let everything outside his gardens fall into the natural state."

Jackson eyed Peaches. How much did she know and how much was she making up? Jackson had the distinct impression she was someone that was very skilled at lying. "What's your real name?" Jackson asked. He was a little surprised by the question himself. He'd thought it, but had not intended to say it out loud.

Peaches smiled. "I wouldn't be a good secret agent if I told you that."

"A good secret agent wouldn't go around telling people she was a secret agent."

The smile widened into a knowing grin. "Interesting point of view." And with that, she headed back down the path. When she was a few strides away, she glanced back. "Alicia. You can call me Alicia."

Jackson smiled and headed after her. When they'd gone a few yards, he glanced back at the house one last time. The feeling of familiarity hit him again. Where had he seen this before?

"I need another drink, where's Oas?" Caprice spoke up suddenly at an unnecessary pitch. She pushed the iPad back across the desk toward Henry.

Henry had been surprised when Caprice agreed to go over the will with him. He'd arrived back at the manor to find Jackson and Peaches inexplicably missing. Calling them was out of the question as he wasn't entirely sure where he'd put his phone so he had to find something else to occupy his time. The will dominated his thoughts and speaking no German himself, he required aid. Caprice and Emma were the only viable options and after the cook had yelled at him, Henry found Caprice. She was, of course, fluent in German, but she also had the attention span of a mayfly. That made the process tedious.

Henry chose the study both because he hoped it would alleviate distraction and he'd taken a liking to the smell of the room. Leather and musky spice. Also the hint of tobacco. Henry didn't see any sign of cigars. Now that he thought about it, each room in the manor had a distinct smell. All different. And always consistent. The drawing room smelled of lavender and vanilla. The grand hall was a softer floral with undertones of vetiver and sandalwood. The conservatory, of course, smelled of roses and other flowers while the saloon had a fresh scent and possibly that of fir trees and maybe black pepper. There was no doubt in Henry's mind that Oas must control the room scents himself. Henry scanned the room until he found a suspicious apparatus hiding behind the bear. He'd have to see if other rooms had one as well.

"Is there a way to call for Matilda?" Henry suggested, hoping to keep Caprice focused.

"I don't know. Oas just makes things work." Caprice pulled out her phone and smashed her fingers on it for a few seconds. "Lydia will know. She understands this house."

"Let me ask you a general question about the will," Henry said, trying to pull the conversation back. "Does it seem unusual?"

"Of course it does. Maybe even sinister. That whole surviving thing? We can't even leave the estate."

"Could that be a mistranslation?"

"No. It's right here."

She flipped a few pages on the screen and dropped her finger down hard on the iPad. Henry winced but the screen didn't crack.

"No mistranslation," she said. "Which I suppose means poor Ramses is out. I'm assuming he'd leave everything to his nephew anyway. He didn't have any other family left."

Her eyes, not for the first time, flickered over the blood spray on his shirt. She hadn't mentioned it yet, but Henry could see she was trying to work out what it meant. He didn't offer the answer.

"Why would your sister have a stipulation like that?"

"I don't know. She's Laundra. Really, I didn't know her that well. Not for a long time at least. God, I need a drink. Where is the butler when you need him?"

"Would you care to make a guess?"

Caprice eyed Henry a moment, leaning back in the leather chair. "No. I wouldn't. And I don't know why she'd leave the estate to the dog. I never even knew she cared about the thing. It's not like she hasn't had other dogs and pets. Although I suppose in the last few years, she hasn't had much other company. We used to spend much more time here but... well... time has a way of slipping by. Fine. I'll make a guess. She'd snapped. Changing her will. Thinking someone wanted her dead. She wasn't herself anymore. I think something had gone wrong in my sister's head." Caprice narrowed her eyes. "Do you think there could be a case to contest the will?"

"I don't know about that," Henry said carefully. It seemed it was an idea that had just hit Caprice. Could that be an act? "What about the scale? The one she uses to determine how the rest of her assets are divided. Anything unusual there?" He flipped through the document on the iPad to the proper place and slid it back to Caprice.

Reluctantly, she took it and read. "Of course Lydia has the highest share. Then Oscar and then myself and Sloan. I'm a bit surprised that Regal is in here, but it's a modest share. Then, of course, the staff, Ramses and Oas having the largest share there. Then the rest."

"Now that Ramses is dead, his share goes where?"

"From what I've read, it just goes back in the pot. None of this gets divided out until the month lapses. So anyone that leaves the estate or dies before then is out." Caprice sighed. "I need a drink."

"You are only confined to the estate until the burial though."

"Yes, and with this now being a murder investigation, who knows how long they'll keep her body."

This time there was nothing Henry could do to keep Caprice focused. She stood and left the room in a dramatic sweep leaving Henry alone. He picked up the iPad and followed her out. They exited into the saloon just as the doors leading outside opened and Jackson entered with Peaches. They were both sweaty and breathing heavily.

Caprice leered at the two then trotted away quickly.

"Where have you been?" Henry asked.

Jackson scanned the room, waiting for Caprice to disappear, before answering. "You seen Oscar?"

"Not recently. Have you seen my phone?"

Jackson plucked the phone from one of his pockets and handed it to Henry. "You left it under the passenger seat of the car. Guess what we just saw?" Jackson smiled that annoying smile he always had when he was proud of himself.

"Why didn't you give it back when you found it?"

Jackson ignored the question and stepped closer. He spoke in a low voice. "You're going to love this," Jackson started then stopped, looking at Henry fully for the first time. "Are you bleeding?"

"No."

"Someone else is dead?"

"No. Ari Björnssen cut himself. You should give me your shirt."

"Why?"

"I'm the detective. I shouldn't be bloody."

"Oh, and the doctor should?"

"Not unreasonable."

"I'm not a medical doctor."

Henry glanced around to make sure none of the family or staff were present. "We haven't really established what kind of doctor you are."

"Not the kind that gets bloody."

"Just give me your shirt."

"I thought you said sleeveless shirts are for toddlers and Richard Simmons."

"I'll take Richard Simmons over Freddy Krueger."

"Dude, your pop culture references are older than you."

"Just give me your shirt."

"It won't even fit you," Jackson protested. "And if I put yours on, I'll rip it."

"You're not that big."

"Why don't we just go find somewhere to buy clothes? Yeah? Unless you want me wearing this forever."

Henry sighed. Jackson was right. The tank top would probably fall right off him. "What did you find out?"

Jackson quickly told Henry what he and Alicia had seen. At first, Henry wanted to chide Jackson for taking the investigation into his hands, but the end result was far too impressive to be upset. Oscar was faking his head injury - at least in part.

"That has to make him your top suspect, right?" Jackson asked as he finished.

"Maybe."

"Maybe?"

"At this point, it's too early to say, but it would have been challenging for him to poison Mrs. Henbit. In that regard, the only one that could have easily carried that out is still the nurse." It was true, but as he said it out loud, a thought caught in his head. Why would he kill his uncle? He did seem truly broken up by the loss, and with the will, he would have stood to inherit more if Razek had lived out the month and then died. If he had killed Mrs. Henbit someone else had to be responsible for Razek's death. Maybe he should look into the drug dealer. "It would be helpful to talk to whoever handled Oscar's accident."

"I think you'd need the Chief Inspector for that. And a warrant," Peaches said.

"I suppose so. I'd like to know who he was talking with as well. But for now... I need to find a few people."

"Who?" Jackson asked.

"Any relative of Ari Björnssen that still lives in Alku and a Raudur Sildsson."

"We could find the first at the pub," Jackson suggested.

"Raudur Sildsson?" Peaches said, raising an eyebrow.

"You know of him?" Henry asked.

"I'm familiar with him."

"Ari believes he provided Ramses with the drugs that killed him."

Peaches shook her head. "Raudur isn't a model citizen for sure, but there's no way he'd risk killing a customer. If word got around that

Raudur's stuff was tainted, he'd be out of business. If Raudur is anything, he's a businessman."

"A drug dealer," Henry said.

"Yes. That is his business. I could ask around though. See if anyone else has died from his product."

"Really?"

"Yeah, no problem. Are you ready to go back to Erfundenborg?"

"No. I'd like to track down Ari's relatives."

"We could drop you off in Alku," Jackson said. "I'm getting a rental car, so I could come back and pick you up once I have that done."

"You don't need a rental car."

"Yes, I do."

Henry tried to think of an argument for his opinion but couldn't come up with anything. And indeed it would be helpful, even with them staying at the Alku Inn. So Henry relented, and the three took their leave of Henbit Manor and loaded into Peaches' orange car. It had been a productive day so far. He wished he'd gotten more from Caprice on the will, but then again, there was only so much he could trust her. He would need to find another source to translate it for him. One question still tugged at his mind. Why had Mrs. Henbit changed the will? Had something happened? Maybe one of the staff would know. Oas wouldn't be helpful but maybe the maid. She was friendly. He made a mental note to ask a few staff members about that next time he visited the estate. For now, he wanted to know exactly why Ari Björnssen had been taken away from Alku.

The layout of the village of Alku was reasonably simple to understand once Henry put his mind to it. The hub was at the bridge. Every road eventually led to that bridge in one way or another. In a way, with all their curves and twists, it was really only one very knotted road. Bike and footpaths cut between the cobblestone roads and provided beautiful views of some very well maintained gardens. The footpaths were well worn just as the buildings and roads were. Everything in Alku felt old. Older than anywhere Henry had ever lived.

Before Jackson left for Erfundeneyja, they'd tried searching for a place to buy a new shirt. The first shop had only sold brightly colored parkas lined with real fox fur. The second had gone out of business and the third had only sold women's clothing. Still, Henry had found one bright yellow shirt that did fit and almost looked like a men's shirt. Under his suit coat it worked well enough. At least he'd thought that in the shop. Now strolling through the streets of Alku, he was having second, third and fourth thoughts.

As he moved further from the hub, the buildings seemed less and less ancient. Even at the edge though, the houses were either brick or stone. Henry wondered how they'd managed to keep the esthetic of Alku throughout the years. But before he could ponder that for long, he arrived at the small cottage he'd been searching for.

Like most homes in Alku, it was made of stone. It sat right on the cobblestone road, a small stone slab patio being the only protection from traffic. Not that there was much traffic. He'd seen few cars on the roads.

Henry stepped onto the patio and knocked on the dark wood door. He waited a moment then knocked again. This time there were sounds inside. A young girl's voice shouted in Verlorlandish. Moments later, footsteps ended with the door flying open. A short man with bright blue eyes and graying hair blinked up at him. He had broad shoulders and a deep chest, but he couldn't be much over five foot tall if that. He wore a pair of dingy overalls and slippers.

"Are you Hafthor Thorssen?"

The man's face screwed up in an expression Henry guessed was wariness. It was only then that Henry remembered what Otto had said about Hafthor, he didn't have a tongue.

"Who wants to know?" a heavily accented voice said from behind him. It was the girl's voice he'd heard before.

Henry looked past the man to a small blond haired girl in the shadows. She glared at him with bright blue eyes.

"I'm Detective Henry Pets. I work out of Erfundenborg." That was a risk. The people of Alku didn't love people from Erfundeneyja invading their village, but it would at least make him a local to the Verlorland Islands and not a complete outsider. "I'm investigating some deaths in Alku."

The man nodded in understanding. He pulled a notepad and pencil out of his overalls and jotted something down. He held it up.

You want to know about Ari? It read.

Henry nodded. Hafthor motioned for Henry to follow and led him to a small living area. The girl waited for them to pass, then shut the door.

There were a few well-built chairs that looked to be hand carved, a small table between two, a shelf of old books and a large stone fireplace with a hearth that curved out into the room. Hafthor sat in one of the chairs by the small table and Henry took the other. The girl stood next to Hafthor. The chairs were remarkably uncomfortable.

"So you are Ari's uncle?"

Hafthor wrote. *That is the question isn't it?*

"Is it?"

Hafthor nodded conspiratorially.

"That's the question that got my dad hit with a fish," the girl said. "I'd say it's important."

"You doubt your brother was his father?" Henry's eyes darted from father to daughter, but he still addressed his question to Hafthor.

Hafthor waggled his head non-committedly. He sighed and turned to his daughter, then motioned with his hands. She nodded. Then he started motioning again. Sign language. Not any Henry had seen before though.

"He says Uncle Björn fell for the Egyptian woman - that's what he calls my Aunt Rashidi - he fell for her the first time he saw her. Uncle Björn was the postman that had to take the mail clear out to..." the girl laughed. "I think the word is hideous... He had to take it to the hideous house out there." She pointed in the direction of the road to the Manor. "He met Aunt Rashidi there. They dated a few years. Dad says he kept telling Uncle Björn to move on, but every time another woman would catch his eye, Aunt Rashidi chased after him again." She paused for a moment, wrinkling her brow as Hafthor continued. He stopped and started again. She finally nodded and began. "So they were off for a few months. He thinks maybe six. One day Uncle Björn got a call and left very fast. He went out to the Henbit Manor. After a few days, dad went out there to find him. He was there with Aunt Rashidi, and they had just had Ari."

"Really?" Henry said, very interested. "I'm assuming he was a baby?"

"Newborn. That's what the call had been. Aunt Rashidi had had his little boy. He didn't look like Uncle Björn of course. He had his mother's dark skin. Maybe not quite as dark but still, not Uncle Björn's pink but he said it was his baby."

"You think someone else was the father?"

Hafthor signed furtively.

"Yes. Björn came home a few days later and told dad they had to leave the Islands. He asked him why and he wouldn't say. He just kept saying they had to go. So he took Aunt Rashidi and little Ari off to Finland and never came back here. None of us saw any of them again until Ari showed up on our doorstep, nearly a full grown man and hit Dad with a fish."

"Could you explain that?"

Hafthor wrinkled up his face and pushed back into his seat. It looked to Henry like he was trying to disappear into the chair. It wasn't a body language he was familiar with, so he merely waited for the man to stop doing whatever it was he was doing.

"It wasn't exactly like that," the girl spoke quietly, this time they were her own words. She glanced quickly from her father to Henry. "Mom says they saw Ari when he came back. He visited and all. Then one time Dad had him over for dinner. Mom says dad was drunk."

Hafthor signed quickly, but the girl ignored him.

"So Dad said what he thought about who Ari's father was and Ari hit him with a fish."

"How did he get the fish? No. Never mind. That isn't important. Do you remember exactly what you said?" He spoke this to the girl then remembered to look at Hafthor.

Hafthor shook his head.

"He was drunk."

Henry kept his eyes on Hafthor. The short man smoldered a bit before convincing himself to go on. He began signing again.

"He says he may have said something about that he thought Ari was Ramses' son."

"I see." Henry choked a bit with the surprise. "So you believe he was Ramses' son and not his sister's at all?"

"He thinks Ari is both of their's."

The girl spoke with such certainty it took Henry a moment to understand the implication of this. Hafthor thought Ari was the result of incest. "Brother and sister?"

Hafthor nodded glumly.

"I can see why he hit you with a fish."

Hafthor went back to his pad and scribbled something down.

Poor fish didn't do anything.

"You were going to eat it anyway... never mind." That wasn't important. "Did you have any sort of proof for any of this?"

Hafthor began signing again. His daughter waited then spoke.

"No, but after Aunt Rashidi died, Uncle Björn made a few comments about Ari that made Dad start thinking about this again. Then Uncle Björn shipped him back here to live with Ramses with some excuse about him being too much trouble."

"What sort of comments?"

"He says he remembers one time Uncle Björn said that Ari never should have been his responsibility."

"Maybe bitter that Rashidi kept the baby at all?"

Hafthor shook his head.

"No. He says it was..." the girl searched for the right word. "More meaningful than that."

Henry thought about that a moment. An incestuous pregnancy could be the reason for such a hasty move from the islands. It would be a secret worth killing for. At least for Ramses or Ari Björnssen. Would Mrs. Henbit have known? Mrs. Henbit had gone to some effort to keep him close, hiring him to be her nurse once he was old enough to leave. And then there was the fateful dinner. The family - or at least Caprice - had been surprised by Mrs. Henbit's insistence that Ari ate with the family that night. Had she been planning on revealing his parentage? Was that the secret she had spoken of? If so was that the reason she'd been murdered? And why would she have wanted the family to know?

There were too many questions but one thing Henry was sure of: he had to find out who Ari's parents really were. So that left him with one critical question: how did he get a sample of Ari's DNA?

"Can I ask you something?" the girl asked timidly.

"Yes," Henry said, pulling himself back to the present.

"Why are you wearing a women's shirt?"

"Of course!" Henry suddenly shouted snatching out his phone. "I need to make a phone call." He didn't wait for Hafthor or his daughter to respond, hitting the shortcut for Jackson. His brother answered on the first ring. "Whatever you do, do not wash that shirt!"

CHAPTER 12

Incessant yipping pulled Oas' attention away from his inspection of Matilda's cleaning. She had dusted all the chairs in the saloon but had neglected to vacuum the upholstery. It was a problem with a room as seldom used as the saloon. Even the chairs collected dust. This was a house that was meant to entertain. The distain the locals had for it, kept it from serving this purpose. Even when family visited, this room remained unused for anything more than a room to walk through.

Oas crossed the vacant room, footsteps echoing up the chamber, and opened the doors. Dandy sprang over his foot and scurried off into the hall. Oas watched the little dog, wondering yet again what Mrs. Henbit had been thinking. The only rationalization Oas could reach was that it did provide employment to the staff past her death. But for how long? Dandy was already seven. He'd known Mrs. Henbit almost his entire life, while she was eccentric and fairly selfish, she wasn't dim or cruel.

The fresh air from the gardens brought in the scents of lilac and grass. It also pulled Oas from his thoughts. He looked outside. No one was there. That was odd. Pip should have been with Dandy.

"Pip," Oas called. Nothing. He looked at his watch and tapped footman. No response. Oas frowned. "Pip," he called out one more time a little louder.

"Monsieur," Matilda's voice came from behind him. "I heard you calling."

Oas turned from the door. "Yes, for Pip. Have you seen him?"

"Not since he left with Dandy."

"He's not answering his watch."

"Did you try tracking him?" Matilda asked.

Oas felt his ears turn hot. Matilda must have noticed because she blushed in turn. It was a secret Oas thought he had kept to himself, that all the staff's watches could be tracked by his. Somehow Matilda had figured out his trick. He didn't reply but turned back to his watch and flicked the screen over to a map. He entered a code and then typed footman. Nothing happened.

"He must have turned it off."

"Why would he do that?"

Oas narrowed his eyes. Pip was an odd boy. He'd had decent references which were good enough for a footman, but he did have a few concerning traits. Enough so that Oas had worried how he would be around Mr. Henbit. For that matter, Mr. Razek and Mr. Björnssen. Fortunately so far there had been no incidents. He'd been polite to Mr. Okumu as well. Other than Pip's hygiene, Oas had had few troubles with the boy. Which was why his absence was strange. Pip was the type to slip away when not needed but to abandon Dandy? No. Pip liked the dog too much for that. He could hardly keep his hands off the thing.

"I could check the gardens?" Matilda offered.

"Yes," Oas agreed. "Please do. I'll search the house. If you find him-"

"I know," Matilda cut in, holding up her wrist and tapping her own watch.

The maid slipped past him and headed out into the gardens. As Oas closed the door, a sharp yipping followed by a crash and a growl that sounded more like Oscar than Dandy broke the silence. Oas sighed. If Oscar killed the dog, they were all in trouble. He made one step for the door before it flew open and Oscar stumbled in. He was soaking wet and dressed only in a pair of form fitting trunks a few sizes too small for a man of Oscar's build. He'd gained a considerable amount of weight since the head injury. Oscar stopped and stared dumbly at Oas. Oas started to question what was going on but decided against it. Someone else could deal with Oscar. He needed to find Pip.

The Inn was what most would describe as quaint. Cozy would have been the perfect keyword to attach to the place. Miss Marigolds had arranged for rooms as she'd told Henry she would. Although the rooms turned out to be one room with twin beds.

"It is our largest room," Mrs. Linna, the tiny innkeeper, said as she ushered Henry and Jackson into the room.

It was larger than Jackson's room at the Candlestick had been, and along with the beds there was a wooden desk, a chest of drawers, a wardrobe and even a large TV that hung right on the wood-paneled walls across from the beds. Through a door on the far side of the room, Jackson could see tiles of various shades of gray in what must be the bathroom.

"The sauna is through the washroom," the woman said pointing to the far door. "If you need anything the phone rings right to the front desk." With that, Mrs. Linna left the brothers alone.

"We have a sauna," Jackson said in near disbelief as he pushed through the room toward the bathroom.

Jackson hadn't managed to find new clothes yet but he had at least swung by Henry's flat to bring him fresh clothes. More importantly, Jackson hadn't thrown away the bloody shirt.

"There's a door," Jackson said, looking into the bathroom. He moved inside. There was a soft creek then Jackson's head popped back out. "It's just a sauna. The bathroom is all ours."

Henry wanted to laughed at Jackson's palpable relief but kept his composure. "Verlorlanders love their saunas. It's the Scandinavian influence. More so in the northern islands. If someone from Alsti invites you to a sauna, be wary. This one should be safe though. Now, did you get the shirt to Chief Inspector Klar?" Henry asked quickly as he dropped the suitcase Jackson had packed for him onto the bed. He began unpacking it immediately.

"Yes. They'll run the tests."

"And compare it to Mr. Razek's DNA?"

"Yes. I told them we wanted to see if Ari was related to the deceased."

"Good."

"Also, Alicia found information on Raudur Sildsson."

"Alicia?"

"Peaches."

Henry looked up from his suitcase. "She told you her name?"

"Yes."

"She's never told me."

Jackson shrugged. "Did you ask?"

"No."

Jackson gave Henry a half smile and shrug he always used when pointing out Henry's lack of social skills.

"What did *Alicia* find?"

"There haven't been any other deaths connected to that guy's customers. The police are hitting him pretty hard right now so Klar might have more."

"Did you get in touch with the Inspector?"

"Briefly. I told her about Oscar. I don't know if she'll do anything about it though."

"He was kicked at the manor, so presumably they would have taken him to the closest doctor."

"Is there one in Alku?"

"A small clinic. I can't imagine they'd have been able to help him there, but it could be a start."

"I could find out in the morning," Jackson said.

Henry eyed Jackson. "What are you doing?"

"What?"

"You're being very helpful."

"Yes. That's because I'm trying to help you."

"Why?"

"You're my brother."

"If I recall correctly, just recently you talked our father into cutting me off to try to get me to go back to Portland."

"Dude, I didn't talk him into anything. He did it. I came here to try to give him reason not too. And now maybe you are actually going to have a real case. If you pull this off, I think I can talk dad into letting you stay."

"I'm a grown man. I can stay without his approval."

"And without his money?"

Henry shrugged, averting his eyes. "Investigating a murder isn't a game. You can't simply pick it up as a hobby."

"Tell me exactly what to do then. I'm good with people. Let me talk to the less important ones."

Henry allowed himself a look at Jackson again. Jackson was good with people. They always seemed to like him for some inexplicable reason. "Are you enjoying this?"

"No," Jackson grimaced. "Don't be morbid."

"Alright. In the morning you can find out if Oscar went to the clinic in Alku. Also, ask them if they have anyone there that does home births."

"What?"

"Ari Björnssen was born at Henbit Manor. I'm fairly sure of that. I've left another message with Doctor Novak, but we might as well cover other bases."

"Alright."

"Also, don't wear that," he said, motioning to Jackson's attire.

"I'll look for clothes in the morning."

Henry shook his head. "Make sure it's something with sleeves. Sleeveless shirts are for-"

"Toddlers and Richard Simmons. I know."

"I was going to say Fred Flintstone."

"And now you're in the 60s."

Henry ignored the jab and crossed to the desk, placing the iPad on the wood. "I wish I knew German."

"I think Alicia does."

Henry raised an eyebrow. "Spending a lot of time with my neighbor?"

"She drove me home. Remember?"

"Right," Henry shrugged. "I suppose I could ask her to read this. She is good at keeping secrets. Mostly."

"You do know she isn't a secret agent, right?" Jackson asked.

"We've been over this. Of course, I know that. Now if you'll excuse me, I'd like to look over my notes."

"I think I'll take a shower and check out the sauna."

Henry made a noncommittal *mm-hmm* without really hearing Jackson. His focus was on the impenetrable text of the will. He'd been working on understanding Verlorlandish and had even picked up a little of the other languages spoken in the islands, but German was something he'd never toyed with. Luckily names were names. He could spot those. There was Caprice Marigolds, and there was Oscar Henbit. He kept scrolling. Finally, he came across a list. Seven names. He didn't recognize any of them, but they looked Verlorlandish. Most ended in *ssen* or *tiri*. That could be the names of the committee for Dandy's trust. He moved his eyes up. There was Dandy's name, not far from the list. He'd have to double check, but he felt good about this conclusion. Would one of these people have had the motive to kill Mrs. Henbit? This board would possibly have a good deal of power, not only on Alku but throughout the islands. But then why kill Ramses? If the motive was to get the land into the care of the trust, that was done. No, it was unlikely any of these people killed anyone. But it would be good to look into it. Did they even know they would be named to a trust? How did they know Mrs. Henbit? Good questions but Henry had more pressing concerns.

A thought hit him. He could send Jackson to look into these people. That would free him up to look more into the family. He wanted to question Oscar again, this time with the possible truth of his condition in mind. It was also pressing on him to find Mrs. Henbit's previous will. What had she changed it from? Did anyone know what the old will had contained? Maybe the motive for the original murder was tied to dated information. There were far too many questions. Part of him didn't want to place anything on Jackson; he wasn't a detective. But Henry had to admit, Jackson was good with people. He might as well use that if it was available.

"Jackson," Henry looked up. The room was empty. He listened a moment until he registered the sound of running water. He briefly considered interrupting Jackson's shower but then remembered how happy Jackson had looked when he'd found out the bathroom wasn't shared. He'd give his brother a little privacy. He could give him the instructions later.

Jackson felt good. The best he had felt since arriving in the islands. He'd showered without fear of being walked in on by a stranger. He'd had time to relax in the sauna. He even slept well despite Henry working well into the night. He was still working the next morning. Jackson wasn't sure if he'd worked through the night or if he'd merely woke before Jackson.

Henry didn't seem to notice Jackson as he dressed, still lost on the iPad. Jackson watched his older brother work for a few minutes. He was completely focused. When they were younger, Jackson had amused himself by throwing things at him when he was like this. He'd start small, a coin, and gradually get larger, a shoe or book, to see how big an object he could use before Henry noticed. Once he'd gotten up to a laundry basket. He didn't throw anything at Henry now though. It didn't seem appropriate. This was, after all, murder. Maybe. Possibly even probably. Was he allowing himself get carried away? Maybe. He had hardly even noticed Henry had stopped dropping the British accent when they were alone.

Jackson felt his phone vibrate and looked at it. He grimaced. Right on cue. He'd been dodging his dad's calls since their last conversation. What time was it in Portland? Midnight? Maybe a little earlier? If his dad was up this late, he'd probably had a few drinks. This conversation could wait.

Silencing the phone, Jackson decided it was as good a time as any to head out. He told Henry he'd be back, without acknowledgment then left the room and the inn.

The morning was warm, and the pub wasn't far, so Jackson decided to walk. The locals smiled and waved as he made his way over the cobbled streets. Traffic was light, but the village was alive. It felt comfortable. Jackson had to admit there was a charm to it.

The pub was crowded when he arrived. Breakfast was in full service, and it seemed most of the village had shown up. Otto greeted him at the door and suggested he take a seat at the bar. There were a few empty chairs, one next to a man he recognized: Constable Sham.

"Morning, dude," Jackson said as he pulled up his chair.

Shame turned and looked Jackson up and down. "Do you own any shirts with sleeves?"

Jackson couldn't help but laugh. "I have a few."

"You know this isn't the Caribbean, don't you?"

"I'm on vacation."

"In Alku. We wear sweaters all year."

"You're not wearing a sweater."

"That's because I'm on duty," he said pointing to his uniform.

"Neither is Otto." Jackson pointed to the bartender. He wore a plain white t-shirt.

"We wear sweaters often."

"Get off it, Sham," Otto bellowed at them. "Only time I've seen you in a sweater was your Aunt Migi's funeral."

Jackson laughed. "I'd wear something else if I had anything. Airport lost my luggage and can't seem to get it back."

"We have shops," Sham said.

"Yes. I've been to a few. What I can't seem to find is ones with normal clothes." Jackson turned to Otto. "Where'd you get that shirt?"

Otto pointed at his plain t-shirt. "Amazon."

"Great."

"Here, hold on," Otto said.

Otto disappeared into the kitchen. A few moments later he returned with a bright blue t-shirt. He tossed it to Jackson. Jackson let it unfold and looked at the front. It had bright red and green words across it. The only one even slightly familiar to Jackson was *Ledtrådssen*.

"What's it say?" Jackson asked.

"Drink Ledtrådssen, be happy," Otto said. "We made them for our keg tapping party."

"Thanks," Jackson said. "How much?"

Otto waved him off. "A gift from Alku to our best tourist. Yeah?" Otto laughed and headed off with two mugs of something.

Alone with Sham, Jackson turned to the constable. "Anything new on the Henbit case?"

Sham shook his head. "I still say it's not murder."

"How about your boss?"

Sham shrugged. "Seems to think the drug dealer isn't at fault. Not sure why she trusts a drug dealer so much but..." Sham stopped and looked nervous. "I mean, I'm sure the Chief Inspector has her reasons."

Jackson nodded. He was used to moments like this. Moments when people accidentally spoke too honestly. It's an effect he seemed to have on people. Sham probably wasn't in the habit of bad-mouthing his boss to anyone, let alone a stranger. He'd moved past the unexplainable trust though and was in danger of clamming up. "Of course. She seems to be a great inspector. Have you found anything on Oscar's family?"

Sham shook his head. "We're mulling over the idea that his papers were fake. Oscar Chu doesn't seem to exist before he married Mrs. Henbit."

"I'd say it's a pretty good chance they are fake."

Sham smirked. "Is that your professional opinion as a rafting guide?"

"I'm not a rafting guide. What are you doing here anyway?"

"I live here. This is my breakfast spot. And dinner. Lunch if I'm not working."

Jackson had forgotten the constable was a native to Alku. That gave him an idea. He pulled out the scrap of paper Henry had given him after his shower. Seven names were written on it. He handed it to Sham. "Do you know any of these people?"

Sham eyed Jackson a moment then causally shifted his attention to the paper. He read, then shook his head. He handed the paper back. "Some sound familiar."

"This isn't a large village."

"Doesn't mean I know everyone."

Before Jackson could press him further, Otto came back to the bar.

"Show him the names," Sham said. "Otto knows everyone."

"What names?"

Jackson handed the paper to the bartender. He glanced it over and frowned.

"They seem familiar but not placing them."

"You know everyone," Sham said.

"Not everyone. Just everyone that comes here. Or I'm related to. Or live near. Or-"

"We get the point," Sham cut in.

"Is strange though. I'm sure I could find them on my wall."

"That would be helpful," Jackson said.

A chirping ringtone sounded from Sham's pocket. He snatched out his phone and looked at the message, groaned and pulled out his wallet. "What's the bill, Otto? I got to run."

"Trouble?" Otto asked.

"At the manor again."

Jackson perked up. "Another murder?"

"No. Someone's missing."

"Who?"

Sham shrugged. "Doesn't say. The Chief Inspector is on her way." Sham paid Otto and gave them both a nod as he exited.

"So, hungry?" Otto asked.

Jackson nodded, but his eyes went after Sham. Henry would want to know about this. "Do you think you could find out where all those people live?"

"Oh yeah. For sure."

"Thanks. I'll be back in later." Jackson took his leave and headed back outside. Working or not, Henry would want to know about this. A part of Jackson reminded himself that he was getting carried away, but another part of him felt a drive unlike he'd ever felt before. He wanted to know who did it.

CHAPTER 13

Raised voices echoed out into the hall as the chauffeur let Henry and Jackson into the house. Jackson wore the shirt from Otto now. Henry had been slightly appeased that he'd at least found sleeves but that had mostly dwindled when Jackson told him what the words said.

Matilda was the only current occupant of the room, but her attention was on the open door opposite the main dining room. As they approached, she turned. Her expression was something between apprehension and confusion.

"We weren't expecting you," she said hastily crossing to meet them.

"We heard there's a missing person," Henry stated.

"Yes. Pip. The footman. It's only been a few hours though."

They reached the door she'd been looking through and entered. It seemed to be another dining room, not nearly as lavishly decorated as the other. Miss Marigolds, Oas, Ari and the Chief Inspector gathered around the table, all stood save for Miss Marigolds.

"He's probably just getting some time away from this damn place," Ari finished as they entered.

"He wouldn't leave while responsible for Dandy," Oas replied. "And he wouldn't risk leaving the estate."

"Then he's probably still on the estate somewhere," Ari said.

Oas was about to reply when he noticed the intruders. "You're here." The statement carried no obvious emotion.

Miss Marigolds turned. Her eyes lit up, and she jumped to her feet.

"No need to get up," Henry said politely.

"I'm so glad you're here. We can't find Pip anywhere."

"We have just started searching," Chief Inspector Klar clarified. "And honestly if it weren't for the other deaths we wouldn't even be doing that yet."

"Exactly," Ari said. "I guarantee you he's found a place to throw back a few beers away from this insanity."

"Ari, if you aren't going to be helpful, why don't you go check on Dandy?"

"I'm sure the dog's fine."

"Do I need to remind you how important it is that Dandy remain alive?"

Ari sighed and lumbered out of the room. Once he'd left, Oas continued.

"It is early but Pip - while not the brightest or best of people - does do his job well. He wouldn't wander off while responsible for Dandy."

"Who was the last one to see Pip?" Klar and Henry both asked at once. Klar gave Henry a sideways glare, but Henry didn't seem to notice.

"Most likely myself," Oas said. "I told him to take Dandy for his walk."

"Does he always walk Dandy?" Henry followed up.

"Often. He enjoys it more than most of the staff."

"And the search?" Henry asked.

Klar turned to Henry with a reluctant casualness. "Constable Sham has a unit out searching the grounds."

"My sister and Regal are searching the rest of the house. We just finished looking through the staff apartments," Miss Marigolds said, motioning to the far door leading out into another wing.

"And your mother?"

"She's resting."

"She imbibed nearly two bottles of wine last night," Oas added.

"What about Oscar?" Jackson spoke up.

They all seemed surprised to hear him, but Miss Marigolds answered. "He seemed a little overwhelmed by the chaos, so I took him to his room."

"I see." Henry thought for a moment. "Do you mind giving the Chief Inspector and I the room?"

"Of course," Miss Marigolds said.

Oas merely narrowed his eyes at Henry. Miss Marigolds said goodbye and headed out, and finally, Oas followed. Henry waited until the door had shut.

"Is this another murder?" Henry asked Klar.

A half grin picked at the corner of her mouth. "You're the private detective. What do you think?"

"The search, has it turned up anything suspicious?"

"The only thing that's suspicious is the dog coming back alone. If it weren't for that, I don't think Oas would even be concerned."

"Why would someone kill the footman?" Jackson asked.

"The will," Klar answered quickly. "His share would get divided up among the others."

"His share can't be that much," Jackson protested.

"It's still money," Klar said. "Honestly, I'm guessing if he is dead, it was an accident. They happen out here. Could have been a fall or rockslide or he could have gotten into one of our poisonous plants."

"Poisonous plants?" Jackson's voice went up a bit as he thought about his own trek off the path to the rundown house.

"We have quite a few," Klar added.

"There have already been two murders," Henry said. "Logically-"

"We still don't know about Laundra Henbit, and Ramses was a drug addict. We're investigating both as murders, but it might prove to be something else."

"So what do we do?" Jackson asked.

"Sham will search until we lose the light. Then we'll give it a night and see if he comes back by morning. If not then we'll be sending out more search teams. For now, though, I'm going back to Erfundenborg."

"One other thing," Henry said. "I was up very late last night and think I found something of interest."

Henry took out the iPad and handed it to Klar. Jackson leaned over to look. Henry hadn't said anything about this to him yet. Jackson really had no idea what Henry had been doing all night.

"What is this?" Klar asked.

"I got the idea from Jackson actually. He found all the Facebook profiles for the family and staff for me. Very helpful. But of course some more so than others. For example the one there, Oscar. You'll note it has nothing from before his marriage to Mrs. Henbit."

"Yes. I've looked over these already."

"Yes but," he held out his hand. Klar looked at it a moment then realized he wanted the iPad back. Henry clicked around a few times then handed it back. "It took some creative searching, but last night I managed to find that."

Jackson moved behind Klar and looked over her shoulder. It was still Facebook, and the photo looked like Oscar, but quite a bit thinner and the name was written in what looked like Mandarin. In fact, all the writing on the page was in the non-western language.

"I've contacted the profile but so far no response. I've also contacted the man's wife. You can see the link to her right there."

Klar stopped looking the page over and turned surprised eyes on Henry. "This is Oscar?"

"I believe so. Seems he's from Taiwan and married."

"How did you find this?"

"I started with one of his older images. A selfie actually. This one here," Henry flipped to the image. "You can see a pandanus palm there." He pointed to a tree with a what looked to Jackson to be a bright orange pinecone type fruit. "Obviously not a tree that grows here in the islands. I then did a reverse image search on-"

"Never mind. I don't need to know. Did you contact him through this profile?" Klar asked.

"Yes. And his wife."

"If in some off chance he is murdering people, do you think contacting him to let him know you found his secret identity would help or hurt us in catching him?"

Henry frowned. Jackson could tell this thought hadn't crossed his mind. It was a weakness his brother had always had, he wasn't good putting himself in someone else's position.

"You're lucky he has brain damage. Maybe he doesn't even remember this."

"Actually," Jackson started, but Henry's eyes cut him off.

"We believe the brain damage could be an act," Henry said.

"Do you have proof?"

"I saw him acting different," Jackson said. "As in normal not the usual different."

Klar shook her head. "I suppose we should speak to him before I leave then. Come on. Let's find him before he disappears too."

Henry readily agreed. It was a good plan.

As they headed for the door, a thought hit Jackson. He tried to dismiss it but it gnawed at him. "Remember when you used to do puzzles all the time?"

"This is not the time to reminisce."

"Yeah, I know. I just keep thinking about you, Chad and those damn puzzles."

"We have other things to worry about."

"All this just makes me think of that. Mrs. Henbit, Nic and now Pip. It doesn't seem to fit. Like your puzzles never fit."

"The puzzles never fit because Chad kept mixing up the pieces to upset me."

"Exactly."

Henry shook his head. "This isn't a game, Jackson. This is murder."

"I know," Jackson said. He could tell he needed to drop the thought. He wasn't even sure why he'd had it.

Oas was just outside the room - Jackson wondered if he'd been able to hear the conversation inside - and was dispatched to fetch Oscar from his room. Jackson wished he was surprised that Henry had sent the messages, but he wasn't. Hopefully, Oscar hadn't seen it yet.

That hope died when Oas rushed back down the grand staircase without the widower. Lydia Marigolds looked up from the seat she'd taken on one of the benches near the stairs.

"Is he asleep?" She asked.

"He's not there."

"Maybe the washroom?"

"I checked. Oscar is not upstairs."

There was an uneasy silence.

"I didn't see him come down," Miss Marigolds said.

"We have been preoccupied with searching for Pip."

"Oscar can't have gone missing," Miss Marigolds said. "Not while we're searching for Pip. That's too much of a coincidence. I'm sure he's around here somewhere."

Klar shook her head and gave Henry a quick glare. "Mr. Pets, why don't you help Miss Marigolds search the main level here. I'll take the maid to search the grounds and Jackson can take the lower level with Oas. I'll get the word out to Sham." Klar didn't wait for a response, she merely whistled at Matilda and headed out the front door.

"We can start in the conservatory. He likes the plants," Miss Marigolds said, addressing Henry.

"Good. Good. After you."

As they exited, Jackson turned to Oas. "How do you get to the lower level?"

"He won't be down there."

"How do you know?"

"Regal and Sloan are searching it already. It's not large. A gym and pool and bowling alley."

"Not large and it has a bowling alley?"

"Only one lane. And of course the saunas."

The stairway to the lower level was hidden in the gap between the two curves of the grand staircase. It appeared to be a mural of a man on a horse chasing foxes, but with a push from Oas, the panel moved back to reveal a curved staircase.

They came down into a large open room with a pool Jackson wouldn't have called small. The air was humid and smelled of chlorine. Voices echoed from a door to the left as the exited the stairwell.

"If he is then at least we'll get more." The voice sounded like Sloan.

"That's horrible." That one sounded like Regal.

Oas motioned for Jackson to follow and the headed toward the voices.

"What's it matter if it's a horrible thing to say? If he's dead, he's dead. We didn't kill him."

"I don't want to talk about him like he's dead. And besides, I don't think his share was large. It's apparently weighted by years of employment."

"Anything will help. Not like you'll be getting any more from OZ Corps."

"Don't bring that-" Regal stopped as he saw Jackson enter the room.

The pair stood in the middle of the gym. Again, modest wasn't what Jackson would call it. It had nearly everything Jackson would have wanted in a gym minus a rock wall. It also looked hardly used.

"Hello," Regal stammered.

"Have you seen Oscar?" Oas said flatly.

"Oscar?" Sloan seemed to be taking a moment to catch up. "I thought we were looking for the creepy little guy with the dark circles around his eyes."

"Yes. Pip. We also are looking for Oscar now."

"We've lost someone else?" Sloan gaped.

"Murdered?" Regal looked genuinely worried now. "What is going on here?"

"Not murdered as far as we know," Oas said. "He wasn't in his room."

"Did you check the washroom?" Sloan asked.

"Of course I checked the washroom," Oas's voice wavered a bit, losing its usual composure.

"He likes the conservatory," Regal offered.

Oas eyed Regal a moment before turning to Jackson. "We should check the bowling alley." He headed out without another word.

Jackson looked back at Regal and Sloan.

"We do hope they're both alright," Regal said.

"You should probably go wait in the hall. We'll finish down here."

Jackson left the two looking very awkward and headed back past the pool. With all this available, how had Laundra Henbit let her health deteriorate so much? Even with a bad back, she could probably have taken up swimming. Not for the first time, Jackson found himself wondering what kind of woman she'd been. Lydia Marigolds seemed to adore her but had been honest about a few of her aunt's shortcomings. She'd married for money then married many more times but never had any children. She doted on one niece though. It was easy to see why Lydia had been Laundra's favorite. Sloan had less personality than a toaster.

Laundra Henbit seemed to be a sad, eccentric woman but generally liked. She'd been a good employer and a good aunt to at least one niece. She seemed to have looked after her friends in the case of Ramses the gardener and even his sister for a few years. And that had extended to Ramses' nephew, Ari. Odd, yes, but kind. Except for the will. The will wasn't kind. Jackson shook his head. It didn't make sense. But often people didn't make sense. Still, it didn't fit. A puzzle piece was missing.

Jackson was almost to the next door when he heard Henry's voice from the stairwell.

"We got him." Henry stepped out - looking over the room once then back to Jackson. "Hurry." He started for the stairs then turned back to the pool. "Very nice pool."

"Sure, where'd they find him?"

"At the airport. He was trying to leave the country."

"Great, we can see if they found my luggage."

"They're taking him to Hell's Mouth."

Jackson shrugged. "Oh well. It was in Iceland last night. Who knows where they put it today."

Oscar sat in the small white room, hands cuffed together and attached to the desk. He squirmed, trying to get comfortable. Everything itched. He let out another long sigh. He'd almost made it. Ten more minutes and he'd have been down the runway.

The door opened, and three people came in. He recognized them right away. The police lady, the detective and the doctor that always wore shorts. He still wore shorts but had a new shirt finally. The woman and the detective took the seats across from him while the doctor leaned against the wall.

"I assume you received my message?" Henry asked.

Oscar laughed. It briefly crossed his mind to put up the act, but he was sure it was too late for that. Brain dead Oscar wouldn't have been able to drive the limo let alone buy a ticket to Taipei. And then there was the fact he'd used his real name and been found with his actual passport.

"What am I being charged with?" Oscar asked.

"In the very least," Klar started. "Illegal entry into the country."

"I came legally."

"No, you came under a false identity."

"But legally."

Klar put her hand on the bridge of her nose and squeezed her eyes shut in frustration. "Coming in under a false identity makes it illegal."

"Are you sure?" Oscar asked.

"Of course I'm sure. I'm the Chief Inspector."

"Of an Island."

"All the islands."

"I don't think it's illegal in Taiwan."

"You're not in Taiwan and I'm sure it's illegal there too."

"We'll just have to agree to disagree on that."

Klar clenched her fists. "You're in the Verlorland Islands. We decide what's legal. It's not something we can agree to disagree on."

"We have other questions too," Henry said. "Regarding the deaths."

"I had nothing to do with them," Oscar nearly shouted.

"You married Mrs. Henbit to inherit her money. Right?" Henry asked

Oscar looked down. Henry waited. Silence built up in the room until the pressure seemed to cave in on Oscar. "Sure. She did the same thing though. No one had a problem with that."

"She didn't pretend to be someone else."

"Or enter the country illegally," Klar added.

"She found me," Oscar said. "Just for the record or whatever. We wouldn't have come up with the idea if she hadn't found me first."

"Online?"

"Yeah."

"As Oscar?"

"I've always used English names for dating apps."

"You were already married though."

"It was my wife's idea. It was an app for rich women to find younger men."

"So you were looking for someone like Mrs. Henbit?"

"Yeah. But not her. I didn't message any of them. I let them message me." It was a point Oscar was proud of. It was obvious by the look on his face.

"Congratulations," Klar said flatly.

"Then you faked the brain damage to get out of the relationship?"

"No," he snapped back. "Not entirely. I did get kicked in the head. And it wasn't an act at first. I was really messed up. It was horrible. But I got better but... hell, I thought with her condition she would just want a husband to look at and spoil or something. I didn't expect her to want to... you know... do stuff."

Jackson squirmed in the back of the room. Even Klar looked suddenly uncomfortable.

"Yeah, exactly. It wasn't pleasant. But that stopped once I was damaged. It was a free pass, I wasn't going to screw that up. I started to get better but, you know, just kept the act going. And it's not like I'm back to normal either. I get these headaches all the time from the damn dog's yipping and I can't smell. Also forget things. A lot. That horse messed me up."

"But you did fake the extent of the brain damage," Henry stated.

Oscar shrugged. "Yeah."

"Then she took too long to die, so you needed to hurry it up," Henry said.

"What?" Oscar gaped. "No. No. I didn't kill her. She was fat. She just died. Right? You think I killed her?"

"It has crossed my mind," Klar said.

"I want a lawyer! Now."

"Alright, I'll see who's available," Klar said and stood.

Henry looked up at her, shocked. "You're leaving?"

"Yes. That's the law. He asked for a lawyer."

"You could convince him not to?"

"That's not how it works. I can't speak to him or be in here without his lawyer now. You can stay. He doesn't have to talk to you though."

"And I won't."

The door shut and the room again fell into silence. Henry kept his eyes locked on Oscar. Oscar turned his head down, stealing occasional glances at Jackson and Henry.

"Where were you when Pip went missing?"

"Ah," Oscar said, looking up quickly. "Can't put that on me. I was in the house all day with Lydia and then the black guy. He was trying to teach me to swim. That was weird actually."

"Why was he teaching you to swim?"

"I think he was trying to be nice. Oscar isn't really able to ask questions like that. It's one of the downsides of his condition."

"The fake condition."

"It's real for Oscar. That's called acting. I made Oscar real. No one suspected."

Jackson raised his hand. "I did."

"He actually did," Henry agreed. "He said so."

"Well, no one important did."

"We could stop by the house on the way back," Henry said. "Agent Orange made curry."

"Dude, I don't want Agent Orange's curry," Jackson replied, the street lights flashed overhead as they drove through Erfundenborg. "I just want a burger from the pub, a shower and then a long sit in the sauna."

Henry smiled, lopsided eyes full of amusement. "You're in danger of becoming a Verlorlander. Maybe not the burger or dude parts but the rest."

"Do you think Pip is dead?" Jackson asked, changing the subject.

"I don't know," Henry answered. He pulled out his iPad and began fiddling with it as he spoke. "He's a wild card still. If he is dead, Oscar couldn't have done it. Which would mean he likely didn't commit the other murders. Oh!" He picked the iPad up and looked at it carefully.

"What?"

"Mrs. Henbit's solicitor in Germany responded. She sent the previous will as well."

"In German?"

Henry paused as he read. "Yes. But she does summarize it here."

"How different is it?"

"Very. Her sister still gets the house in Cape Town. There's a decent sum for her husband. A very good sum for Ramses and a surprisingly large amount to Ari. Also a good amount for Oas. But everything else goes to Miss Marigolds."

"Really?"

"Yes."

"And the dog?"

"Not in the will at all."

"Really?"

"Yes. I wouldn't have said it if it were otherwise. Stop asking that."

"Who knew about this will?"

"The solicitor was unsure."

"You know what this means, right?"

"Of course I know what this means. If this was the will people expected, Lydia Marigolds would have the most to gain for her Aunt's death."

"Talk about a favorite niece. What did Sloan get?"

Henry read some more. "A boat."

"Hell. Maybe Sloan killed her out of spite."

"I doubt that."

"Me too. Just thought it would be funny."

"It wasn't." Henry paused to make sure Jackson understood. "What I'm wondering is why Ari receives more than Ramses who had been a nearly lifelong friend. In fact," Henry put his finger close to the screen and scanned the document again. "His is the largest outside of Miss Marigolds."

"She really liked the guy."

Henry frowned and leaned back. "Why would she leave nearly everything to one niece and a former employee's son?"

"She did keep him close," Jackson said. "Next room and all that. Maybe they were..." Jackson trailed off. "I mean with Oscar faking the brain condition."

Henry thought for am moment. "Possibly."

Jackson shook his head. "I don't think so. I don't get the vibe from Ari. It's more... like... respect. Maybe? Or... he talks about her like an aunt or a grandmother maybe. Maybe she knew Ari was Ramses' son?"

"We're still assuming that," Henry pointed out. "But assuming that's true, I don't know how Ari being the result of incest would make her choose him to inherit so much."

"Maybe she felt sorry for him?"

"Or maybe she knew something else about him," Henry mused. "We need that DNA test."

"We need dinner. I didn't even get lunch today."

"Dinner would also be good."

CHAPTER 14

"Where's Oscar?" Caprice asked as she kicked Dandy away from her chair. "This dreadful dog will not leave me alone without him dropping food everywhere."

"He's been arrested," Lydia replied.

The rest of the family had decided to join her in the conservatory for dinner to the annoyance of Oas. Lydia wasn't exactly pleased to have the company either mostly because her mother kept reminding her she was the only reason they had to juggle their plates and wait on drink refills. It had been Regal's idea. Lydia did appreciate the thought. Of all her immediate family, Regal was the most empathetic.

"I don't remember that."

"It was two days ago."

Two days. There had been little movement on the case since Oscar's arrest. Pip was still missing too.

"Did he kill Pip?" Caprice asked as if reading Lydia's thoughts.

"Pip is just missing, not dead," Sloan snapped.

"Just asking," Caprice said, waving her mostly empty drink.

"Most likely he didn't," Regal added. "I was with him from the time Oas last saw him until Dandy returned without him. "He didn't murder anyone that we know of. Oscar just isn't Oscar."

"What does that mean? Don't be coy. How do I get a refill without the butler?"

"It was a fake name," Regal said. "He's actually married to a woman in Taiwan. They've arrested him for faking his entry papers."

"Really now? I bet you he did it then. Killed everyone. Covering it up. Well, with that settled perhaps we should start making arrangements to get out of here."

"Our tickets home aren't for another week," Sloan spoke up. "Not to mention we can't go before the time's up. Or the burial. Whichever comes first."

"And I do believe the police want us to stay until they're done," Regal added.

"Baaa," Caprice said waving her empty champagne flute. "When did you say this happened? The things with Oscar. Or whoever."

"Two days ago."

"I must have been drunk."

"You were," Sloan replied.

"And I still would be if that dreadful butler were here."

"I think I'm done," Lydia said with a sigh, putting her plate down beside the chair. "Excuse me."

Caprice continued with her inane babbling as Lydia left the conservatory. The last thing she heard was her mother saying they shouldn't have bothered joining her for dinner if she was going to leave them in the middle of it. Lydia didn't look back.

She didn't have a destination in mind yet, but she couldn't stand another moment with her mother. It had been like that most of her life. Even as a child. She'd never been a great mother really, especially after her father died. This house had been an escape from that though over the years. And now her mother had invaded that. Her and death.

The house felt so different now. Empty yet crowded. She passed on through the saloon and on into the great hall. Lydia placed a hand on one of the marble pillars near the grand staircase. She wondered if the house would ever feel the same again.

Her thought was interrupted as the doors opened. Laki Ünwichtigbock entered followed by Constable Sham. The chauffeur was covering footman duties with Pip missing, a task Laki grumbled about often but usually in Verlorlandish. Lydia had actually forgotten about Laki until he'd started covering for Pip.

Laki nodded and introduced Sham then quickly headed back out. It was a typical occurrence now. Sham led the team searching for Pip and was the primary police presence around the house. Lydia was disappointed Henry wasn't with him, not that he often was. She hadn't seen him since Oscar had fled. She wondered if that meant Oscar had done it.

"Have you found anything?" Lydia asked.

"No, ma'am. Just coming to tell you we're pushing out further into the heath so you won't be seeing us so often."

"Unless you find him."

"Of course," Sham nodded politely. "Could you tell the others?"

"Yes."

"Thank you, ma'am."

Sham nodded again and turned to the door.

"Have you heard from Henry? I mean, Mr. Pets?" She wasn't sure she should ask the constable that. She wasn't exactly sure how to interact with the police or the detective really. She knew she was technically a suspect, but she was also the one that would pay Mr. Pets. Still, she wanted him to remain objective, so she'd given him his space. She was curious though.

"He's still making a nuisance of himself. Been in to see *Oscar* once or twice."

"If you see him tell him..." Tell him what? Hello? That wasn't right. "Good luck."

"I will," Sham said hastily then let himself out.

Henry knocked sharply on the door. Again.

"I don't think they're home," Jackson said.

Henry sighed. "I know."

Jackson had finally found a place in Alku to buy more clothes but Henry wasn't sure how much better they were. The shop sold traditional Alku workwear which meant sweaters and something like canvas lederhosen called tyrätstutterbuxters. Jackson had balked at the sweaters but for some idiotic reason loved the tyrätstutterbuxters. Today he wore an evergreen colored sweater with a traditional Alku fish pattern woven in light blue. The tyrätstutterbuxter were dark grey and possibly used. He'd gone from looking like a lost frat boy to a lost Alku tradesman.

Henry knocked one more time. "I have left dozens of messages for Dr. Novak. All she has to do is call me back." He knocked harder.

"I don't think you'll find them home."

"You just said..." Henry started then realized this had been said in a far different voice. He turned. Behind Jackson stood, or rather hunched, a very old woman with a large red hat. She hung over her walker with a pleasant smile on her overly made up lips. "Oh, hello."

"You want the doctor?" The old woman asked.

"Yes, I'm Detective Pets. I have need to speak with her. Do you know Dr. Amelia Novak?"

"Oh yes. I live just across the street."

"Do you know when she's normally home?"

"Yes but I think they've gone on vacation. Haven't seen them in days. Their car's gone too. It's always taking up so much space on the street. They should have a garage with a car that big. Are you the Detective Pets that found Fanney's mink?"

Henry smiled. "Yes, I am."

"Oh bless you. She was so worried about the poor creature. Not me, mind you. Such an ugly thing. Well, I do hope you find the doctor."

"Could you do me a favor?"

"Of course."

"If you see her, could you call me?"

Henry exchanged numbers with the elderly woman then he and Jackson climbed back into the rental car.

"Fanney's mink?" Jackson asked.

"It was one of my first cases."

Jackson laughed. "Where to now?" Jackson asked.

Henry thought for a moment. "No messages from the Chief Inspector?"

"One text. They've arrested the drug dealer. Unrelated charges. We could question him though."

"I don't think that would be helpful."

"Neither do I."

"Oh?" Henry said with a slight smile. "Please tell me why."

"Two deaths and one missing person that's most likely dead. I doubt a small-time drug dealer did all of that."

"So while you're in the detecting mood-"

"That's not a word."

"I know it's not a word. I'm being creative." Henry cleared his throat. " So while you're in the detecting mood, who do you suspect?"

Jackson looked at Henry a long moment. Henry could tell he was being analyzed. Jackson did that. All the time really. Henry felt a little pride in the fact that he seemed to be the one person Jackson didn't really understand.

"Fine. Okay. I think the key is the will. If we find out why Mrs. Henbit changed her will, we find out why she was killed."

"Interesting. I think the key is in the old will."

"What do you mean?"

"When I know, I'll tell you. Still, you haven't answered my question. Who do you think did it?"

Jackson shook his head then leaned back and looked up at the ceiling. He thought a few minutes before he spoke. "I think Oas could kill someone if he had to but not his boss. Matilda couldn't hurt anyone. I doubt Regal could either. Sloan... she could if she felt she had no other choice. Caprice maybe but she wouldn't do it herself. Ari, yes. If he was angry. The cook... she's a tough one. Haven't got a good read on her. Oscar... I don't know. I feel like he's smart enough to know waiting for Mrs. Henbit to die was the safe option. Am I forgetting someone?"

"You still didn't exactly answer. And yes. You forgot two people. Miss Marigolds and the Chauffeur."

"Lydia hired you."

"No one is above suspicion. No one."

"Who's the other one?"

"The Chauffeur."

Jackson shook his head. "I don't remember him."

"He's easy to forget. Let's go. Maybe Peaches has found something interesting."

"Alicia."

"You do know that name could also be fake, yes?"

Jackson frowned.

"Hadn't thought of that, had you?"

"No."

"See, that's why I'm the detective."

"Can't say I've found anything more interesting than you already know," Alicia said, handing the iPad to Henry.

Henry had left it with her for the day to look over the wills, both of them, hoping she could find something useful. After finding out she spoke Mandarin - and her actual name - Jackson had suggested they see if she could read German. She could.

"Does Lydia Marigolds know how much she lost with the new will?"

"I don't know," Henry said taking the iPad.

"She'd be pretty pissed if she knew," Agent Orange said from the kitchen where he was cooking something that smelled like fish and lemon Pledge.

He was dressed in a lumberjack outfit complete with a large fake beard. Alicia wore an unflattering pantsuit and heels. Jackson almost asked for an explanation to both but thought better of it.

"You wanna stay for dinner?" Orange asked. "We have extra."

"No," Jackson said quickly. "I think we need to get back to Alku. Right, Henry?"

"I'm in no hurry."

Jackson frowned and sniffed the air. He raised his eyebrows at Henry. Henry merely looked at him, baffled. Subtlety was wasted on Henry.

The food was better than it had smelled. Not by much though. Agent Orange did take off the fake beard to eat, and once again Jackson considered asking what it was all about but decided against it.

"So, are there any other Pets?" Alicia asked. "Or just the two of you?"

"Yes. Or no. Not Pets," Henry said.

"Our last name is Ruck," Jackson said. From the smile on Alicia's face, he guessed somehow she actually knew that. "We have a younger brother. Chad Ruck."

"Never trust a Chad," Agent Orange said.

"What?"

"It's a motto I have. Saved me from a lot of bad decisions. Chad's are always trouble."

"He really is," Jackson said shaking his head.

"Will you invite him out?"

Henry's eyes went wide a moment. "I don't think that would be safe."

"For?"

"For the islands."

"He can't be that bad," Alicia said with a chuckle.

"He once dropped a brick on a nest of baby bunnies," Jackson said.

"How old was he?"

"That was two months ago. You should have seen all the milk. And the sound..."

"I received the brains," Henry started. "Jackson received the brawn. And Chad ended up with the crazy."

Jackson laughed. Not really because of the joke but because he knew that's how Henry saw him. Still to this day, Henry thought Jackson was only good for hitting things. That had been their relationship for quite a while. Jackson would beat up the kids bullying his older brother. Henry was rarely grateful. Eventually, people stopped picking on him though. Then Henry had moved off to college and without him around suddenly Jackson found out he wasn't as stupid as he'd always thought. Sure, he couldn't recite the names and birthdays of every president of the United States and couldn't memorize every book he read, but he wasn't dumb.

A buzzing cut off Jackson's train of thought. The conversation had moved on to mutual friends that Jackson didn't know. He fished out the phone and sighed, Jackson's dad's face filled the screen.

"Excuse me."

"I haven't been avoiding your calls," Jackson said forcefully, sinking down onto Henry's sad bed.

"I've been calling for days now."

"I know."

"And you haven't been answering." His dad's voice was high with emotion.

"We've been busy."

"Busy getting him home?"

"He has a case. A real case."

"Don't tell me you're buying into it. You've always followed your brother around blindly. I should have sent Chad."

"You know that wouldn't work. And I don't blindly follow him around. There was a murder. Two actually. Maybe a third. He's getting paid to investigate it."

"Paid? Real money?"

"Yes."

"How much?"

"I didn't ask."

"Then ask."

"He's not using your money now."

"Everything he owns is mine."

"Dad, he could actually have something here. He's making headway. His investigation has actually lead to an arrest." It was true. Oscar would have made it out of the country if Henry hadn't told Klar about him.

"An arrest?"

"Yes. Not the murderer. But he uncovered someone scamming the family."

The line was silent a moment. "But not the murderer?"

"He'll find out who did it. I think he could make this work. The detective thing."

"He better."

"He will."

"If you're covering for him-"

"I'm not covering for him."

"I'll be disappointed."

Jackson sighed. That wasn't a word he wanted to hear from his Dad. He was a man of very active disappointment. "I understand."

"I have things to do. We can continue this conversation later."

"How's Chad?"

His dad groaned. "Don't ask."

"What did he do now?"

"Have you heard of something called fentanyl?"

"Damn it."

"I have to go. Call me when Henry's solved the case or bring him home."

The call ended. Jackson fell back into the bed and sighed.

"Everything alright?"

Jackson turned to the door. Alicia stood there, watching him, silhouetted by the hallway light.

"Yeah," Jackson said, standing up quickly. "Our dad is... he's... how much did you hear?"

"More than you'd like. Comes with the job."

At least she was honest. Well, for the first part at least. "He's not too excited about Henry's life choices."

"He's a grown man."

"Who's never exactly made his own living."

"That is a problem."

Jackson shook his head. "Our dad sort of creates his own gravitational pull. Once you're in his orbit, it's pretty damn hard to get away unless he ejects you."

"Is this you getting away?"

Jackson laughed. "No. I'm visiting."

Alicia didn't reply. Jackson couldn't see her face, but he felt like she was giving him a skeptical look. Maybe that was just his own emotions. Was he escaping? No. He'd go back. But right now he was very glad that of all his family, he was with Henry.

"Did you need something?" Jackson asked when the silence between them grew awkward.

"Yes. Henry's on the phone with someone at Hell's Mouth. He wanted me to get you."

"Why?"

"They found the footman."

Once again, Jackson found himself looking at a dead body. This one was more unsettling than the gardener's had been. At least it should have been. Somehow it didn't make Jackson as uncomfortable as the previous body. Was he already getting used to it?

A hiker had found the footman, Pip, in the woods outside Henbit Manor. It was ground Constable Sham and his team had covered, but the body had rolled under a dead tree and had only been found when the hiker tried to use the tree as a place to relieve himself. The reason the dogs hadn't even found him took more explaining.

"What killed him?" Jackson asked.

Sham looked at him sideways with a look that nearly shouted, *Isn't it obvious?* What he said was, "Muukalane haetta poisoning."

He pointed to one of Pip's arms. It was bloated - more than the rest of him - and covered in oozing red sores. His hand was even worse, purple and black, puss seeping from a wound in the palm.

"I've never seen a reaction this severe," Henry said.

"What is muuka... muuka..." Jackson shook his head. "What is that?"

"Muukalane haetta. A plant," Klar answered. "It grows on Alku. The oil on the thorns is poisonous."

Jackson took a step back and looked around at the foliage. "It does that?"

"Not to locals," Sham said. "Anyone that grew up on Alku has a natural tolerance. It will only give us a rash. That's why it's called muukalane haetta."

"I don't speak Verlorlandish," Jackson reminded them.

"Stranger danger," Sham translated.

Jackson raised an eyebrow. "That means something very different where I come from."

"I think the closer translation is danger to strangers," Klar added.

"So if I get scratched by one of those thorns, that will happen to me?" Jackson asked.

"Maybe but probably not. You would need to get an antidote quickly. Most tourists survive now. Maybe get a few scars. But a few people are overly susceptible to the poison. In those cases, this is the result."

"Even then," Klar put in. "This is extreme."

"So he's been right here all this time?" Jackson asked. "You had dogs out here sniffing for him, right?"

"Breath in," Henry said to Jackson.

Jackson took in a breath, bracing for the smell of the body. Instead, the overwhelming scent was something sweet and musky with a hint of pine.

"The oil has a very strong odor," Henry said.

"Drug dealers use it to mask their products all the time," Klar added.

"They use a poisonous oil to mask the scent of their products? That seems safe."

Klar merely shrugged.

"So," Jackson said slowly. "Is this murder?"

"As suspicious as another death out here is," Klar shook her head. "I think he took the dog for a long walk, grabbed the wrong branch and died before he could signal for help."

"His watch was dead before he left the house," Henry added. "He couldn't have signaled anyone for help."

"So this is an accident?"

Henry nodded. "I have to agree that is probable. Except..." Henry looked around, studying the landscape. "Assuming he is on the extreme end of reactions to muukalane, he would have been dead within minutes of exposure."

"Yes," Klar agreed.

"Why's he this far away from the house?"

"Confusion," Sham spoke up. Henry turned and gave him an expression that said go on. "One of the first side effects is confusion. Even in mild cases, people can end up wandering off or forgetting they've been poisoned. My uncle almost lost his leg because he went home and fell asleep after getting scratched."

"And this plant is just out here?" Jackson asked with growing nervousness.

"Yes," Sham said. "But the thorns are bright reddish orange. You can't miss them."

"He did," Jackson said pointing to the body.

"Assuming Constable Sham is correct," Henry cut in before Sham had a chance to respond. "He would still have needed to wander off the grounds. I doubt Henbit Manor has muukalane haetta in the gardens."

"I asked Oas about that," Klar said. "He said Pip often took Dandy out on the trails. If we made our way back toward the house from here, we could probably find the trail he was using."

"I see," Henry said softly. "I suggest we let the family know quickly about the nature of this death. Two murders caused enough worry. It will be good for them to know there wasn't a third."

"Thank you, Mr. Pets," Klar said in an overly kind tone. "I had planned on doing that myself. I think we can handle things from here. The two of you should get back before it gets dark. Wouldn't want to stumble into the same muukalane haetta plant as our victim here."

Henry took his leave and struck out toward the manor. Jackson followed quickly, eyeing the plants.

"Killer plants. You didn't tell me this island had killer plants."

Henry sighed. "His reaction is one in a thousand. Even if you aren't local, most people would be fine as long as they received medical attention within a few hours. And even beyond that, most likely they'd only lose a limb."

"That makes me feel so much better."

"Good."

"That was sarcasm."

"You know I hate sarcasm."

"Yes, I do."

They continued on in silence. Jackson watched the path closely. The light was beginning to fade, and he was not going to be caught in the dark. He picked up his pace.

"This is a big coincidence," Jackson said. "If he came out here a lot, what are the chances of this happening right now?"

"Coincidences do happen. Baring someone hiding in the underbrush wielding muukalane haetta branches, an accident is the most likely scenario."

"That could happen," Jackson said. "Local attacks him with a branch."

"Look around us," Henry said, motioning to the short brush around them. "Do you see good hiding places?"

Jackson looked around. They were fifty yards from Klar and her men now, but it was easy to spot them still. There were no significant trees in this area, just thin underbrush and wildflowers. The hills were soft and rolling. It would be difficult to hide.

"More than that," Henry said. "None of our suspects could have been this far from the house at the time of his death. The most likely explanation is an accident so until I find something else that points another direction, this death would merely be a distraction."

Jackson nodded.

"Now that doesn't mean I won't keep my eyes open. And also so should you, that there is muukalane haetta." Henry pointed to a deep green bush two feet from where Jackson was passing. It was unremarkable in every way except for the vivid reddish orange, three inch long thorns. They glittered in the light with a viscus oil that nearly dripped from the ends.

Jackson quickly moved away, eyeing the glossy death spines. "Let's get back to the village."

CHAPTER 15

One thought stuck in Jackson's head over the next few days: he had to make sure Henry solved this case. Henry was a machine. Focused. He moved from one task to the next. He'd also taken to the iPad. Jackson had looked through it. Henry had taken the blueprints of Henbit Manor and made an interactive map of the family and staff's movements around the murders and Pip's disappearance. That was less important now, but he'd done the work before his death had been ruled accidental. He'd also filled in the blueprints with renderings of all the furniture, art and in same case simple objects. How he could hold all of that in his head was beyond Jackson, especially for a man that lost his phone multiple times a day.

But Jackson knew he fell short on one key thing: people. He didn't get them. He was continually baffled by their actions. Jackson wondered if that was why he didn't think the change of will was essential to the case. He didn't understand people, so he didn't notice glaring changes in their behavior.

Instead, Henry was focused on finding out as much information on the suspects as possible. This included: the shockingly massive debt held by Regal and Sloan, some suspicious activities around Emma Fischer's former restaurant, and too much information on Pip's extended family. They were almost all Nazis of one flavor or another. Even though he was now dead instead of missing, he was still technically a suspect.

"Any luck with the names?" Jackson asked Otto as he sipped his Ledtrådssen Rauchbier. It was quickly becoming one of his favorite beers.

"Names?" Otto asked blinking.

"The list of names I gave you a few days back."

"Oh yeah," Otto said in a slow draw. "Completely forgot about that. Mind writing them down again?"

Jackson shook his head but made sure to keep smiling to let Otto know they were still friends. Maybe not quite friends but Jackson saw more of Otto than anyone other than Henry. Alicia had been by a couple of times, always with something for Henry that could have been easily relayed over the phone. Jackson didn't mind. She was good company.

Once Otto found Jackson some paper, Jackson found the names on his phone again and wrote them down.

"This might be important."

"I won't forget this time. Only had six beers today," he said with a smile then looked Jackson up and down. "That's the third tyrätstutterbuxter I've seen you in."

It was a statement but Jackson could hear the question in it. "Apparently no one sells jeans in Alku. It was these or those wool capris the fish market sells."

"Ah, no, you need to go to the Nýt Jutta."

"What?"

"Nýt Jutta. The place with all the computers."

"Computers and jeans?"

"New things."

"Jeans are new things?"

"They were at one time."

"So was the wheel."

"Alku doesn't change quickly. You still don't have your suitcase?"

"It's in Jacksonville, Florida now."

"Ah! So back home."

"Not exactly."

Jackson finished his beer and headed out into the street, waving at a few of the usual pedestrians. The people of Alku had a routine and stuck to it rigidly. He felt a little swell of pride that he'd begun to make the transfer from an intruder to at least someone that could be waved at, although Otto said it was mostly due to the clothes.

Jackson entered the inn and nearly missed Mrs. Linna behind the counter. Her eyes hardly cleared the top when she wasn't on her apple box. Her little hand waved up barely high enough to see, and Jackson gave her a well-practiced *good evening* in Verlorlandish. It wasn't until he was in the stairs that he realized he'd said *thanks for the beer*.

His ears were still a little red when he opened the door to their room. Henry jumped up from his seat at the desk, iPad in hand, and spun on Jackson.

"Good. You're here. Let's go."

"Go? I was going to hit the sauna before-"

"Forget the sauna. We need to get to Hell's Mouth."

"In Erfundenborg?"

"It hasn't moved," Henry said, snatching up his ill-fitting suit jacket and putting it on while juggling the iPad.

"I've had a few beers."

Henry shook his head in disapproval. "I can drive." He pushed past Jackson without any more explanation and headed down the hall.

Jackson sighed. Maybe it was time to ask if they could have two rooms. Although Jackson was not moving if the new room didn't have it's own bathroom. It also had to have a sauna. He was getting used to that luxury.

"What's at Hell's Mouth?" Jackson asked as they pulled away from the inn.

"The Chief Inspector has new information for us."

"What information?"

"Sham wouldn't say. I don't think he knew."

"Think something's happened with Oscar?"

"Hopefully not. I'd be happier if he stayed out of this case from now on."

"You don't think he did it then? Any of the murders?"

"No."

"Alright, why?"

"Logically he had a better chance of his plan succeeding if Mrs. Henbit died naturally."

"People aren't always logical."

"I know that," Henry said in a bitter tone.

"It couldn't be easy for him to act like an idiot all that time."

"It works for Chad."

Jackson let out a surprised laugh. "Dude."

Henry smiled at his own joke.

"Alright, I'm temporarily lifting my joke ban."

"You don't get to ban jokes."

"Yes I do. But forget that. What I'm saying is he could have gotten fed up and tried to hurry things along."

"True."

They were into the open countryside of Erfundeneyja now. The shadows were long in the late sunlight.

"Miss Marigolds and Ari Björnssen had the most to gain from Laundra Henbit's death," Henry said.

"But why would Ari kill his uncle?"

"There are too many questions," Henry replied. "Maybe we'll have a few more answers soon."

Hell's Mouth was a buzz of activity when Henry and Jackson arrived. Three officers nearly ran them over as they entered the building. They were hardly greeted before being sent off to find Klar's office on their own. She was on the phone when they arrived but finished quickly. As she hung up, she motioned for them to come in.

"This place seems different," Jackson said. "Busier."

"We have bodies."

"Someone else has been murdered?" Henry asked, holding back his excitement only just.

"Not in Alku. Here. Outside Erfundenborg. Two bodies washed ashore. Most likely tourists that fell off a cliff while sightseeing. It happens too often. But we won't know for sure until we identify them. It's never good for the islands to lose tourists." Klar shook her head. "Someday we'll have to install hand railings on all our cliffs.

"How often does it happen?"

"As I said, too often. Because of our dead tourists, I won't be able to do anything with the information I have for you. At least not until we've identified them. So I hope you know what to do with this." With the final word, she handed a folder to Henry.

Henry opened it quickly and looked over the page inside. Jackson peered over his shoulder, but his brother was moving too much for him to read.

"Just as I suspected," Henry finally said.

"What?" Jackson asked.

"Ari. He is Ramses Razek's biological son."

"Damn," Jackson said. "So we got incest."

"No," Klar said, brow creased. "Read the other page."

Henry raised an eyebrow then turned the page. His expression dropped. "What is this?"

"The second test."

"What second test?" Jackson asked.

"Apparently you weren't exactly clear when you asked for the DNA test, so the lab tested it against both of the deceased."

"I'm sure I told them to check it against Ramses," Jackson said. He tried to think back. "I'm sorry if I was confusing. I didn't mean to waste anyone's time."

"You didn't waste anyone's time," Henry said, looking up. "They are both matches."

"What?"

"They are both matches."

"He's related to Pip too?"

"Not Pip. The other deceased. Laundra Henbit was Ari's mother."

Jackson let the words sink in then said the first thing that came to mind. "So no incest?"

The last light of dusk faded, shrouding the guest house in darkness. Ari pulled the door open and stumbled inside. He wiped the sweat from his brow with his sleeve. It came away dark with grime. It had been a long day. He had helped Ramses with the gardening before, so he knew what he was doing. It was a laborious task caring for the entire estate alone, but it kept his mind off things. Things he didn't want to think about.

Oas had told him he would hire a new gardener once the estate was settled but until that time, the butler appreciated the job being done more than he disliked Ari going outside of his duties, not that he actually had any anymore. Laundra Henbit had died. He knew it would happen sooner or later. But he'd hoped it would be later. He'd hoped it would at least not happen until he had a chance to tell her he knew.

What would she have said? Now Ari would never know. Uncle Ramses... no, not uncle. His Dad had been angry at Björn for telling Ari, but at the same time, he'd been relieved. It had given them time to be father and son. It had been the best years of Ari's life. And he'd been able to care for his mother, even if she hadn't known that he knew.

As he stumbled up the stairs one thought stuck in his mind. It was the same thought that stuck there so often now. Had she planned on telling everyone that night? Was that why she'd asked him to stay for dinner? Was that the secret she was going to tell?

Laundra Henbit had gone to great lengths to hide her affair with his father. She'd gone to even greater lengths to hide her son from everyone. She'd paid his mom and dad... No, she'd paid his Aunt and Uncle a great deal of money to take him away to Finland and lie to him for the rest of his life. Was that what she regretted? Ari punched the wall, unable to contain the frustration. The plaster crumbled around his massive fist. He pulled it free, debris falling to the floor. Now he'd have to fix that.

Ari growled at himself and walked down the hall to the bathroom. He started the water for the tub then headed back into the hallway and crossed to his room. It was small. Even for a normal sized man, it would have been small. He couldn't bring himself to move into his dad's room though. He dropped onto the bed and pulled his boots off one at a time. Dirt poured out as he dropped them. He should have taken them off outside. Too late now though. He peeled the rest of his filthy clothes off and went back into the bathroom. He lowered as much of himself as would fit into the water, nearly overflowing the tub. He'd have to do this a few times to get clean, but he'd given up on the shower head. It didn't even make it to the middle of his back, and he was done taking kneeling showers. It would be quicker to use any of the showers in the main house, but he didn't feel like seeing anyone. He wanted to wash off the day and fall asleep, hopefully without dreams. Even the pleasant ones left him feeling empty in the morning.

Ari leaned his head against the wall and closed his eyes. The water was hot which would do nothing to stop his sweating but felt good on his muscles. His mind wandered back to the years he'd spent in Alku. He'd been born here, on the manor. Not many people knew that. Björn. Dr. Novak. Maybe Oas? Ari wasn't sure of that though. All the others were dead. Rashidi, the aunt he'd called mother. His real mother, Laundra. Even his Dad, Ramses. They were all dead.

He must have dozed off because he woke with a start. Had he heard a creak? He forced one eye open, then the other. Before he could process what they'd seen though, pain hit him in the right arm. Ari turned his head. Something was stuck in his arm. With a shout he pushed himself up, colliding with the figure hanging over him. His eyes blurred. He couldn't focus on the face. There was a scream. It wasn't his. Ari's arm wrapped around the intruder. He squeezed tight. His right arm throbbed. His legs were weak. They slipped on the wet tile, and he felt all his weight moving forward. He kept moving. He was falling. They crashed to the floor with a sharp crunch then the world slipped into darkness.

"Do you have any idea what hour it is?" Oas huffed blocking the entryway as best he could. From behind him, Caprice's forced laughter echoed through the hall.

"It's 9:16 and I don't think the house is asleep quite yet," Henry answered.

"That is too late for visitors," Oas protested.

"That may be so, but I need to speak to Ari Björnssen immediately."

"He's not even here."

"Where is he?"

"The guest house of course."

"Thank you. Now, can we cut through the house or do we have to walk around?"

Reluctantly Oas let the door open. Henry and Jackson followed the butler through the hall. Caprice's laughter came again, now inside it seemed to be emanating from the upstairs.

"Having a party?" Jackson asked.

"Mrs. Marigolds may be, but we are not."

They passed through the rest of the house only coming across Matilda who was doing her best to shoo Dandy toward the hall.

"Just pick up the damn thing," Oas muttered.

"He smells."

"Then he needs a bath."

"I do not bathe dogs."

"Then find some bacon. He'll go anywhere for bacon. Ask Miss Fischer if she has any."

They exited the house and Oas started out across the lawn.

"We can make our own way," Henry said.

"I insist," Oas said flatly without looking back.

They crossed the rest of the lawn in silence as they approached the grove. Lights could be seen between the trees. As they neared the house, they could see they were emanating from both first and second levels. Oas rapped on the front door then waited. He knocked again, this time with more force. Still nothing. Exasperated, Oas lifted his wrist and tapped the watch a few times. Waited. Still nothing.

"He must be sleeping. He works long hours," Oas said, turning away.

"The lights are on," Jackson pointed out.

"We do need to speak to him tonight," Henry insisted.

Oas tensed visibly but took the doorknob and turned. The door didn't open. "It's locked," he said, surprised.

"Maybe Ari doesn't trust the rest of you," Jackson suggested.

Oas didn't acknowledge the comment. He took out his keys and selected the correct one.

The house looked much the same as it had before. The lights were on in the living room but not in the adjoining rooms. No one was in sight.

"Mr. Björnssen," Henry spoke out loudly to the empty room. "It's Detective Henry Pets. I have a few questions for you."

Jackson eased over to the first dark doorway. It led into what might be a small dining room. It was dark but with enough light to see it was empty. The same was true of the kitchen.

"Do we go upstairs?" Jackson asked.

Henry frowned.

"Ari is not a pleasant man to wake," Oas said.

"I'll remember that. Thank you," Henry said without a tone of appreciation. "You can wait here. Jackson." Henry motioned for the stairs.

"You want me to go first?"

"Yes."

"Why?"

"You know. The brawn thing."

Jackson shook his head but didn't try to argue. If they were headed for trouble, Jackson didn't think it would matter which one of them Ari got ahold of first. "We could call Constable Sham."

"I'm sure he's merely sleeping. I seriously doubt he would attack us."

"Then why did you need me to go first?"

"I can be wrong."

"Great."

The light in the hall was on, and lights also spilled out from the spare bedroom and the bathroom.

"If he's asleep, he sleeps with the light on."

"He could be very tired," Henry suggested. Henry turned back to the hall and called out, "Mr. Björnssen."

"What are you doing?" Jackson said in a hushed voice.

"Letting him know we're here. Maybe wake him before we get to his room."

Jackson nodded. That wasn't a horrible idea. No response came, so the pair eased on down the hall. They passed the spare bedroom. It was empty.

"Look," Henry said.

Jackson did. He saw nothing unusual. "What?"

"The boots. The dirt. It looks freshly spilt."

Jackson gave Henry his best skeptical scowl. "How can you tell it's fresh dirt?"

"Do you want me to explain? I can."

"No."

Henry stepped into the room and picked up a filthy t-shirt. "It's still wet."

"That's just gross. Do you want to smell his underwear too?"

"That won't be necessary. But we can assume he undressed recently."

"Great. So we're looking for a naked giant man."

Henry stepped back behind Jackson and shoed him forward. They reached Ramses room next. The door was closed. Henry glanced at Jackson before putting his hand up and knocking.

"Mr. Björnssen. I need to speak with you."

Jackson's attention moved to the final doorway. The bathroom. The door was slightly ajar, letting the light inside pour out. Had he heard something from there? While Henry continued knocking, Jackson moved toward the bathroom, straining to hear. Maybe a low groan? Or it could have been the pipes. Jackson placed his hand on the door, hesitated. If the man was taking a bath, this was going to be one hell of an awkward conversation.

Jackson pushed the door slowly. If Ari was in there, he was going to give him plenty of time to see them coming first. The only sounds came from Henry. Jackson considered knocking but he was committed. He pushed the door open the rest of the way. What he saw inside took him a long moment to process. Only a moment though, then adrenaline hit.

Jackson dropped to his knees beside the prostrate bulk of Ari. "Henry," he shouted as he tried to take in everything at once. Ari was naked and wet. Blood ran from somewhere. It had stained the floor but only a little. Less than a nosebleed even. The wound couldn't be serious. It wasn't until Jackson put his hand on the man's carotid artery that he saw the second body. One hand was the only thing visible, stuck up just under Ari's face. Jackson started back when he saw it but forced his hand to stay put until he was sure he'd felt a pulse.

"What is..." Henry's voice came from behind him.

"Call 911."

"They don't use 911," Henry replied.

"Then call whatever it is you call here. He's not dead. And get Oas. There's someone else under here."

"Under where?"

"Him. There's someone under him."

As Henry's footsteps rushed off behind him, Jackson followed the trail of blood. It came from Ari's arm. He turned it out carefully. There was a needle jabbed into the crook of his arm. It had been torn partially free, blood running from it. The syringe was only partly emptied. Jackson snatched some toilet paper from next to him, wrapped it around the needle, then pulled it free, careful not to let any more of the substance get injected into Ari's arm. He sat it next to him then grabbed a towel from the wall. He ripped a strip off and wrapped it securely around the wound.

"What is this?" This time it was Oas' voice.

"Help me turn him over. There's someone under him," Jackson shouted.

"Under?" Oas gaped.

"Yes. Under him. Why do I have to keep repeating that. Help me turn him over."

Oas moved toward Jackson as footsteps rang behind them. Jackson could hear Henry's voice. He seemed to be speaking to someone, Jackson hoped it was some form of help. He didn't focus on the words though, only the task at hand.

Jackson caught Oas' eye to make sure he was paying attention but a chirp from the butler's watched grabbed it away. Oas lifted his wrist to his face.

"That can wait," Jackson said.

"Matilda, we are quite busy here," Oas said in a voice that sounded far too calm.

"Sorry, sir. But I can't locate Miss Fischer."

"That is not important right now."

"Dude, help," Jackson shouted back again.

Oas finally dropped down beside him. He looked Ari over. "This will be awkward."

"Don't think about it."

"Could you maybe track her for me?" Matilda's voice came from this wrist. Thankfully, Oas ignored it this time. He carefully reached across Ari and reluctantly found a handhold.

"He's very slippery."

"Shut up," Jackson growled trying not to think about that. "On three." Jackson grabbed Ari by the shoulder and torso and counted down. On three, they heaved. Between the water and the grime on his body, they almost lost control. Jackson strained his muscles to turn the bulk in their favor while doing his best to support Ari's neck. It took more than a little maneuvering and some uncomfortable moments to get Ari turned onto his back, but they eventually managed it. Oas immediately dropped a towel over the man.

"To preserve a little dignity," he said.

Ari let out a low groan.

"He's alive," Oas gasped.

"Yes," Jackson said. "I already knew that."

They both turned to the much smaller body that had been under the man. From the angle of her head, Jackson doubted she was alive. Henry stepped into the room behind him. The conversation he'd been having cut off.

"That's," Henry said. "Unexpected.

"Oas? Did you hear me?" Matilda's voice came again.

"Yes," Oas replied.

"Did you page Miss Fischer?"

"I don't think that will be necessary."

"Why not?"

Oas looked from Jackson back to the body.

"I believe we found her," Oas said.

"Could you ask her about the bacon?"

"The bacon will have to wait."

CHAPTER 16

It took every one of Chief Inspector Klar's officers plus Jackson to help the EMTs carry Ari down the stairs and to the waiting ambulance. Jackson huffed next to Constable Sham as it raced away. His sweater was soaked. Jackson didn't know if it was from sweat, bathwater or both. He'd also managed to get blood stains on his favorite tyrätstutterbuxter.

"He is a big man," Sham said.

"If he dies after all that," Jackson said between deep breaths. "I'm going to be pissed."

Sham actually chuckled. Jackson glanced around. A few more officers milled around them, but there was no sign of Henry. Jackson took his leave of Sham and headed back to the guest house.

Henry and Klar stood in the upstairs hall, attention turned into the bathroom. Jackson crossed to them. The cook's body lay in the position Jackson had found it. A young woman with a camera carefully picked her way around it, taking photos. She was doing her best to avoid the mess of blood and water spreading over the tiles as well as the broken shards that Jackson guessed used to be a hypodermic needle.

"Cause of death seems obvious," Henry said.

"Death by squashing," Klar said.

"More specifically I meant broken neck."

"Could also be from the head injury. Not all that blood came from Ari's arm."

"I suppose squashing works for now then," Henry said. "Any chance you've found any more on Laundra Henbit's cause of death?"

"No. And let's focus on the dead person on hand."

"Right. Of course."

"Do we know what she injected Ari with?" Jackson asked from behind them.

"Looks similar to the heroin we found in Ramses Razek's room," Klar said. "We were lucky she didn't get it all into him. So was he, likely enough."

"You think she dosed Ramses too?" Jackson asked.

"No," Klar said firmly. "He went for a walk after injecting himself. A short walk but a walk. I doubt that would have been his first activity if he'd been forcibly injected. But I would bet good money she added the rat poison."

"We can infer that Miss Fischer wanted it to look as if Mr. Björnssen followed in his father's footsteps," Henry added.

Klar looked to be about to correct Henry but stopped. Father was correct. Ramses hadn't been Ari's uncle.

"So," Klar said. "Did this woman know Ari was Mrs. Henbit's son and is that why she tried to kill him?"

"What would she gain?" Jackson asked.

Henry nodded. "I think we need to see Miss Fischer's room immediately."

After Chief Inspector Klar gave the photographer a few instructions, the three left the guest house to Constable Sham and struck out across the lawn to the manor, collecting Oas on the way. Henry hadn't let the butler leave the guest house since they found Ari and Miss Fischer. Jackson had let Matilda know that there'd been an incident in the guest house. By now it was safe to assume most of the house knew something had happened.

"Who else knows Miss Fischer was out here?" Henry asked as they approached the back of the manor. The question was addressed to everyone.

"Matilda may suspect," Oas said. "She knew where I was when I informed her I'd located Miss Fischer." Oas shook his head and sighed. "She was very good cook."

"She was probably a murderer," Jackson said.

"True," Oas agreed. "But a very good cook. We've had trouble keeping cooks."

"I've heard," Henry said. "Why exactly did you dismiss the previous cook?"

"He'd been recommended by Dr. Novak."

"And?"

"His specialty was healthy cuisine. When Mrs. Marigolds suggested we take on Miss Fischer, Mrs. Henbit jumped at the opportunity."

"I'd been told there was quite a fight."

"With Dr. Novak. Not Mrs. Henbit."

"Maybe the cook was trying to kill Mrs. Henbit with the food," Jackson said with a chuckle.

"Not the time," Henry hisses. He paused and scratched his chin. "Could we back up one moment."

"We're almost to the house," Oas pointed out.

"Not physically. The conversation. When Matilda spoke to you back in the guest house, she asked if you could track Miss Fischer for her. What exactly did she mean by that?"

Oas's expression went more vacant. Klar spun on the butler.

"You track your employees?" Klar asked forcefully.

Oas cleared his throat. "I do have the ability to locate the staff's watches. Assuming they have them on then-"

"And we're just hearing about this?" Klar growled.

"I didn't think it was pertinent."

"Pertinent that we know the exact location of every member of this household."

"Only the staff and only if they are in fact wearing their watches."

"Which they have to wear at all times," Henry stated.

"Yes."

"Is there a log somewhere?" Henry asked.

"I can make reports of previous movements."

"Does anyone else have access to this?" Klar asked.

"They shouldn't."

"But they could?"

"Only if they accessed my personal computer."

Klar shook her head. "I would like to access that myself."

"As would I but for now we should not waste time," Henry said, picking up the pace. "If the maid knows Miss Fischer was in the guest house, anyone else may also know."

"What are you afraid will happen?" Jackson asked.

"I'm afraid a killer may get away," Henry replied.

"Our killer is dead already," Klar said.

"Miss Fischer may have done the killing but she's not the one responsible for this."

"You think she was a hired killer?" Klar asked, turning a skeptical look on Henry.

"I'd prefer to leave this conversation until later. Oas, once we are in Miss Fischer's room, you may inform the rest of the house about Miss Fischer's death and Mr. Björnssen's hospitalization."

"I think I'd prefer to do that," Chief Inspector Klar said.

Henry looked at Klar as if he'd forgotten about her. "Right, yes. I suppose that is appropriate."

"Let me make one thing clear, Mr. Pets. You were right about these being murders, but this is still my investigation."

"Of course."

"Good," Klar said as they reached the doors to the saloon. "Now I've got two unidentified bodies in Erfundenborg waiting for me so let's make this as quick as possible."

"Then we are not informing the rest of the household yet?" Henry asked.

"Of course I am," Klar said. "Just wanted to make sure you know it was my call, not yours."

"I see."

Klar shook her head. "Oas, could you bring everyone together in... one of your larger rooms. I don't care which."

"I believe the drawing room would be appropriate," Oas said.

"That's fine," she replied then turned to Henry. "Try not to touch too much before I get there."

Miss Fischer's room was not large, but Jackson did take pains to point out she had her own restroom. All the staff bedrooms shared a wing. Each resembled a studio apartment save for the lack of a kitchen. The room was tidy and sparsely decorated. It looked rather like an Ikea catalog. None of the wall hangings were personal, merely generic decor. Henry had a feeling it had all been purchased from a single spread in a catalog.

"What are we looking for?" Jackson asked.

"Something to connect Miss Fischer to the individual who hired her."

"Who do you think it is?"

"I'm very close."

"Who?"

"Not yet. We need evidence."

"You can tell me. That won't spoil the evidence."

"I'm not ready yet," Henry said turning in a full circle. He stopped facing the desk. There was a small but bulky Acer laptop on it. Henry crossed to it and flipped it open.

"Didn't the inspector say not to touch anything?"

"She said not to touch too much," Henry corrected. He tapped the trackpad, and the screen blinked on to reveal a mess of windows. "No password. Convenient. Jackson, see if you can find her email or maybe even text messages." Henry waved Jackson over to the desk and continued his scan of the room.

"Then what?" Jackson asked as he sat down in front of the desk.

"Who would want to hide that Laundra Henbit had a son?"

"Someone that thought it could get in the way of their inheritance."

"Exactly. That is not Miss Fischer so we can assume for now she did not go into this on her own. So, who benefits the most from this staying secret?"

"With the will, no one."

"But they didn't know about the will."

"I guess the family then."

"Precisely. Oscar Henbit, Caprice Marigolds, Lydia Marigolds, Sloan Okumu and Regal Okumu. All had a motive. Sloan and Regal have massive amounts of debt, and with Sloan losing her sports career and Regal's failed film endeavor, they need any money they can get their hands on. Caprice has lived off her sister's wealth for years. She doesn't even own her own house. The same could be said for Miss Marigolds, a young woman that as far as I can tell has never so much as held a job."

"She'd have to be incredibly dense to hire someone to investigate her own murders."

"Possibly. But with those suspects in mind, only Miss Marigolds or Oscar could have arranged for Mrs. Henbit's murder with the cook in person. The others would have to have contacted her while out of the country. That is what you are looking for."

"You think she'd have left that kind of stuff on a laptop?"

"If we're lucky. If not..." Henry shook his head.

"Alright, but why would they keep killing people after the will was read?"

"I think we can assume both Ramses and Ari Björnssen were aware that Ari was Mrs. Henbit's son. Ramses argued with the solicitor after the reading of the will. Maybe he was expecting his son to be acknowledged in the will. If he had talked then suspicion could have fallen on the killer. Maybe Mrs. Henbit's death would have been reinvestigated."

"But killing Ramses did exactly that anyway. Are you sure you're looking at this the right way?"

"What do you mean?"

"Listen, dude. I'm telling you. It makes no sense. Laundra Henbit was not the type of person to leave her house to a damn dog for any reason. She cared about her niece."

"And Ari?"

"Yes and him. I don't know why she gave him up, but she still took care of him. And she was going to leave quite a bit to him. This new will makes no sense."

"People make no sense! That's how the world is. People do things for no reason at all. It's not logical. There's no order to it. They just do things."

"Only if you don't understand them."

"And you do?"

"Of course I do."

"Really? Then maybe you should be the detective. Who do you think did it?"

"I don't know," Jackson threw his hands up. "But none of this makes any damn sense. There is something wrong with the will."

"It was witnessed by two people. People Mrs. Henbit knew well."

"Then we should talk to them."

"We've tried. That doesn't matter right now. If we can link Miss Fischer to one of the members of the family, then it doesn't matter why Mrs. Henbit made a new will. We're here to find a murderer, not to question an eccentric old woman's intentions. I believe I may just know who that murderer is but I need proof."

"Who?"

Henry raised a finger. "Not yet. When I have proof."

"Dude-"

"No."

"I'm telling you nothing fits. I just keep thinking about Chad and the puzzles. You're trying to smash pieces together that don't belong. I think you'll get the wrong answer if you keep doing it."

Henry stopped scanning the room. He turned his lopsided eyes on Jackson. His expression was entirely too neutral. "It has been fun having you tag along with me, Jackson. But this is my job, not yours. I'm the detective. You are a rafting guide."

"Dude, I'm the vice president of an international adventure retreats and outdoor gear and apparel company, and you're a pet detective."

"I think you should go. I can handle this. And Vice President's shouldn't call people dude."

Henry didn't say any more. He stood in front of Jackson, waiting. The brothers locked eyes, neither wanting to flinch first.

"Am I interrupting something?"

Both spun on the door. Klar stood there, leaning against the frame, one eyebrow raised.

"I take it she didn't leave a *this is why I did it* note?" Klar asked.

"Not so much," Henry said. "You've informed the household?"

"Yes. They took it as well as can be expected. Lydia is crying. Caprice is drunk. And all of them seem to think they'll be next."

"Jackson, you're good with people. Why don't you try to alleviate their fears?"

"How should I do that?"

"You're the one that understands them. I'm sure you'll figure it out." With that, Henry stepped toward the desk. Jackson moved out of his way. "We should look into Miss Fischer's financial records," Henry began, glancing back at Klar. "I think they could be quite informative."

Jackson edged past Klar as they traded places. He looked back a moment at Henry. He was focused on the computer now. A dozen insults tumbled through Jackson's thoughts, but he put them all away. He'd already hurt Henry enough. And Henry was right, it was his job. Jackson didn't know what he was thinking getting so caught up in it all. He left the detective and the inspector and headed back past the other staff rooms and into the curving hallway leading back to the main house. Maybe Henry would find the answers tonight. His brother could solve the case, and he could leave. That would be for the best. It shouldn't have come as a surprise, their relationship had never been close, but it did. They'd often fought as kids. They'd largely ignored each other as teenagers. As adults, they got along when they weren't together. It should have been more surprising that they'd managed to do this well. If he stayed any longer, they'd be falling back into fighting like children. Jackson wasn't going to let that happen.

CHAPTER 17

Otto dropped a pint onto the bar in front of Jackson's scrambled eggs and salmon. Jackson looked up at the bartender mid-bite.

"A little early for that," Jackson said.

"Don't worry. It's my own breakfast porter. And you look like you need it."

Jackson nodded reluctantly. He could use a beer. The night had been tense. Henry had hardly spoken to him. The morning hadn't led to cooler heads. Or maybe it had led to too cool of heads. Henry had given him the cold shoulder from the moment he'd woken up, so Jackson sat out to get breakfast on his own.

"Heard about the murder out at the manor last night," Otto said.

"Not exactly a murder," Jackson said.

"How's that?"

"Honestly, probably shouldn't say. This is Henry's territory, not mine. Better if I just eat my breakfast and keep my nose out of it."

"Then you're not interested in those names still?" Otto asked.

"Names?"

"Yeah." Otto pulled a folded sheet of paper from his pocket. He spread it out next to Jackson's beer. "Those names you gave me. I've got them all tracked down for you. Well, more or less."

Jackson pulled the paper to him. He'd forgotten about the list of names. It was the names of the locals that would serve as oversight of the trust for Dandy. "Don't happen to have addresses for them?"

"It's fairly simple there. All but two are at the same address."

"Really? Where?"

"The Alku cemetery."

Jackson didn't finish his breakfast. He did down most of the beer quickly before paying Otto and rushing out toward the Inn. Jackson didn't know what this meant, but he knew it was important. Henry would want to know.

His brother was right where he'd been when Jackson had left, at the desk, pouring over the iPad.

"Dude, you need to look at this."

"I'm not a *dude*."

"Don't get stuck on that. This is-"

"Not now."

"I think you'll want-"

Henry turned, he gave Jackson a look that Jackson thought was supposed to be intimidating but mostly made him look like an angry toddler. "What I want is to focus on my work before the Chief Inspector arrives and not be bothered by a half drunk frat boy that talks like a beach bum and thinks short shorts are appropriate attire for every occasion."

"This is your work," Jackson forced the paper into Henry's hands. "Otto tracked down the committee members."

"I don't feel that's relevant at this point."

"All but two are dead."

"Dead?" Henry finally sounded slightly interested. "Killed?"

"No. All natural causes. Heart attack. Cancer. Stroke. Henry, they were all old. Like over ninety."

"Why would she pick dead people? He must have mixed up the names. Maybe they have children or grandchildren with the same name."

"No. And she didn't pick dead people. They all died after the will was made. Except for two and they're both in a hospice in Erfundenborg."

Henry looked at the page a few moments in silence. Then he sat it down and turned back to the iPad. "That is very interesting but again, not relevant."

"Not relevant? Why would Mrs. Henbit chose people that were dying to watch after her dog?"

"We've been over this. People do things that make no sense."

"Not like this."

"Exactly like this. We've found the evidence we needed. First, Oas's employee tracking has let us confirm that Miss Fischer was in the guest house a day after Laundra Henbit's death. That would have given her the opportunity to poison Mr. Razek's heroin. Also, we have found money connecting Miss Fischer to one of the family members, not to mention multiple incriminating text message between the two." Henry smiled. "My suspicious have proved to be correct and now I have the proof."

"Who was it?"

"Not yet."

"What?"

"I will reveal that in good time."

"Seriously? Just tell me."

There was a knock at the door. Henry put the iPad down and stood. Jackson gave Henry an annoyed look but turned to the door and opened it. Constable Sham stood on the other side.

"Where's the Chief Inspector?" Henry asked.

"Outside. She's ready to head out."

"And Oscar?"

Sham rolled his eyes. "Yes, we have him."

"Ari Björnssen?"

"He almost died."

"I would like him to be there."

"We're sending a constable to the hospital with another tablet. You'll have to settle for a video conference with him."

"That's not ideal..." Henry shook his head. "But it will have to do."

"What's going on?" Jackson asked.

"We're about to unveil a murderer."

"Dude-"

Henry shot Jackson a glare full of vitriol.

"I mean... Henry. You can't do that."

"And why not?"

"This list. Shouldn't we look into it first?"

"We don't need to do anything. I am going to go finish this case while you stay here. I'll be back when it's over."

"But-"

"That's it, Jackson. Don't argue. Just stay here."

"You're making a mistake."

"Yes. I did make a mistake. I should never have taken you with me."

With that, Henry stepped around Jackson and left the room. Sham gave Jackson a last half amused look then shut the door behind them. Jackson stood in the room alone. He sighed. At least he could go have another breakfast beer.

Once again the Henbit household gathered in the study. Oas had informed everyone that they would be convening there after breakfast on request of the Chief Inspector. It had taken some convincing to get them all in one place, and a bit of alcohol in the case of Caprice but they were all there now. Everyone but Matilda. Oas checked his watch again. He'd sent her to bring Dandy inside almost an hour ago. Now she wasn't responding to his messages. He could see she wasn't far from the house though. He could check on her.

As he lowered his wrist, a beep sounded. Not a message. The door. Matilda would have to find her way back herself. Oas excused himself and headed out through the drawing room, bypassing the saloon with the narrow passage that led right to the grand hall. He crossed the large doors and pulled them open.

"Good morning," Chief Inspector Klar said.

"It is morning," Oas replied. He nodded to Henry Pets. Constable Sham was behind them. Between him and an extraordinarily tall officer, was Oscar. He was handcuffed and lacked his usual absent stare. Looking at him now, Oas could hardly believe he'd fallen for the man's ruse. "Almost everyone is in the study."

"Almost everyone?" Henry asked.

"Matilda is collecting Dandy."

"I would like everyone to be there," Henry said sadly. "But I'm sure we can start without her." He waved Oas forward. "Let's get going."

All eyes turned on the door as Henry followed Oas into the study. They sat in very much the same places they'd sat days earlier while Ms. Veratiri had read the will. There were more empty spaces now though. Lydia smiled weakly at him from her prominent seat. Henry merely nodded back. There was a slight stir as Sham led in Oscar. Caprice made a disgusted noise and leaned in to whisper something to Lydia.

"Hi," Oscar said, waving one hand the best he could.

"What is he doing here?" Caprice asked.

"I wanted the entire family here for this," Henry said.

"He's not family," Caprice said.

"I did marry her," Oscar said. "And all that goes with that."

"And what is this anyway?" Caprice asked again before Oscar could elaborate.

"You will see soon enough," Henry said then he turned to Sham. "Is it ready?"

"Give me a minute," he said a bit annoyed as he sat Oscar down. "Where's your iPad?" Sham asked. Henry's eyes went wide as he patted down his jacket. Sham shook his head. "I don't have another one.

Oas cleared his throat. "Would any tablet do?"

"Yes."

"If you will excuse me," Oas said with a slight nod.

As he left the room he glanced again at his watch. No new messages. He straightened his suit jacket and briskly made his way to his room.

"There hasn't been another murder has there?" Lydia asked looking around, counting all those present.

"No," Henry responded quickly. "No one else has died." Henry had settled the family and staff but waiting for Oas to return had added an unneeded speed bump. Just when he was wondering if he'd have to find a way to stall, the butler returned.

Oas handed off the tablet to Sham and in a brief few minutes Sham was done.

"Ready," Sham said handing the tablet to Henry.

Henry took it. A very bleary-eyed Ari filled the screen. His hair was disheveled, and it was obvious someone was holding the tablet above him. He wasn't even sitting up.

"Can you hear me?" Henry said.

"Yes. Why is this happening?" Ari asked.

"You will understand everything presently," Henry said. He looked around the room and settled on an empty chair. He crossed to it and placed the tablet on the seat, making sure it was tilted toward the desk. Once he was satisfied, he crossed back to the desk and took his place standing in front of it.

"First. I would like to go back to the night of the first murder."

"Haven't we talk about that enough?" Caprice asked.

"Please, no interruptions."

"Do we have to do this?" She asked, addressing her question to Klar.

Klar shrugged. "You hired him."

"I certainly didn't."

"I did, and I want to hear what he has to say," Lydia said in the firmest tone she was capable of making.

"Thank you," Henry said. This time he did smile at Lydia. "Laundra Henbit gathered all of you in one place. Why? To share a secret. And a warning. She wanted everyone to know one of you was planning her murder."

"That's ridiculous."

"Mother, please," Lydia said.

Caprice rolled her eyes and tilted back her Long Island ice tea.

"Now. Let's move forward. Forward to last night. Mr. Björnssen." Henry turned to face the tablet. Ari looked back at him with one eye half closed. "Tell me about last night."

"I don't feel good."

"We are aware of that. But please, last night."

"What about it? I tried to take a bath, and the damn cook stuck a needle in my arm. Now I'm here."

"Inelegant but yes. That is what happened. Emma Fischer entered the guest house at 8:23. She then waited until Mr. Björnssen was in the house and in a vulnerable position before attempting to inject him with a lethal mix of heroin and rat poison. However, Mr. Björnssen stopped her from injecting the full dose and in the struggle that followed, he fell on her, breaking her neck."

"That's horrible!" Lydia shook her head.

"Yeah, it was," Ari mumbled from the tablet. "I know. I was there."

"Wait," Regal cut in. "The cook tried to murder the nurse but then the nurse killed the cook by falling on her?"

Henry thought through that a moment. "Yes. That is basically it."

"Why would Emma do something like that?" Lydia asked.

"That," Henry said dramatically. "Is the question."

"Are you going to answer it?" Sloan asked, slouching down into her chair. She gave off an air of disinterest.

"Yes. But not yet. First, we have one more murder to discuss. The gardener, Ramses Razek."

At the back of the room, a hand went up, catching Henry's attention. It was the chauffeur.

"Yes, Mr. uh..." Henry searched for his name and came up blank.

"I'm Laki."

"He's the chauffeur," Oas added.

"Yes, I knew that part. Do you have a question?"

"Yes. I thought Ramses just did too much drugs and the Misses had a heart attack."

"That is what we were led to believe. And had Miss Fischer succeeded with Mr. Björnssen, she would have hoped we saw that as another accidental death. But there have been no accidental deaths. We are dealing with murder." He let the word hang in the air for as long as he dared to add to the effect of the moment. It was decently effective.

"So Pip was murdered?" Laki asked.

Henry once again turned back to the chauffeur. For a man that had so far been entirely forgettable, he had quite a bit to say suddenly. It was annoying. "Okay, one accidental death. We can forget about that one for now though. The pressing question is this. Why would someone want not only Laundra Henbit but also Ramses and Ari dead?" Henry looked each member of his audience over in turn.

"Are we supposed to answer that?" Sloan asked.

"Do you have a supposition?" Henry asked back.

"I'd guess money."

"That is possible. Money is often the motive, and Mrs. Henbit had a good deal of money. It could have been a motivation for you and Regal, to help with the crippling debt."

"We're not in debt," Sloan retorted.

"We all know you're drowning in debt, dear," Caprice said, punctuating the comment with a roll of her eyes.

"Well, we don't have to tell everyone," Sloan growled.

Henry waited to see if anyone else wanted to add a comment. When no one spoke, he continued. "But what about Ramses and Ari?"

"Fewer people to inherit so more for everyone else," Constable Sham answered.

"Possibly."

"But none of us knew we'd get anything until the Misses was already dead," Laki spoke up again. "Emma couldn't have known she'd get anything from her."

"Precisely. So why would Miss Fischer want to murder Mrs. Henbit?"

The room fell silent again. Lydia sat on the edge of her seat, waiting. Sloan kept her disinterested slouch. Caprice eyed her empty glass, fingering the lip absently. Oas stood at attention near the door, no emotion readily apparent. He did sneak a look at his watch though.

"It wasn't me," Oscar said from his chair. "I think that should be obvious."

Laki perked up and looked from Oscar to the others. "He's not..." Laki started then trailed off not sure how to end the question.

"My brain's fine," Oscar said.

"Did everyone else know that?" Laki asked.

"Did we all know that Oscar is an oriental con artist trying to steal my sister's fortune?" Caprice sneered, tapping her empty glass. "Yes. We all knew that."

"Mother," Lydia said. "You can't call him that."

"It's what he is. A con artist!"

"No, I mean oriental."

"That's only offensive if it's a good person."

"I don't think it works like that." Lydia blushed with embarrassment.

"Uh, yes. So," Henry interjected. "Moving right along. Yes. He is a con artist. And he has been faking brain damage since the incident. But..." Henry let the word linger a moment. "He did not kill anyone."

"How do you know that?" Caprice asked narrowing her eyes at the detective.

"To answer that, we first need to investigate why Laundra Henbit was murdered."

"Oh good grief," Caprice muttered. "I need another drink."

Oas made no move to fulfill Caprice's order.

"Why would someone need to murder a woman so close to death already? What could have been so pressing as to warrant murder?"

"The secret," Lydia answered avidly.

"Precisely," Henry said. "Mrs. Henbit invited the entire family together because she wanted to come clean on a secret she had been carrying with her for years. A secret that someone else wanted to ensure Laundra Henbit took to her grave. Wanted it so much that this person paid Emma Fischer to poison her."

"But why kill Ramses or Ari?" Lydia asked.

"Because Ramses knew the secret. The secret that led to murder. Murder to conceal that Laundra Henbit had a child."

Lydia gasped. Sloan and Regal looked at each other. Regal raised an eyebrow and Sloan shrugged. Even Ari suddenly looked alert in his hospital bed.

"No," Laki said from the back. "Who would even..." he trailed off, glancing at Oscar. Oscar turned bright red. "From Oscar?"

"No," Oscar said shooting up. "There's no way. I'd know if she'd had a kid."

"Oscar was not the father," Henry said. "Was he, Caprice?" With that, he turned on Caprice Marigolds. She nearly dropped her glass.

"What?" She gasped.

"There's no more denying it, Mrs. Marigolds. You were the one that convinced your sister to fire her cook and hire Miss Fischer."

"It's Ms. Marigolds. And that proves nothing. So I knew her before. So did Lydia and Sloan. Regal even. I've known a lot of people that haven't killed anyone."

"Did you know that Miss Fischer saved all her text messages on her personal computer? All of them. From two different phone numbers, actually."

The blood drained from Caprice's face.

"We have the DNA test to prove Laundra Henbit did indeed have a child. That is definitive. Furthermore, we have transcripts of your agreement to help Miss Fischer obtain this job to keep an eye on your sister. We have also found evidence that you paid Miss Fischer a sizable sum of money. What exactly were you paying her to do, Mrs. Marigolds?"

"Ms. Marigolds."

"That hardly seems important right now," Oas muttered.

Lydia was nearly on the verge of tears. She choked them back to speak. "What are you saying?" Lydia asked. "What's he saying, mother?"

Caprice turned away. "Maybe I paid her to keep an eye on my sister, not to kill her."

"You knew your sister was a mother, didn't you?" Henry asked.

Caprice kept her eyes turned away. Lydia jumped up and moved in front of Caprice. She forced Caprice to look at her. "What did you do?"

Caprice burst into tears. The glass slipped from her hand, shattering. She fell into Lydia's arms.

"I never wanted you to know. I didn't want anyone to know. Not ever. I didn't want anyone to die, but I couldn't let you find out. You're my daughter, and nothing will change that. Nothing. Ever."

Henry blinked. "Say that again?"

Caprice turned on Henry, eyes blazing. "You had to ruin everything! Lydia is mine! Not her's. She didn't want her. She was going to let her be adopted by a stranger until I convinced her to let me take her. I had to hide on this damn little island so my husband wouldn't find out I wasn't even pregnant. That child was family and I sure as hell wasn't going to let a stranger raise a member of our family. I upended my entire life for Laundra. For Lydia. Then Laundra did everything she could to make Lydia love her more than me."

"I..." Henry started. He looked to Klar. She looked back, just as confused.

"Wait," Ari said from the tablet. "She's saying Lydia is Laundra's kid too?"

Now Caprice spun on the chair with the tablet. "Don't play dumb. You knew. You told me you knew her secret. That's why I had to have you killed."

"No," Ari said, forcing his eyes open. "I meant me. I was the secret."

Now it was Caprice's turn to blink. "Come again?"

"You knew," Ari replied. "You told me you knew why she wanted me close."

Caprice gaped a moment. "She wanted to keep you close because she liked burly men. I assumed you were servicing her needs."

As one, the occupants of the room recoiled. Ari lost a few shades on the tablet.

"You thought I was having sex with my mom?" Ari's voice cracked.

"She wasn't your mother!"

"Ari is the son of Ramses Razek and Laundra Henbit," Henry said. "That is what you murdered her to hide... yes?"

"Him?" Caprice gasped. "But..."

"Okay, I'm confused," Laki said once again holding his hand up. "How many kids did the Misses have?"

"Only the two," Oas said. "Just the two."

"Of course you knew," Caprice hissed.

"Wait, Lydia isn't my sister?" Sloan gaped.

"I'm not?" Lydia asked.

Laki laughed, a huge smile on his face then he cocked an eyebrow. "No possibility I'm her son too?"

"No," Oas said flatly.

"Alright," Klar said. "I think this has gone on long enough. Sham, get Oscar. Caprice, if you don't fight us, we can do this without handcuffs."

"Wait!" Lydia shouted. She stood up, shaking. She took in two deep breaths before turning on Caprice. "How is this true? How is Aunt Laundra my mother?"

Caprice looked away. "I'm done talking about it." She didn't say anymore or even look at Lydia. Instead, she strode away toward the door. "Let's get this over with."

Lydia watched as Klar followed Caprice out before crumpling back into her chair. Sham also moved in to take Oscar as the others began to move out of the room. Soon only Henry, Lydia, and Oas were left. Oas looked almost emotional.

Henry crossed the space between him and Lydia. "Miss Marigolds, I am very sorry about this."

"Sorry?"

"I knew that Ari was Laundra's son. I didn't know about you. If I had-"

"You did your job," Lydia said. "You found..." she trailed off, tears flooding her eyes. "I can't believe it. Did you really do a DNA test?"

"That was on Ari. Not you. Again, we had no idea about you."

"Maybe she's wrong," Lydia said hopefully.

"I think Caprice would know."

"She isn't wrong," Oas said. "You are Mrs. Henbit's daughter."

"Hey," another voice spoke up. Henry turned to the empty chairs. The tablet sat where Henry had sat it with Ari's face on it.

"Sorry, forgot you were there," Henry said.

"So, I have a sister?" he asked.

"It would appear so," Henry replied, picking up the tablet.

"Why..." Lydia started. "I don't understand any of it."

"Your mother was a..." Oas searched for the right word. "Singular woman. I don't think she believed she could be a mother."

"Who's my father then?" Lydia asked. "Mr. Razek?"

"No," Oas said. "He was only Ari's father. The rest is a longer story."

"I'd like to hear it."

"I think I should go for now," Henry said. "I have questions for Caprice."

"Of course," Lydia said, standing. "Thank you. I..." Lydia searched for words. "This is all just too much. But thank you."

"You're very welcome, Miss Marigolds."

"Call me Lydia."

Henry smiled then handed Lydia the tablet. "I... uh... maybe the three of you have things to talk about. Lydia," Henry gave another awkward smile then left Lydia with the butler and her brother. He didn't want to leave her, but it wasn't his job to make her feel better. It was his job to find a killer. He had done that. His job was done.

CHAPTER 18

Jackson tilted back his beer and drained the mug. He needed to stop. He'd had enough by now, but he wanted the distraction. Why did he let himself get so caught up in this? And why was he so sure Henry was missing something important? He shook his head and dropped the mug back on the bar.

"Mrs. Linna said I'd find you here."

Jackson turned. Henry stood behind him looking as disheveled as ever. "Hey."

"Mind if I join you?"

"Of course not."

Henry sat down, and Jackson signaled to Otto to bring more beers.

"Back to no sleeves?" Henry asked, motioning to Jackson.

Jackson glanced down. He'd gone back to the clothes he'd arrived in. "It fits better," he said. "So, how'd it go?"

"Good. Mostly. With a few surprises. I forgot my iPad."

Jackson chuckled. "Yeah. I saw it in the room."

"You could have called me."

With a half smile Jackson dropped a phone in front of Henry. "It was on the sink."

"That would explain this," Henry said, pulling a toothbrush out of his jacket pocket.

"You going to tell me who did it?"

"Caprice."

"Did she confess?"

189

"Sort of. Enough I think. She swears she didn't poison Mrs. Henbit but she's confessed to hiring Emma Fischer to kill Mr. Razek and Mr. Björnssen. She did tell us something we didn't know though."

"Which was?"

"Apparently Laundra Henbit was not only Ari's mother but also Lydia's mother."

"Seriously?"

"Yes."

"Damn," Jackson said as Otto dropped new pints in front of them. Jackson took his up. "Well, congratulations on solving your first case."

Henry picked up the remaining pint and clicked it against Jackson's. "Thank you."

"I'll let Dad know. I'll get him to turn your credit card back on."

"I don't know if I'll be needing it," Henry said. "Lydia is paying my standard fee plus a very large bonus. Not to mention the notoriety this case will bring me. It will be all over the islands."

"Still, I'll see what I can do."

"I think I'd rather you didn't." Henry cleared his throat and took a deep swig of his pint.

The words caught Jackson off guard. It wasn't what he'd expected. Henry had always used their father's support reluctantly, but he'd never turned it down. His interests had never been exactly profitable. His age showed through the boyish features as he sat there sipping his beer.

"I do think we should vacate the Inn though. With the case over, I don't want to keep imposing. If you want to stay with me, I could get a cot or something."

"Actually," Jackson said. "I'm flying out tonight."

"What?"

"You're doing good here. I don't want to be in the way."

"You don't have to leave. With the case over I could show you around the islands."

Jackson smiled and shook his head. "There'll be another case. Like you said, with the notoriety from this case, you'll have work stacking up. Anyway, I need to get back. I've been gone too long already." That was at least partially true. It was easier to say than the real reason.

"I'm sure Dad can handle things a little longer."

"I've booked the flight."

"It could be moved."

"If I stay, we'll just find something else to argue about."

"What? No, we won't."

"Dude..."

"Jackson, you are not a-"

"Exactly. See what I mean?"

Henry started to say something but stopped and merely shook his head, a smile of understanding on his face.

"I love you, brother, but maybe it's better for us to have an ocean between us," Jackson said.

"I'll miss you."

"I'm sure I can stop by on my way to Munich one of these days."

"That would be nice."

The brothers turned to their respective pints and drank in silence. Henry gave Jackson a sideways look as he drained his.

"Will you be driving yourself to the airport?" The question had a passive reproachfulness that only Henry could pull off.

Jackson shook his head and chuckled. "Don't worry," he said pulling the rental car keys from his pocket. He slid them over the Henry. "Alicia's picking me up. You mind returning the car for me? I've paid out the rest of the week so you could use it for the next few days."

Henry took the keys and thanked Jackson. They stumbled through broken conversations about family and the sad under-appreciation of saunas back home until Jackson's phone buzzed. It was Alicia. Jackson fumbled through his Verlorlandish currency and laid a smattering of bills on the bar. He said goodbye to Otto with a few promises to visit next time he was in the islands then stood.

"Let me know when you get another case," Jackson said.

"I will. Tell Chad hello," Henry replied.

Jackson frowned. "If he hasn't gotten himself arrested." He waited beside Henry a moment. "So are you gonna stand so I can hug you or just gonna sit there?"

Henry reluctantly stood and gave his brother an awkward hug. They said their goodbyes, and Jackson left Henry at the bar.

Henry watched Jackson leave then adjusted his shabby suit and sat back down. Maybe he'd buy a better fitting suit with some of the money he now had. His money. Before he could decide if he wanted tweed or something classier, his phone buzzed. Henry fished it out of the suit pocket. It was Lydia.

"Hello?"

"Henry?" Lydia sounded like she was on the verge of tears.

"Yes. What's wrong?"

"There's been another one."

"Another one?"

"A murder. Someone's murdered Matilda."

Jackson watched Alku shrink behind them in the side mirror of Alicia's orange car as they crossed the bridge to Erfundeneyja. The village of Alku disappeared into the dense fog growing over the islands as evening settled in. He'd miss the village. He'd miss the beer. He'd miss Otto and even the inn. He'd certainly miss his own personal sauna. He supposed he'd miss Henry too, despite everything. Henry had been right. He'd solved the case. Jackson had nearly derailed everything. What had he been thinking?

"Jackson?"

Jackson shook off the thoughts. "What?"

"I asked how she hid two pregnancies."

"Oh, right. Sorry. I guess her size helped. She was very obese. Makes it easier to hide a little more weight."

"I guess that makes sense. Still... that's a lot of work to hide two kids."

Jackson nodded, but his thoughts had wandered off again. He looked out the window at the open countryside of Erfundeneyja.

"What's going on in there, Dr. Jackson?" Alicia asked.

"Let's drop the doctor thing," Jackson groaned.

Alicia laughed. She wore what Jackson could only think of as a whaler's outfit, complete with a yellow rain slicker. "So what's on your mind, not doctor Jackson?"

He sighed. "Family."

"We'll keep an eye out for Henry."

"I think he's going to be fine," Jackson said. "Just trying to figure out how I feel about... I don't know. Everything."

"Everything is a little hard to tackle. Maybe start smaller."

"We've never been close, Henry and me. Maybe as kids. I don't know. I always had friends but him... not so much. He's always been a loner. For some reason, I just don't feel right leaving him this time."

"Why's that?"

"I have no idea. Something just doesn't feel right."

"Fair enough," Alicia said with a nod. "Speaking of family, mind if we stop and scoop up my brother on the way? He needs a lift into the city."

"Your brother's visiting?"

Alicia laughed. "No. My brother. Agent Orange."

Jackson looked at Alicia and cocked an eyebrow. "He's your brother?" He searched for the right words. "You don't look that much... uh... alike."

She laughed again. "Half-brother. Same mother, different fathers. Obviously, mine had slightly more African heritage. It happens."

"Obviously," Jackson agreed. If Lydia and Ari could be sister and brother so could Alicia and *Agent* Orange. "So..." Jackson again chose his words carefully. "Seeing as I might never see either of you again, I have to ask."

Alicia raised an eyebrow and let her hazel eyes move to him.

"The outfits. What exactly is going on there? I mean, they're strange enough alone but, I can not for the life of me figure out how they go together. I mean, he dressed like a lumberjack and you had a Hillary Clinton look. The nun and the dog costume. Not to mention the burka and the union jack briefs."

"That last one is just what he normally wears on his days off."

"That explains everything."

Alicia laughed again. Jackson liked her laugh. It was raw and uncontrolled.

"Okay," he said. "Just tell me what you could have possibly been doing with one of you dressed as a dog and the other a nun. Just explain that one. And don't say secret agent stuff."

Alicia shook her head. "Fine, can you keep a secret?"

"Seeing as I'm leaving the country, yes."

"We aren't secret agents."

"I knew that."

"You're very astute," Alicia said with a wry smile. "I'm a journalist. There's a convent up on Heilaguryja that I needed to blend into. Hence the nun attire. And the dog costume was because my brother had a furry convention to go to."

Jackson waited for Alicia to laugh but her face stayed completely serious.

"That's not a joke?"

"No. He's really into the furry thing." Alicia sped on before Jackson could inquire any more about that. "I'm here on a long-term assignment. There's been a uniquely high uptick in crime on the islands and I'm trying to figure out why. He's mostly here to keep me company. It's good to have family and he's never been one to keep a job long. He's a stripper at the moment, hence the lumberjack costume and creative underwear. You'll love what he's wearing tonight."

"Stripper? Really?" Jackson couldn't imagine why anyone would want a stripper that looked like Alicia's brother.

"It's a niche market."

"I'd guess so." Curiously satisfied, Jackson settled back into his seat. The entire situation remained decidedly surreal but pulling the two oddities apart did make each slightly less insane. Slightly. He found it dubious that Alicia needed to dress like a nun for journalism but it was at least plausible. "Do I have to still call him Agent Orange?"

"Dom. Just don't tell Henry. For some reason, Dom thinks it's hilarious that Henry thinks we're really secret agents."

"He doesn't. He said... uh... something about snaps." It clicked. "Oh, the stripper clothes."

"They snap off. Still, Dom is Dom. He thinks it's funny even if Henry's only pretending. It saves me having to explain our wardrobes at least."

Jackson nodded. The conversation wained after that. Soon the lights of Erfundenborg shone softly, diffused in the haze. Jackson decided he was also going to miss Alicia. Probably not Dom though.

Henry let out an exasperated shout as he sped toward Henbit Manor, one hand on the wheel and the other holding his phone up. It was the tenth time he'd been greeted by Jackson's voicemail. The phone was ringing so he had it on but he wasn't answering. He waited for the greeting to end this time.

"Jackson, call me back. There's been another murder."

He ended the call and dropped the phone onto the seat between his legs. He sped through the main gate and pressed down on the gas as much as he dared. The house materialized out of the fog. He recognized the family limo and Constable Sham's vehicle out front. There was also a Volvo he believed belonged to Ms. Veratiri. Henry skidded to a stop next to Sham's vehicle and jumped out of the car, snatching up his phone. He looked at the screen. Jackson hadn't called back.

"They're all inside."

Henry turned around. Laki, the chauffeur, stood behind him looking unnaturally pale.

"Are you feeling alright?" Henry asked,

"Not entirely to be honest. Don't murders usually stop after the murderer's been caught?"

"That is generally the goal," Henry replied. "What happened?"

Laki shrugged. "They found her out back. I haven't gone inside since they found her."

"Why not?"

"One of them's a killer, right? I think I might be safer out here."

"Three of our victims have died outside," Henry said absently. In his head, he tried to sort through all the information he had. What had he missed?

"Don't say that," Laki whined.

"That belongs to Ms. Veratiri," Henry said, pointing to the Volvo. It wasn't exactly a question. "When did she arrive?"

"Maybe a few hours after you left. She came to update us on the will, seeing as there are fewer heirs and all that."

"She was here when they found Matilda?"

"She arrived just after. So, where would you say is safe?"

"I can't say."

"Maybe I just stay next to you? Yeah?"

Henry frowned. "I don't know if that's necessary."

"I don't mind."

Henry wanted to protest but didn't know how to do it without being rude, so he let the chauffeur follow him to the house. The door opened before he even knocked. Oas greeted him curtly and ushered him inside.

"Where's Lydia?" Henry asked. The grand hall was empty save for them and Dandy, who pranced around the room yipping.

"The family is with Ms. Veratiri in the study."

"And the body?"

"We left it alone. The constable is there now."

"And Inspector Klar?"

"Has not arrived. Apparently, they identified some bodies in Erfundenborg. She's giving a press conference presently."

"Ah, the dead tourists."

"I think they ended up being locals," Laki spoke up. "That's what I heard."

"I'd like to see the body," Henry said.

Henry followed Oas through the house and out into the gardens with Laki staying close to his shoulder and Dandy yipping after them. As they crossed the lawn in the dim light, the shape of the hedge maze emerged from the fog. They skirted the maze until they came to the arched opening. Oas led them inside.

"In the maze?" Henry asked.

"That's why it took us so long to find her," Oas replied. He watched his watch closely, apparently using it to navigate the twists and turns. Dandy darted back and forth, yipping.

"Could someone take the dog back to the house?" Henry asked.

"I'm not going back there," Laki said.

"Can you navigate the maze yourself?" Oas asked Henry.

"No," Henry sighed. "Fine, just make sure he doesn't disturb the body."

As they rounded the final shrub, Constable Sham came into view. He turned with a start at their footsteps.

"Oh," he said with relief. "It's you."

"If you could wait here," Henry said to Oas and Laki.

"Really?" Laki said.

"Oas isn't going to kill you with me and Sham right over there," Henry pointed out.

Laki reluctantly agreed and Henry took the last few strides to Sham's side.

"Cause of death?" A sweet and musky scent with a hint of pine hit him. "Is that muukalane haetta?"

"Yes. I'd bet my life on it."

"Just like Pip," Henry mused. He bent down next to Matilda. She lay face down, head turned to one side. Her eyes stared blankly. One arm stretched out in front of her. Sure enough, it had the same red sores and the hand was black and purple, puss seeping from a wound on the palm. "Exactly like Pip," he said with surprise.

"Yeah."

Henry glanced around. The hedge was pristine, the grass between the walls cut short. There were no bright pink thorns anywhere to be seen. "Muukalane? In here?"

"I agree. It makes no sense. But that is muukalane haetta poisoning. And it's just as bad a reaction as the last one. That should be rare."

Henry rubbed his temples. This made no sense. This couldn't be an accident. Which meant that Pip was likely also murdered. But why? It made no sense.

"It couldn't have been Miss Fischer," Laki asked.

Henry turned back. Oas and Laki stood where he'd left them. Laki kicked at the dog yipping at one of his ankles.

"Seeing as she was already smashed before this."

"Yes," Henry said absently. He turned his eyes to Oas. "Who found her?"

"I did," Oas said. "When Dandy returned to the house without her I located her by..." Oas glanced nervously at Laki.

"Tracking her watch?" Henry prompted.

"Yes."

"Who was the last one to see Matilda alive?" Henry asked.

"Also me. I sent her to bring Dandy in from the gardens just before you arrived."

"Who else was outside at that time?"

"No one. Miss Marigolds and Mr. and Mrs. Okumu were already in the study. Mrs. Marigolds was in the great hall with me inquiring about drinks."

"Matilda was still in the hall when I came inside," Laki spoke up quickly.

"That is true," Oas confirmed.

"Someone had to be here to poison her."

"Maybe Caprice had hired someone else too?" Sham offered.

"It makes no sense. Why would she want the maid dead?"

"More money?"

"After she's already been arrested?"

"She didn't know she'd be arrested," Sham pointed out.

Henry shook his head. "No, something's wrong. Where's Inspector Klar?"

"Press conference in Erfundenborg. She'll be on her way once that is completed," Sham said.

"Alright, no one touches the body..."

As if on cue, Dandy let go of Laki's pant leg and bounded right toward Matilda's body.

"Get the dog!" Henry said, trying to block the path.

Laki reached for Dandy but completely missed. Dandy bounded right under Henry, missing both of his flailing arms. Sham dropped down and snatched the dog by the collar. The dog made a yelp. No. It wasn't the sound a dog made. Sham was the one that yelped. He dropped Dandy and stumbled back, looking at his hand.

"Sham, the dog!"

Dandy nuzzled Matilda's hand.

"It cut me," Sham said. He held out his hand. There was a puncture wound right in the palm.

Henry looked closer. The skin around it was red and beginning to blister. The wound looked just like the one on Matilda's hand. Henry looked from Sham to the dog. It had the studded collar he'd seen it wearing since the reading of the will. He looked back to Sham.

"I feel..." Sham wavered on his feet.

Henry caught the constable before he hit the ground.

"Someone call... whatever it is you call here. And nobody touch the dog!"

CHAPTER 19

"Come in," Dom greeted Jackson and Alicia as they opened the door.

He wore what could only be described as a sexy cowboy costume. Now knowing what it was for, Jackson could only shake his head, wondering how he hadn't seen it before. There were snaps up the sides of the tightly fitted jeans for ease of tear away. Jackson tried to remember if the lumberjack outfit had been the same way. Henry had seen them. That is what Henry did. He always saw the details Jackson missed.

"I made meatballs."

"We're in a bit of a hurry," Alicia said. "When's your flight?"

"We still have a few hours," Jackson said.

"Good," Dom smiled. "Time for meatballs then."

"Don't you need to be somewhere?" Alicia asked.

"Cancelled."

"Then why are you still wearing that?"

"Would yous rather I take it off?"

"No," Jackson spoke up. "It's fine. Let's eat some meatballs."

The three settled around the small table. Jackson pulled out his phone to double check the time.

"Oh crap," Jackson said.

"What?" Alicia asked.

"I have twelve missed calls from Henry. Hold on a minute." There was only one message from the twelve calls. Jackson hit the message and put the phone to his ear.

"Jackson, call me back," Henry's voice played. "There's been another murder."

The message ended there. Jackson looked at his phone. He wasn't sure what he was looking for, but it seemed the right thing to do.

"Everything alright?"

"Someone else is dead."

"Thought the case was solved," Dom said.

"Me too," Jackson replied. "I'll be right back."

Jackson stood up and crossed to the front door. He tapped call back as he went. Henry answered on the first ring.

"Jackson!"

"What's going on?" Jackson replied.

"The dog. They're killing people with the dog."

"What?"

"I can't explain. No! Don't grab it. Just leave it. No one touch the... sorry, Jackson?"

"Yes. What's going on?"

"I was wrong. I don't know how but I was wrong. Someone is still killing people."

"Who's dead?"

"The maid."

"How?"

"Muukalane haetta. They used the dog to poison them with muukalane."

"Them?" Jackson asked.

"Pip and Matilda. They were both killed with the dog. It doesn't make any sense. I was sure it was Caprice. She admitted to it. But... this doesn't make sense. Why Pip and Matilda?"

"I don't know," Jackson said honestly. "What do you need?"

"I have to figure this out. Sham's been poisoned as well. He might live but... I don't know what do do, Jackson. I don't know."

Jackson suddenly realized Henry wasn't using his British accent. "Okay. Hold on. I'm coming."

"Thank you," Henry said. "No, don't touch it-"

The call ended. Jackson stared at the screen. It went blank.

"What's going on?" Alicia asked from the doorway.

"I think I need a ride back to Alku."

Twilight began to wane. It was too early to be this dark, but the dense fog pressed in on the manor. Lydia watched the changing light from the study window. She tapped nervously at the glass in an absent-minded rhythm.

"Could you stop that," Sloan moaned from one of the brown leather chairs.

"I wonder what's taking so long," Lydia said.

"You won't see anything out there," Sloan replied. "That window doesn't even face the maze."

Lydia turned from the window with a hint of a glare. The room had a deceptively comfortable soft orange glow. It didn't seem to be the proper place to be waiting for news of another murder.

"We are just about done here," Ms. Veratiri said from behind the desk. "Would any of you like more tea?"

"I've had enough," Sloan said. It was unclear if she meant the tea or the situation at large.

"No thank you," Lydia said, placing her own cup on a nearby end table.

Ms. Veratiri nodded and flipped through a few pages. "Honestly, the changes will be fairly simple."

"Really?" Sloan said.

From his position near the door, Regal's attention shifted back to the woman.

Ms. Veratiri nodded without looking up. She was once again dressed in blue. A slightly darker shade and with a higher collar than the previous suit. It was once again completed with long gloves and tall boots, this time they were a vivid pink.

"So mother is still getting her share?" Sloan asked.

"That remains to be seen. If she's convicted then no."

"And Oscar?" Sloan asked.

"His will be redistributed seeing as Oscar technically isn't even who he really is. And of course, Pip Skarsgård, Emma Fischer, and Matilda Desrosiers will not be receiving anything either. But since there are pending criminal proceedings with Mrs. Marigolds, I will wait to calculate all the numbers. For now, just know that the three of you plus Oas and the chauffeur are all still inheriting something."

"And Ari," Lydia added.

"Yes," Mrs. Veratiri. "I forgot about him." The slip seemed to aggravate the solicitor. "And at this rate, maybe they'll be a few more vacancies before I need to run the numbers."

The three other occupants of the room turned their full attention on Ms. Veratiri. She didn't seem to notice.

"Excuse me?" Regal finally spoke up.

She looked up, then blushed. "Sorry. That was an attempt at a joke. I've never had the knack."

"Don't try again," Sloan said harshly.

"I suppose it could feel as if someone were weeding out the heirs," Mrs. Veratiri said. "I'm sure there's another explanation though. Anyway, that's all for now. I'll wait for Oas before I go, but you're all dismissed."

No one moved for a moment while Ms. Veratiri began placing all her papers into her leather binder. Sloan was the first to go. She sighed heavily then pulled herself from the seat. She headed for the door and Lydia followed. Regal fell in after them as they exited. None spoke until the drawing-room door shut behind them.

"That was ominous," Regal said.

"Completely out of line," Sloan added.

"And that tea was horrible," Regal added.

"That's so much more important," Sloan said sharply.

"Sorry," Regal replied.

"It's not like mother was killing people to get more money, she was trying to..." Sloan glanced at Lydia who was only just holding back tears. "Well, it was still horrible, but she wasn't killing people for money at least."

"Yes," Lydia choked out.

"What about the maid?" Regal asked.

"An accident? They said a plant killed the footman, right? Who knows what's out there."

"Two accidents?" Regal asked.

"What are you saying?" Sloan asked as she led them into the saloon. The room was shockingly white after the study.

"What if someone is trying to get more money by knocking off a few of us?" Regal spoke the question softly, but it still echoed in the large room.

"Who would do that?" Sloan balked.

"Someone that wants money," Regal replied.

Sloan stopped and turned on her husband. "Who? You? Me? Lydia?" She spoke Lydia's name with a mocking tone indicating the level of absurdity that thought held.

"There's also the butler and the..." Regal thought for a moment. "What's the other man do? The stout one."

"Oh, of course, the butler did it," Sloan said with bemused sarcasm. "I'm going for a swim." Sloan turned and headed for the great hall.

Regal waited until she was gone before turning to find Lydia who was sitting in one of the less than comfortable looking chairs. "Are you staying here?" He asked.

"Yes," Lydia said. "Henry will come back through here, I think."

"Do you want company?"

"No. I'll be fine."

Regal nodded. "I'm sure Sloan is right. No one is trying to kill anyone."

"Of course," Lydia said in a voice that didn't give any indication as to her level of belief.

Regal didn't move right away, looking from Lydia to the doors leading to the gardens. Silence loomed over the room, and Regal shifted awkwardly. Finally, he nodded mostly to himself and turned to leave.

"I'll be in my room if you need anything. I think I could go for a nap."

With that, Regal left Lydia alone.

"So the dog killed someone?" Dom asked from the backseat.

It was the third time he'd asked the question. It was beginning to dawn on Jackson that there was a good chance Dom was very high at the moment. Thinking back, there was a good chance Dom had been high in every interaction he'd had with him. They were nearing the bridge to Alku now. Jackson was trying to think, but Dom was making it very difficult. And for some reason, he kept thinking about what Alicia had just told him about her and her brother's strange wardrobes.

"No. The dog was used to poison two people. Apparently."

"Dog poison?"

"Muukalane haetta. Somehow. He didn't explain."

"Ah," Dom said. "Dangerous stuff. That stuff got them two that washed up the other day. The lady on the news said so."

"Great," Jackson replied. Then the string of words Dom had spewed out clicked together. "Wait, what two people? The tourists? I thought they died on Erfundeneyja."

"They washed up here, but muukalane only grows on Alku so they must have stumbled into it there. Oh, and they weren't tourists. It was some doctor and her husband."

"Doctor?" Jackson asked. Realization dawned on him and he spun around to look at Dom. He still wore the stripper cowboy getup including the stupid hat. "What doctor?"

"Uh..." Dom thought. "They live 'ere, but they were Polish or something like that."

"Novak? Was it Doctor Novak?"

"Yeah. That's the one."

"Shit," Jackson said, turning back around.

"Who's that?" Alicia asked.

"Laundra Henbit's doctor. They were friends too, I think. At least enough that they witnessed her will."

Alicia cocked an eyebrow. "That can't be a coincidence."

"Four people connected to Laundra Henbit killed by muukalane haetta. No. I don't think so. And they lived on Erfundeneyja, not Alku."

"There were two others, right?" She asked. "Two other murders?"

"Yes. One was killed with heroin tainted with rat poison. But then that killer died trying to do the same to a second person. She got crushed when he passed out on top of her."

"Bad way to go," Dom said.

"He was naked too."

"Eh," Dom cocked his head. "Maybe she enjoyed it then."

"Two methods of murder," Alicia said, nodding slowly.

Two methods of murder. Two different ways of killing. The pieces didn't fit. Caprice had admitted to hiring Miss Fischer to kill Ramses and the attempt on Ari. The others though, they didn't fit at all. The doctor and her husband, the footman and the maid. It didn't make sense. And then, of course, Mrs. Henbit herself. They still didn't know what had been used on her. Caprice hadn't admitted to that one either. "Puzzles," Jackson muttered mostly to himself.

"Puzzles?" Alicia asked.

"Yes," Jackson said, a thought solidifying in his mind. "Puzzles. Henry used to have these puzzles he'd try to put together. Usually architecture for some reason but that's not important. He could never finish them because Chad would mix up the pieces. He'd have half of the Empire State Building and half of the Chrysler Building. But he'd keep trying to make them work while Chad would just laugh."

"Okay."

"It's two different puzzles. Two types of murders. Maybe three if you put in Laundra Henbit."

"Which you should, seeing as that started it all."

"Caprice is responsible for the gardener and the attempt on the nurse. That makes sense. But someone else is killing the others. Like the dog and nun costumes. They don't make sense together but if you pull them apart, well... there's a break down in the metaphor but still. Someone else killed the footman and the maid."

"Why?"

Jackson shook his head. The bridge to Alku appeared out of the fog. The village lights shone behind it. "We need to go to the pub."

"The pub?" Alicia asked.

"I could go for a pint," Dom added.

"Yes, the pub. I need to see something."

* * *

Sham cried out in pain. Again. He'd fallen to the grass, all too near Matilda for Henry's comfort, both because of the smell of death and the possibility of contaminating a crime scene. Henry placed a hopefully comforting hand on Sham's shoulder as he knelt down beside the constable. That should be comforting. He'd read it somewhere at least.

"This reaction is far more severe than should happen for a native of Alku," Oas spoke casually like he was making a comment about the weather.

"Statements like that are not helpful," Henry nearly shouted. "Stop just stating what we all can see and find the damn dog!"

"You've been unclear as to whether we should not touch the dog or catch it for you," Oas said. "So far you've said-"

"Get the dog but don't touch the collar. Wear gloves or something. Where is it?"

"I believe it headed for the house," Oas said.

"Holy hell." Henry jumped up. "You two get Sham out of the maze and wait for the ambulance." Henry jumped up and started down the maze.

"You're leaving me with him?" Laki gulped.

"You'll be fine, I..." Henry looked ahead then turned back. "Damn it. I don't know how to get out of here."

"I can help," Oas said.

"Fine. First, help me out of here then go back and get Sham out of here."

"You're leaving me alone?" Laki asked, eyes wider.

"Holy hell. You're a grown man. Say here. Don't touch the dog. You'll be fine."

"So don't go after the dog?" Oas asked.

"Just do the last thing I said and ignore whatever I said before. Move! Lives could be at stake."

Jackson burst into the pub with Alicia and Dom on his heels. The usual patrons jumped at the intrusion. Otto looked up at them from behind the bar.

"You're back," Otto said, surprised.

"Do you remember those names I had you look up?" Jackson asked.

"I think so. Is everything alright?"

"No. Show me," Jackson said pointing to the plaques on the wall.

Baffled but also intrigued, Otto dropped what he was doing and crossed to the wall. Jackson followed. The red-bearded man took in the entire spread as one then slowly moved in closer. He eyed a few before pointing to one. Then quickly pointed out three more.

"Wait, slow down. That one," Jackson said pointing to the first name Otto had indicated: Leo Eliassen. "Who's his nearest living relative?"

"That's a tough one," Otto said. "Never married and no children. Let's see. His brother is also dead. He was on your list too. Aleksi Eliassen."

"He have children?"

"Yes. One. She died young. His wife too."

"So... who is left?"

"Cousins. If I had to make a guess..." Otto stepped back and checked over the sprawling names. "Closest that still lives around here would be her." Otto pointed to a name.

Jackson leaned in. The name took him by surprise. Lenna Veratiri. "Is that the lawyer?"

"Solicitor. Yes."

The next name up the tree caught Jackson eye next. Vera Ansatiri. "This one," he said pointing to the name. "That's Ms. Veratiri's mother?"

"Yes."

"She's a painter?"

"Was. Died ten years back. She never adjusted too well after old Mr. Henbit kicked them out of the Ledtrådssen house. Really she died then, just took a few decades for her body to realize it."

"Ledtrådssen house?"

"Yeah. Elias Ledtrådssen home. His people lived there for generations. But it was on the land Mr. Henbit wanted to use for the manor, so they all had to move into Alku. That was before my time. I do remember my ma saying that Vera stopped painting after they moved. I think her painting of the Ledtrådssen house was her final one. Her daughter has it at her office. It's... nice. A little kitschy for my taste."

It clicked into place then. The ruined house. The one he and Alicia had followed Oscar too. Jackson knew why it had felt so familiar. It was the house from Ms. Veratiri's painting. "So Ms. Veratiri is a descendant of Elias Ledtrådssen? She got kicked off the Henbit Estate?"

"Oh yes. She's very proud of that. The first part. Not the second so much."

"Show me the rest of the names."

Otto did. One by one they traced them. In every case, they connected back to Elias Ledtrådssen and every one also connected to Ms. Veratiri. She was the nearest living relative to every person on the committee of Dandy's trust.

"Holy shit," Jackson said as Otto traced the final name to Ms. Veratiri.

"What does that mean?" Otto said.

"It's like a... expression of surprise," Dom explained.

"No, I know what shit means. I watch Netflix. What does this mean?" he motioned to the wall.

"It means that the only living person that can authenticate the will is the one that gets the trust for the entire Henbit Estate."

"That's the entire island," Otto said. His eyes went wide, and he leaned close to Jackson. When he spoke, it was hardly a whisper. "You mean that jackass is going to own everything?"

"Not exactly own, but close enough."

Alicia stepped up beside Jackson. She glanced around to make sure they didn't have the attention of the room. "What exactly do you think this means?"

"Everything I've learned about Laundra Henbit does not line up with the will she left behind."

"You never even met her," Alicia said carefully.

"Yes, but people are people everywhere."

"I think I read that on a fortune cookie once," Dom chuckled.

"I've seen her previous will. It made sense. Then she suddenly goes to a new lawyer-"

"Solicitor," Otto corrected.

"Whatever," Jackson shook his head. "She throws out everything from the old one and makes a bizarre will that leaves everything to a dog, screws over her kids and creates a loophole that encourages the beneficiaries to kill each other."

"I will give you that the will is very strange," Alicia said.

"Four people could verify that the will we read is real. Mrs. Henbit dies, and before anyone can speak to them, the two witnesses die of muukalane haetta poisoning. The same poison that two of the beneficiaries died from. Mrs. Veratiri is the only living person that knows anything about the will."

"So..." Dom tried to put it together.

"I think Mrs. Henbit went to Ms. Veratiri to make a will that would come clean about her children. That's why she was in a hurry. For some reason, she thought someone wanted her dead and didn't want that secret to go to her grave. She made a new will with Ms. Veratiri then when she died, Ms. Veratiri gave the family a fabricated will that would give her control of the entire island," Jackson said.

"She has always hated that estate," Otto said. "Her father burnt down the old Ledtrådssen House when they lost it to Mr. Henbit, you know.

Actually died doing it."

"Holy hell," Jackson gaped. "That's motive enough for murder."

"So what do we do now?" Dom asked.

Jackson tried to think through the options. He had to tell Henry, but would Henry listen? What proof did they have? "If we could find the will. The real will."

"You think she would have kept it?" Alicia asked.

"Who knows. But if so, that could be a start."

"I saw her driving out the Henbit Estate earlier so you could probably snoop around her place a bit if you wanted," Otto said casually. "I'm sure she left the back door unlocked."

"She's out at the Henbit Estate?" Jackson nearly shouted.

"Yes," Otto said cautiously.

Jackson felt his stomach drop. "I have to call Henry." Jackson grabbed his phone and quickly hit Henry's contact. It rang twice then went to voicemail. Jackson groaned and hung up. Quickly he tapped out a message and sent it. "Alicia, I need to get out to the estate, now."

"What about the will?" Alicia asked.

"Screw the will, Henry's out there with a psychopath."

"Good call. Dom-"

"Right, if I find anything, I will let yous know," Dom said with a nod.

"What?"

"Yous want me to stay and find the will."

"No, I was going to just tell you to finish your beer."

"Right, I could do the other though too."

Alicia looked from Dom to Jackson. Jackson looked to be paralyzed by conflicting thoughts. Finally, he shook his head. "Let's just stop her from killing anyone else. We can let someone else find the will later."

"Fine," Dom said reluctantly. "I'll drive."

Lydia's head snapped up. She hadn't meant to doze off. She wondered how long she'd been waiting. What had woken her? She looked around the room. It was still big, white, and empty. The only sounds were... what was that? She strained to hear. Her head felt extraordinarily foggy. Eventually, she picked out the noise, faint yipping. It came from outside. Dandy wanted in. Reluctantly, Lydia stood to cross the room. The room spun. She held out a hand to steady herself. Why was she so tired?

Once the room settled into its proper place, Lydia took one careful step at a time to the door. Her footsteps echoed out around her. They seemed strangely muffled. Everything felt muffled.

Lydia opened the door. Dandy pranced about a few times yipping the darted under her. Lydia reached down to pet the dog. The world spun, faster now. Lydia reached out to catch herself. She was falling. Her head smacked something hard. Lydia closed her eyes.

CHAPTER 20

The small figure in the doorway fell. Henry's stomach dropped. The person was far too small to have been Sloan or Regal. It could only be Lydia. Henry pushed himself harder. His oxfords weren't made for running, and his ill-fitting pants threatened to trip him up, but he kept running.

He bounded up the stairs and fell to his knees next to Lydia's body. She lay crumpled in the doorway in a limp heap.

"No, no," Henry stammered. He had been too late. He'd been wrong and now Lydia... He had failed.

Henry grabbed Lydia's hands, looking at each. Maybe he could stop the poison. It took some work to get enough light on each. They looked... healthy. No red not to mention black or purple. There was no wound. There was blood, not from the hands though. He looked Lydia over and found the source. A small cut on her head. It bled minimally. He scrutinized his surroundings. The door frame. Halfway up was a bit of blood. She'd hit her head while falling. Quickly Henry checked her over. He couldn't find a wound anywhere else. Her breathing was normal. She merely seemed to be asleep.

"Is everything alright?"

The voice startled Henry. He jerked his attention into the room beyond them. Ms. Veratiri stood there, fumbling with a leather binder.

"Give me a hand. I need more light."

Ms. Veratiri stuck the binder into her purse and crossed to Henry. Carefully, they moved Lydia into the saloon.

"She looks to have knocked her head," Ms. Veratiri pointed out.

"Yes," Henry answered absently. Lydia wore a white blouse and jeans. The white had a few spots of blood from her head but showed no sign of any other wound. The jeans showed nothing. Maybe she hadn't been poisoned. Why had she fallen then?

"We could take her to her room," Ms. Veratiri suggested. "I'll call a doctor."

"Yes, I think that would be good. "Have you seen the dog?" Henry asked, suddenly remembering why he'd come to the house.

"No."

"That's good. If you do, leave it alone. Let's get Lydia upstairs."

He could at least keep her safe from the dog if she hadn't been poisoned yet. Ms. Veratiri was surpassingly strong. It was not nearly as difficult for them to carry Lydia up the stairs as he should have thought. The bleeding had stopped on her head wound, and she continued to breathe regularly. Shortly they had her in her own bed. She seemed to be resting comfortably.

"I'll get the doctor on the line," Ms. Veratiri said as she retreated from the room.

"Yes, and again, don't touch the dog. Call me if you see it. Tell the others the same."

Ms. Veratiri gave him an odd sideways look that Henry couldn't begin to understand. He hardly even registered it at the moment. Then she nodded and left the room, shutting the door behind her.

Henry checked Lydia's pulse and breathing. Everything seemed fine. She was sleeping. Whatever had caused the fall, it wasn't muukalane haetta. It could have been another drug.

It was dark outside. How long had he been here? Klar had to be on her way by now. Henry pulled out his phone to check the time. It was past nine. He also had over a dozen missed calls from Jackson. There was a message too.

Veratiri is the killer, it read.

Henry frowned. Was that a joke? Surely Jackson was on his way home by now. He clicked call back and waited a moment. Jackson answered on the first ring.

"Holy hell, I thought you were dead," Jackson nearly shouted.

"I'm fine. We've had some developments here that required my attention." Henry gave Lydia one last look. She seemed fine. He did need to find the dog before it killed anyone else. Henry headed for the door. "Is your flight delayed?"

"Forget the flight. Are you near Ms. Veratiri?"

"No, she's calling the doctor. Lydia had a bit of an accident. I'm sure she's fine." Henry grabbed the door handle and turned. It stuck. He looked down at it and turned again. It didn't budge. "That's odd."

"Okay, do not go near her. Or maybe do but have Sham arrest her or something."

"Jackson, this is not the time for games," he said. Again, he tried to open the door. It was jammed tight.

"Henry, I know I'm not a detective, but you have to believe me. That doctor? Novak. She's dead. So is her husband. They died of muukalane haetta poisoning."

Henry forgot about the door a moment. "Muukalane?"

"Yes."

"How? It only grows on Alku."

"I don't know that, but they are dead."

"It couldn't have been the dog."

"What?" Jackson choked.

"The dog. Its collar is poisoned somehow. That's what killed Pip and Matilda."

"That's twisted. Still. All four were muukalane. I'll explain more when I get there but for now, please trust me, Ms. Veratiri is a killer."

Henry nodded to himself. "I think she's locked me in Lydia's room."

"What?"

Henry pushed against the door. It didn't budge. "Yes. I am certainly locked in here."

"You have to get out," Jackson said. "I'm on my way, just hold on."

"Of course," Henry said. He looked around the room. There were many windows, but they weren't on the ground floor. "I think I'm going to need both hands."

"Call me if anything happens," Jackson said.

"I will," Henry said, then he ended the call. Ms. Veratiri. Why would she be the killer? Jackson had to be wrong. Still, she had locked Henry into the room. From the outside. That was suspicious. Henry crossed to the nearest window. It slid open with little effort. He leaned out then leaned right back in. It was a very high second floor.

"Keep breathing," Laki suggested.

"Of course I'm going to keep breathing," Sham gasped.

Oas and Laki supported Sham between them. His arm had swollen more, but it wasn't turning purple. His breathing had become more strained, however. They rounded the last bend in the maze. It was dark now, and without moon or stars, they were left to navigate with the light from Laki's phone. They stepped out of the maze. The house glowed out of the fog.

"We should get him to the house," Oas said.

"What if the dog's in there?" Laki asked.

"Don't touch him," Oas stated.

Laki muttered to himself as they crossed the grass. It was wet from the fog and slick. Oas listened for sirens but heard nothing. Sham needed medical help, quickly. The last thing they needed was for a local to die on their estate. He was already unsure of where they stood with the heir to the estate being used as a murder weapon. Dandy, of course, hadn't meant to kill anyone, but the end result couldn't be argued. The citizens of Alku had never appreciated their presence. After all of this, they might try to drive them all out for good.

A figure moved in the doorway.

"Has the ambulance arrived?" Oas shouted.

"Not yet." It was Ms. Veratiri's voice. "Who's hurt?"

"Constable Sham. He's been poisoned."

"That's very unfortunate," Ms. Veratiri said, her voice wavering. "Quite unfortunate. Quick. We can find a place for him to lie down. There's tea in the billiard room."

"I don't think I need tea," Sham muttered between clenched teeth.

"Tea helps everything," Oas replied.

"I do agree with you on that point," Ms. Veratiri said with a smile.

The tires of the orange box of a car squealed as they turned into the Henbit Estate. The vehicle threatened to tilt, but Dom kept it upright. They sped up the drive and screeched to a stop right in front of the house next to Jackson's rental car. Jackson sprang out before Dom had the ignition off.

"Wait," Alicia shouted, climbing out behind him. "What exactly are we going to do?"

Jackson shrugged. "I don't know. Stop her from killing people."

"We don't even have anything to protect ourselves."

"I do," Dom said pulling two revolvers from his cowboy holsters.

"Those aren't real," Alicia said.

"Ah, but she doesn't know that."

Alicia sighed. "Fine, give me one." Dom tossed one over the car. Alicia caught it. "Okay, let's go in."

The three walked up the steps, while Jackson sent a quick message to Henry to let him know they'd arrived. For once, there was no one there to open the door. Jackson almost knocked but thought better of it. He grabbed the handle and pulled. The door didn't open.

"It's locked," Jackson said.

"Maybe yank it open," Alicia suggest.

"I'm flattered you think I could do that, but this is solid oak. Or something like that."

"I got it," Dom said. He stepped up to the door, lifted one booted foot and kick. The door didn't budge, but the buttons up his jeans snapped open. Dom quickly dropped his leg and grabbed the edges of his stripper jeans. "Never mind."

Alicia looked around the entry. Her eyes stopped on the balcony to their right. "This way," she said. She stepped up to the banister and looked out over the edge. Before anyone could say anything, she jumped up on the ledge and stepped out, foot landing on the nearest windowsill.

"What are you doing?" Jackson asked.

Alicia edged out onto the ledge and looked onto the window. "This should work." With one swift kick, she shattered the window. A few more kicks and she had an opening big enough to crawl through. With a motion to follow, she disappeared inside.

Jackson quickly made his way to the edge of the balcony.

"We could wait for her to open the door?" Dom suggested.

"I'm not waiting," Jackson said as he climbed over the railing.

"You're not even wearing proper shoes," Dom said pointing to his sandals.

"You're wearing stripper pants. Besides, if I couldn't climb in sandals then I wouldn't deserve to be a Ruck."

"A what?"

"Ruck. That's my last name."

"I thought it was Pets."

"I already explained this." Jackson shook his head. "Are you coming?"

With that, he made his way onto the windowsill. He edged over to the broken part of the window and carefully ducked inside. A piece of glass grazed his thigh as he crawled in and for once he wished he wasn't wearing shorts. With a crack of glass, he landed on the broken pieces of the window. Another shard cut into his foot. He bent down and picked it away before stepping out of the debris. No sooner had he stepped away, Dom landed behind him.

"This is a very nice room," Dom said, looking up at the "candlelit" chandelier.

"Where now?" Alicia asked.

"Henry was upstairs. We should look for him."

The rattle of a door came from across the room. All three turned. Jackson recalled it as the door to the billiard room. It shook again. Someone was trying to get out. Jackson held up a finger. Someone knocked. Not forcefully. It was a polite knock. Jackson finished crossing the room and took hold of the knob. He turned and pulled. The door stuck.

"Hello?" A polite voice spoke from the other side. It was Oas.

"Oas?" Jackson asked.

"Yes, who's there?"

"Jackson. What are you doing?"

"The door is stuck. I can't unlock it."

Alicia was beside him now. She crouched and looked at the lock. "Something's broken off in here."

"Is the dog in there with you?" Jackson asked.

"No!" Oas exclaimed. "But Sham has a fever."

"Fever?"

"Also, I think something might have been in the tea," Oas said. "Laki has fallen asleep, and I am finding it difficult to stay awake myself."

"Okay, hold tight," Jackson said. "If you see Ms. Veratiri, just stay away from her."

"Seeing as we are locked in here, I don't think we will being seeing anyone."

Jackson turned back to the room. "Dom, try to get this door opened. Alicia, come with me."

"Should I try kicking it?"

"Do whatever you think," Jackson said.

"Within reason," Alicia added quickly.

Jackson and Alicia left Dom to handle the door as they exited out into the great hall. It was vacant. Jackson turned a full circle. "Okay, I'm open to suggestions." He checked his phone, nothing from Henry.

"We could check upstairs and see if..." Alicia stopped and sniffed the air. "Do you smell smoke?"

Jackson breathed in deeply. There was a definite hint of smoke. "Fireplace?"

"The one in the dinning room is fake," Alicia said. She kept sniffing and walked toward the stairs. Jackson followed. She started up one of the twin staircases the stopped. Slowly she came back down and headed between them. She pointed to the mural. Smoke leaked out from where the bottom met the floor. "What's behind that?"

"Basement. It's a gym and pool. Also a bowling alley."

"I could live here," Alicia said with a laugh. "Apart from the murder, that is."

"That does decrease the appeal."

They moved between the stairs and stopped at the mural. Jackson pushed. It moved back to reveal the stairs and a good amount of smoke.

"That can't be good," Alicia said.

The two quickly moved down the curved staircase. The smoke began to build as they reached the bottom. They came out into the gym area, and both scanned the room. Alicia squinted at the doorway to the pool.

"Is there something in the door there?" She asked.

"Go check," Jackson said. "I'll follow the smoke."

The smoke seemed to be coming from the restroom. Jackson weaved through the nearly unused exercise equipment, rechecking his phone. Still nothing from Henry. He reached the restroom door and pulled it open. Smoke billowed out. He coughed as he took in a lung full. There was still no sign of flames, so Jackson pulled his shirt up over his nose and moved inside. It was hard to see as he crossed the white tiled floor. He stuck his head into the showers. Nothing. That would have been too easy. Light flickered past the showers, however. He moved in, eyes stinging. He tried to breathe through the shirt, but every breath was full of smoke. Past the showers, he saw the doors to the saunas. An orange light flicked inside.

Jackson rushed through the room. The wooden door wasn't on fire yet so he grabbed the handle and yanked it open. Dark smoke clogged the air. He tried not to breath. Flames jumped up in front of him. Jackson stepped toward it and smashed his toe on something. He looked down. Through the smoke, he could just make out the shape of a sharp dark rock. There were more scattered about. Jackson moved in more carefully now, inching toward the flame. It was in the back. A mostly burned towel lay across the heater. Fire licked the wooden walls. Jackson snatched up an unburnt corner of the towel, yanked it up and tossed it out behind him. It did little to stop the burning. Fire still flickered up the back wall.

Jackson jumped back out of the sauna, coughing to catch his breath. He looked around for a solution. No fire extinguisher. There were showers though. He ran toward them, stomping out the bit of burning towel as he went. He yanked of his tank top and turned on the nearest shower. Once the fabric was wet, he ran back to the sauna. Taking in one deep breath, he jumped inside. He smothered the flames in the wet shirt. The flames hissed and died. His lungs ached, but the fire was gone. Jackson stumbled out of the sauna and moved back to the shower. He let the cold water wash over his hands a moment before pulling on his singed tank top.

The gym air seemed fresh and clean after the restroom. Jackson bent over and let the coughing fit pass before making his way to Alicia. She looked up from where she crouched next to the pool door.

"Were you putting out a fire or going for a swim?" Alicia asked, looking him up and down.

"I thought I was going to die in a sauna," Jackson said.

"It happens."

Jackson saw the body laying next to Alicia. "What happened?"

The wet long blond hair told him it was Sloan. She lay in a puddle of water, dressed in a swimsuit.

"She's alive. Maybe drugged though. I can't wake her up. I think she fell here."

"We should get her upstairs," Jackson said. "The fire's out, but there's still a lot of smoke." Jackson started coughing again.

"Yeah, we should get you out too."

A climb down from the top floor was not going to happen. Henry had exhausted every option that way. With work, he could make it to the roof of the corridor leading to the conservatory, but there was no way he could make it to the ground. Slowly he edged back to the window to Lydia's room. His last chance was to reach another bedroom. He'd have to use the decorative edge crossing beneath all the windows. He sighed and bent down to take off his shoes and socks. The oxfords would be too slick for this. Once he had his feet free, he stepped to the ledge.

Henry breathed in deeply and started to move across. Suddenly, he wished he'd spent more time climbing with Jackson. Sweat rolled down his face. His dress shirt was soaked through. Jackson had tried to teach him to climb. He'd taken him to Joshua Tree and Yosemite. Both were beautiful but Henry had been content to watch the stars or read a good book in the shade. Both his brothers were built for adventure, admittedly Chad's was often the less than legal kind. Not Henry. He was made for thinking.

Inch by inch he moved toward the next window, fingers gripping the brick. He tried not to think of how far up he was. How much it would hurt to fall. Instead he put his mind back to the case. How had he missed the truth so completely? If Jackson was correct, Doctor Novak and her husband had been murdered. The two people that could verify the will were dead. Why hadn't he pushed that harder? It had seemed so simple once he'd narrowed in on the family secret. Two murderers? That just wasn't fair. He was supposed to be the one that figured things out. How had Jackson done it?

Henry's hand touched glass. He forced himself not to hurry the last bit. Carefully he moved in front of the window. With one hand he pushed on the glass. To his great relief, the window slid open.

The room was dark. Henry couldn't tell who it belonged to, but the door was open. Henry raced across the room. The hall was empty. Lydia's room was to his right. He checked the door as he exited the room. It was locked still. The lock itself looked to have been tampered with. For now, he could leave her. Lydia should be safe inside.

As he moved toward the grand stairs, something caught Henry's attention. Smoke? Yes. He smelled smoke. Henry dashed the rest of the way, hitting the stairs at a full sprint. His bare feet slapped on the marble stairs.

"Henry?" Jackson's voice shouted up at him.

Henry glanced around. There was movement near the stairs to the basement. Henry bounded down the rest of the stairs and turned. Jackson and Alicia had Sloan hanging between them. She was unconscious and dripping wet, dressed only in a swimsuit. Jackson was just as wet, and his tank top had large holes burnt in it.

"What happened to Sloan?" Henry asked.

"Not sure," Jackson said. "Where's Ms. Veratiri?"

"I don't know. Is she dead?" Henry asked, pointing to Sloan.

"No," Alicia answered.

"Lydia's been drugged," Henry said. "Maybe Sloan too."

"The tea," Alicia said.

"What?"

Jackson nodded and coughed a few times. "Oas said he thought there was something in the tea."

"Where's he?"

"Trapped in the billiard room with Sham and Laki."

Henry nodded. "We need to find Ms. Veratiri."

"I can take care of this one," Alicia said. "Go find the damn lady before she tries to burn this place down again."

Jackson helped Alicia get Sloan to the ground then headed for Henry.

"Wait," Alicia said. "Take this." She tossed her gun to Jackson.

"Is that a gun?" Henry balked.

"It's fake."

"Well, that just brings up even more questions."

"Later."

"Also, why are you wet?"

"I had to put out a fire. Why are you barefoot?"

"I had to climb between windows."

"Just go find the damn solicitor!" Alicia yelled at them.

"Right, of course."

The brothers agreed and moved off to the next room. A quick search of the staff dining room led to nothing. Jackson followed Henry on into the study. It too was empty. Henry glanced at a few empty tea cups. He bent down and sniffed one.

"I would venture to guess this is how Lydia and Sloan were drugged."

"Maybe Regal too," Jackson said pointing to a third cup.

"I haven't seen him."

"It's a big house."

Henry nodded, and they moved through the room. There was nothing of note in the drawing room, so they passed on into the saloon.

"Maybe she left," Jackson said.

"Perhaps," Henry replied.

"She was trying to burn the entire place down."

"I think she would hang around to make sure it worked."

"True."

"I know the dining room is empty. She's not in the billiard room either," Jackson said.

"That leaves the library and the wings," Henry replied.

A yip startled them both. Henry would have jumped out of his shoes if he'd worn any. Dandy sat at the far side of the room. He yipped at them again. Jackson started toward the dog.

"Careful," Henry said. "Those spikes on his collar are full of muukalane haetta oil."

"That's just cruel," Jackson said. "She didn't even care who got killed."

"I think she always intended to kill them all eventually. What made you guess it was Ms. Veratiri?"

"The names. The names of the committee. I checked them out after I found out Dr. Novak was dead. All the dead committee members had the same next of kin."

"Ms. Veratiri?"

"Yes. And she's a descendant of Elias Ledtrådssen. Her family used to have a house out here."

"That's..." Henry trailed off a moment. "That's very good deduction."

"I think she fabricated the entire will. She made one that would give the island back to her family."

"Very good work," Henry said, then grinned. "For a rafting guide."

Jackson laughed. Dandy made a loud yip and ran for the door across from them.

"We should get the dog, right?" Jackson asked.

"Yes. Make sure it doesn't kill anyone else.

The two rushed across the room and entered the library. Dandy was across the room already, disappearing into the adjoining corridor. They followed. As they entered the curving hallway, Dandy's yipping echoed back at them. Henry couldn't help but feel a pang of jealousy that Jackson had managed to find all that information before him. But if he hadn't... how would this have gone differently? Would he have figured it out before the house caught fire? He hadn't been wrong, exactly. The cook had killed Mr. Razek and tried to kill Ari. She'd likely killed Mrs. Henbit too, somehow. How could he have guessed there were two different cases tangled up in one? That was a statistical anomaly.

They stepped out of the corridor into the conservatory. It was dark, lit only by a few soft strings of small decorative lanterns hanging on the tops of the windows. Dandy yipped away from them, bounding for the far windows. In the dim light, a figure stood by the windows, obscured by shadows. Henry held a hand out to stop Jackson and put a finger to his lips. Jackson understood.

Dandy ran up beside the person across from them. The figure bent and picked up the dog with one gloved hand. The other hand moved to the dog's collar. Henry caught the urge to warn of the danger. With a soft click, the collar fell free and hung from the woman's hand. She put the dog down and opened her purse, then dropped the collar inside.

"That's a cruelly genius device there," Henry said.

The woman spun around with a shout of surprise. The dim light shone on her face now. Ms. Veratiri gathered her composure.

"Is it?" She asked.

"Did you make it yourself?"

"I don't make dog collars."

"I'm afraid I'm going to need to have it," Henry said.

Ms. Veratiri looked from Henry to Jackson. Jackson held the gun. It wasn't pointed at Veratiri yet.

"You killed four people. Maybe five if Sham doesn't survive."

"He'll live," Ms. Veratiri said. "He has our blood."

"You were going to burn him to death," Jackson added.

Ms. Veratiri's mouth twitched but she said nothing.

"Why did you hate them so much?" Henry asked.

Ms. Veratiri turned and looked out the windows. "On a clear day, you can almost see our house from here." She pulled off one of her gloves slowly and put the hand on the window glass. "It had such a beautiful view. On a clear day, you could see so many stars. We'd count them. Together. This was our home. It was not theirs."

Ms. Veratiri pulled her hand back and thrust it forward. The window shattered. She yanked her arm down sharply. "They don't belong here. This is our island."

"Jackson!" Henry shouted.

Jackson was already in motion. He was at Ms. Veratiri's side when she fell, catching her before she hit the ground. Blood ran freely from her wrist. Jackson pulled his shirt off for the second time and wrapped the wrist tightly. Ms. Veratiri struggled to get her arm away, but Jackson wrapped his arm around her, pinning both arms down. Ms. Veratiri yelled something in Verlorlandish and spat at him.

"She's spitting on me," Jackson complained.

"You're already soaked," Henry pointed out.

"Not with spit."

"Well you already smelled like smoke. You need a shower anyway."

Jackson sighed and looked down at the wounded arm. "I really like that shirt."

Henry moved to Ms. Veratiri's side. He pulled her purse away from her and looked inside. The collar glinted in the light. There were also two leather binders inside. Henry plucked one out and opened it. Ms. Veratiri muttered at them.

The document was a will. Laundra Henbit's will. He put it under his arm and took the other out. It also seemed to be a will. Also Laundra Henbits. Henry sat down the purse and opened both. It was hard to see details in the light, but it was easy to tell the number of pages was not the same. They both had Laundra Henbit's name on the front. One at a time, he turned to the final page of each. Only one had signatures. The other ended with merely a page of text. That's how she had managed to get the signatures. She had taken the final page of the original will.

"You kept the real will?" Henry said.

"I don't know what you're talking about," Ms. Veratiri said weakly.

Henry put them back in the purse and snapped it shut. "We should get her medical attention," he said. "Can't have her bleeding to death on us."

CHAPTER 21

Henry watched from the front steps as the officers climbed into the back of the ambulance with Ms. Veratiri. They shut the doors, and the vehicle pulled away. One had already taken Sham away. He was stable, but his arm was in danger of being lost. They'd also taken Matilda's body.

Chief Inspector Klar spoke a few words to her remaining officers and then headed over to the house. She nodded at Henry and Jackson as she approached, looking one over then the other. Henry knew they were quite the sight. He hadn't found his shoes yet, so he was still barefoot. Jackson wore only a pair of blood splattered and singed shorts and his sandals. His left hand was also bandaged. The burns weren't severe but could get infected if not cared for well.

"The two of you have looked better," Klar said.

"It was an interesting night," Henry replied.

"That's what I gather. I'm going to need statements."

"I assumed so," Henry said.

"How' the rest of the household?"

"They're awake now," Henry said. "Oas is making them all tea in the dining room. Although I can't see many of them wanting more tea after all this."

"How did you put it all together so quickly?" Klar asked. "It wasn't until we were on our way out here that I even started to suspect the Novaks' death might be linked to all this."

Henry glanced at Jackson then looked back to Klar. "I had some help."

"Two killers," Klar said, shaking her head. "It's hard to believe."

"But true."

"Do we know which one killed Laundra Henbit?" Jackson asked.

Henry shook his head. "I would guess Ms. Veratiri, but I don't know how."

"I have the answer to that one," Klar said. "We got back the new report on her. I'm afraid that one was natural causes."

"Are you sure?"

"As sure as we can be," Klar said. "She died because she was a very unhealthy woman that refused to take care of herself."

Henry shook his head in disbelief.

"But I suppose we're fortunate that Lydia thought she'd been murdered. It could have taken us far too long to look into this without her. But for now, which one of you is first?" Klar asked.

"I'll go first if you don't mind," Jackson said. "I'd like to get a shower soon and maybe some new clothes."

"You left your tyrätstutterbuxters at the inn," Henry suggested helpfully.

"I think new shorts will be fine," Jackson said.

As Jackson headed off with Chief Inspector Klar, Henry climbed the steps to the house. The door hung open so he walked inside. It was bright, His eyes took a moment to adjust. Someone stood there waiting for him. It was Lydia.

"How's your head?" Henry asked.

Lydia patted the small knot on her left temple. "It's fine. Still a bit dizzy from the tea. The other tea. Not this tea." She said indicating her drink.

"More tea?"

"Tea helps everything," Lydia said. "Unless it's drugged."

"I suppose I could agree with that."

"I think I need to thank you again. And it is good to know that maybe mother... or I guess Aunt Caprice... didn't kill Aunt... I mean... this is so confusing."

"I have news there, actually," Henry said. "Laundra Henbit wasn't poisoned. She really did die of natural causes."

"Are you sure?"

"I seems to be so."

Lydia shook her head. "I was sure she'd been murdered."

"Maybe she thought she would be. But it does seem that is not the case. Mrs. Marigolds and Ms. Veratiri merely took advantage of her death to carry out their own plans, Caprice to keep you a secret and Ms. Veratiri to... well, kill everyone."

Lydia nodded slowly. "It's all so strange. I don't even know how to get my head around it."

"I agree. Maybe you should get some rest."

"Yes. That would be good."

"I'll say goodbye for now then," Henry said.

"Just for now, yes?" Lydia asked giving *now* a very clear enunciation.

"Yes. Of course."

"Good. Then how about goodnight instead of goodbye?"

"I like that," Henry blushed. "Goodnight, Miss Marigolds."

"Goodnight, Mr. Pets."

Lydia smiled and stood a step back, stopped, lunged forward and hugged Henry. He stumbled back, surprised a moment, then recovering, he hugged her back.

"Thank you," Lydia whispered then released the detective. With one last smile, Lydia headed up the stairs.

Henry watched until she moved out of sight. He wouldn't say anything tonight, but soon she would no longer be a client. He felt like he would want to see her again after that.

"Found your shoes."

The voice came from behind him. He turned to see the man he now knew was named Dom. He still wore the sexy cowboy outfit, Henry's shoes held out in his hand.

"Not the socks though."

"Socks are easy to replace," Henry said, taking the shoes from Dom. "Come on. I think we can leave the household alone for now."

The usual crowd at Otto's had thinned. Jackson wasn't even sure how late it was. His phone had died sometime after leaving the Henbit Manor but before Dom had insisted on buying drinks. Luckily Otto was able to find another shirt from the Ledtrådssen Rauchbier keg opening. This one, to Jackson's surprise and Henry's chagrin, was even a tank-top.

"There's one thing I don't get," Dom said for the tenth or twentieth time.

"Yes?" Henry asked with the patience of a saint.

"Her endgame there only worked if every single person in the house burnt inside it. If even one of them escaped, they would have known something was up."

"They were all drugged. It took hours for them to wake up," Alicia explained.

"Ari!" Jackson said, eyes darting to Henry.

Henry nodded. "I have a feeling Ms. Veratiri wasn't thinking all that clearly at the end."

"She was carrying around the legitimate will," Alicia spoke like that should end the conversation.

"You should have seen her eyes," Jackson said. "I mean they were always a little off but she was full on crazy person eyes at the end there."

"People are messy," Henry said. "Sometimes they don't make any sense."

Dom shrugged.

"I should get this guy back home," Alicia said. "I expect to see you again before you try fleeing the country again, alright?" Alicia eyed Jackson.

"Of course," Jackson replied.

"Good. We'll take our leave then."

There was a quick goodbye and one hug too many then the brothers were left alone with their pints.

"I think I've had enough for the night," Henry said, eyeing his.

"I can finish it," Jackson said.

"I think you've had enough too," Henry said.

"Come on," Jackson grinned. "We stopped a psychotic killer."

Henry laughed. Jackson raised his pint.

"To the Ruck brothers. Or uh... Mr. Pets and Dr. Jackson."

Henry shook his head but humored his brother with a clink of glasses. He even sipped a bit more of the beer.

"I'm sorry you missed your flight," Henry said. "Hopefully you can get it rescheduled."

"I'm sure I can, but I thought maybe I could stay a few days longer."

Henry smiled. "I'd like that."

Two or six beers later, the two paid Otto and thanked him for keeping the pub open before walking out into the night. The inn was a short walk, and the streets were empty.

"What will Dad say?"

"I'll deal with Dad."

They walked in silence a minute before Henry spoke again. "That was very lucky, you stumbling on the importance of those names there. And finding how they connected to Ms. Veratiri. It's not usually that simple."

"Simple? That was simple?"

"The luck part. Usually, it takes more deducing."

Jackson decided not to point out that it was his deducing that there was something strange about the will that had led him to look harder into the names. Henry was the detective. He'd let him enjoy this night. He could rub it in his face later. For now, he just wanted a shower. And possibly a sauna. Although he would keep all towels far away from it.

CHAPTER 22

Despite the late hour, sunlight lit the streets of Erfundenborg as Jackson left the Candlestick. He'd begun to adjust to the long days of the Verlorland summer in the weeks since they'd helped bring in Ms. Veratiri. He'd enjoyed getting to know Erfundenborg but missed the room at the Alku Inn. He'd so far managed to keep a vacant room on the other end of the shared restroom, but he would shower in more peace knowing a stranger couldn't walk in at any time. He also missed Otto's beer.

Henry stood outside 48841F Bilun waiting as Jackson pulled to the curb. Henry jumped into the car almost before Jackson had stopped.

"Dom made us sausage kolaches," he said holding up a bag dark with grease.

"Why?"

"He said they make good pre-drinking food."

"Are they good?"

Henry looked at the bag. "I thought maybe you could try them first."

Jackson eyed them suspiciously a moment before trying one. They weren't bad. They also made Jackson feel like his arteries were clogging with every bite.

"Have you ever seen a man dressed as a sexy clown?" Henry said unprompted.

"No," Jackson said quickly. "I have not seen that."

"I have. It's worse than you'd think."

"You could move?"

Henry shrugged. "Rent isn't cheap." Henry bit into another kolache. "Besides, then you'd have less reason to run into Alicia."

"I think we could manage it."

When they reached the bridge to Alku, Jackson almost felt like they were coming home. That was, of course, ridiculous but he felt it just the same. The streets were so familiar. Jackson felt a little lighter entering the little village knowing no horrible murders awaited them. Today there was only one reason for the visit: beer.

Otto's Pub was packed when the brother's arrived. More than the usual crowd was present. Jackson recognized quite a few of those milling about including Mrs. Linna from the Alku Inn and Lydia's chauffeur, Laki.

"Do you see Lydia?" Henry asked.

"Not yet. She is short though."

"Jackson!" Otto's voice boomed over the din. The red-bearded man beckoned them to come over to the bar.

Jackson didn't hesitate. It took a little longer than usual to navigate, but they managed to squeeze through the crowd. They pushed their way up to the bar. Constable Sham made space for them with a small smile. He'd made a nearly full recovery, only losing two fingers. He'd taken it mostly in stride even though he'd have to relearn almost everything with his left hand.

Otto dropped two pints down in front of them full of a frothy amber brown beer.

"Let me introduce you to the award-winning Eyja Suum Saison."

"Congratulations," Jackson said then took a gulp. He raised his eyebrows. "That is good."

"Might be my favorite," Otto said with a smile. "Saved this for you."

Otto pulled something out from under the bar and lay it in front of Jackson. Jackson grinned. It was a tank-top with the words *Eyja Suum Saison* over a smiling face that looked quite a bit like Otto.

"Don't encourage him," Henry groaned.

"I got one for you too," Otto said, pulling out a second shirt.

"Thanks," Jackson said. "I will wear it proudly."

Otto looked around to make sure no one was looking. "Here, come look at this."

Otto waved them behind the bar, and through a tiny door, Jackson hadn't even noticed before. There was a small office on the other side. It was as cluttered as Jackson would imagine Otto's office should be. He pointed one stubby finger at a framed piece of paper.

"What's that?" Jackson said, leaning forward.

"That there says I now officially own this pub," Otto said. "I'm the first landowner in Alku too by the way. Just by a hair, mind you, but still the first."

Jackson once again congratulated Otto before they headed back into the pub.

Since solicitors had verified the validity of the will Ms. Veratiri had kept from the family, Alku had begun to change. The will had confirmed that both Lydia and Ari were her children and left the bulk of her estate to them. They had immediately begun the process of letting citizens of Alku buy back their property. They kept the exact amounts they were asking for quiet, but after a few more pints Otto confided in Jackson that he'd purchased the pub for a few kegs of beer and the rights to name Otto's next two beers.

"They haven't been too creative with the names yet. The suggestions were Lydia Lager and Ari Ale. I think we can do better though."

It had gone a long way in easing tensions between the Henbit Estate and the citizens of Alku. That and maybe some collective guilt over one of their own going on a murder spree and almost burning the manor down with most of the household inside. Jackson had heard that Laki's family were even talking to him again.

"Speaking of Lydia," Otto said nodding to the door.

Ari and Lydia stood just inside the door, Ari towering over the crowd and Lydia hardly visible. Henry's eyes lit up instantly.

Ari spotted Henry and Jackson and headed toward them, Lydia in tow. People had a way of naturally making a path for the giant man, so they reached the bar much quicker than Henry and Jackson had. They greeted each other pleasantly, then Ari's expression grew serious.

"I never really thanked you properly," Ari said to Henry. "Without you, I might be dead."

"I wish I could have helped more," Henry said. "And Jackson did have quite a bit to do with the actual saving your life part."

"Thank you as well then," Ari said.

"No problem," Jackson replied. "Just maybe lock the bathroom door before you take another bath."

Ari laughed loudly then ordered them a round of beers. Henry and Lydia smiled awkwardly at each other. Jackson watched the two for a moment then turned to Ari.

"Ari. Would you mind showing me... uh..." Jackson tried to think of something, but between the sausages and beers, his mind was a little sluggish. "It's over here. Come on."

Jackson tugged at the man's arm, not budging him an inch but Ari hefted himself up and followed.

"Show me what?" Ari asked.

"Nothing, just keep walking."

"You're a strange man."

"I know. I'll explain when we are out of earshot," Jackson said quietly.

Jackson glanced back in time to see Henry lean in closer to Lydia. She was talking, smiling brightly. Jackson hoped Henry wouldn't say anything too stupid.

"You know, Mr. Pets," Miss Marigolds said as the crowd seemed to fade out behind her. "This is the first time I've seen you outside the estate."

Henry turned that over a moment. It was. He had only seen the Henbit heirs once since the events of the night of Ms. Veratiri's arrest. Jackson and he had been invited to deliver the new will to the family with Chief Inspector Klar. There had been a modest inheritance for both Sloan and Regal Okumu. It was quite a bit more than a boat this time. Solicitors would have to help figure out what to do about the money and property left to those that had died, those that had proven to be illegitimate (Oscar) or arrested for conspiracy to commit murder (Caprice Marigolds). Most likely it would fall to her surviving children. Other than that, Oas had received a decent sum, and Laki Ünwichtigbock had even inherited one of Laundra Henbit's vehicles.

It had been strange being back to the house. Sloan and Regal Okumu had joined them on Skype from back in South Africa leaving the house fairly empty. Mr. Björnssen was still living in the guest house leaving the main house to Miss Marigolds and the only remaining staff, Oas and Laki Ünwichtigbock. It was a very different place now.

"I suppose it is," Henry finally replied. "And please, call me Henry."

"I will, Henry," she smiled. "And you can call me Lydia."

Henry smiled back then he let it drop suddenly.

"What's wrong?"

"I... uh... I do think there is one thing I should tell you. Now that you aren't a client."

Lydia raised an eyebrow and waited.

"It's just that... it's uh... well... I don't know how to say this but I'm... uh... not entirely... uh..."

"British?" she asked.

Henry blinked. "Yes." He cleared his throat and leaned closer, continuing without the faux accent. "Did Jackson tell you?"

"No," she grinned. "Not to be disparaging or anything but you could use a little coaching on the accent."

Henry leaned back, trying to judge Lydia's expression. She wasn't mad. Not that he could tell. "How long did it take you to-"

"Not very long," Lydia said. "I did go to school in England."

"So did I."

Lydia laughed. "I suppose you learn more about accents studying theater than... detectiving?"

"You didn't say anything."

Lydia shrugged. "I like the accent," she said with a smile. "Although we will need to work on it before your next case."

"We?"

"Well, as you said, I'm no longer your client."

Lydia grinned with more warmth than Henry had thought one smile could hold.

"Come on," she said, grabbing his hand. "I want you to meet some people."

"Who?"

Lydia looked around. "Everyone?"

"What?"

"How am I supposed to give this island back to people if I don't know who they are? Come on. It'll be fun."

Henry didn't know if it exactly sounded like fun but if it meant spending more time with Lydia, it would be worth it.

Jackson watched the stars from his perch on the hood of the rental car. He was starting to think he might need to arrange for something more permanent. Maybe a short-term lease. He also needed a new place to stay. Maybe on Alku.

The beer tasting had wrapped up hours ago, and most of the crowd had wandered off into the night. When enough had left that it was becoming strange that Jackson was giving Henry and Lydia such wide berth, he'd decided to get some fresh air. The air was cooler than inside, and even here he could smell the open countryside. The stars stretched out above him.

The stillness was interrupted by a buzzing from Jackson's pocket. He fished out his phone and looked at the screen. It read Randy Ruck right above the stern face of his father. Jackson took in a breath and reached for the green button. He stopped just before hitting it.

Their dad was irritated his little scheme to get Henry home had failed. He was even less thrilled that Henry didn't even need his help anymore.

And then there was the matter of Jackson himself returning home. That wasn't a conversation Jackson wanted to have right now. His dad could wait. Tonight he was enjoying the moment.

"There you are," Henry's voice shouted over to him.

Jackson sat up, pocketing his phone. Henry strolled down the street in his ill-fitting suit, smiling stupidly. "Haven't seen you all evening."

Jackson gave his brother a large genuine smile. "Got into an interesting conversation with Laki about engines."

"Really?"

"No. It was a horrible conversation. But I did find out Ari's going back to med school, despite being insanely wealthy. He really wants to be a doctor."

"Lydia's staying here, in Alku. I think she's going to make this her home."

"That's good."

"Yes."

"When will you be seeing her again?"

"Tomorrow evening, actually."

Jackson laughed. "You don't mess around."

"I have no idea what you're talking about."

Henry sat down on the hood next to Jackson.

"You should probably tell her you aren't British."

"She figured that out already."

"Ah, good," Jackson said. "When?"

"I'm pretty sure the first time I spoke."

Jackson laughed, harder than he intended.

"What?"

"Maybe you should drop the British thing then?"

"Lydia is going to help me with it."

"She's encouraging it?"

"I think she likes it."

Jackson laughed again.

"If you keep laughing-"

"Sorry, sorry. Just wasn't how I saw that going."

"Maybe you don't know everything about people."

Jackson nodded. Maybe he didn't. He never would have guessed Lydia had figured Henry out, especially not that quickly. That was impressive. Or not. The accent was horrible.

"How would you feel about me staying, I don't know. Maybe another month or two?" Jackson asked.

"At the Candlestick?"

"No. Somewhere with a private bathroom. And a sauna."

"You do know a sauna almost burnt down the Henbit Estate?"

"Yes, I was in there."

"My point exactly."

Jackson decided to ignore the diversion and get to the point. "I think that Erfundenborg might actually be the perfect place for our European headquarters. It would be good to get a better feel for it."

"Really?" Henry asked.

Jackson nodded.

"I think I'd like that."

"Good. And if you get another case, maybe I could tag along again?"

"Of course. You could be useful if I need to punch or chase anyone," Henry said with a perfectly straight face. "Or climb. I am not doing that again."

Henry eyed him a moment, trying to decide if this had been a bad idea. Henry smiled.

"Was that a joke?"

"Yes."

"I'm reinstating my joke ban."

"I'll stop making jokes when you buy yourself a suit."

"Only if you buy one that fits."

"My suit is perfectly-" ringing cut Henry off. He patted his pockets.

Jackson chuckled and pulled a phone from his shorts pocket and handed it to Henry. "You left it at the bar."

Henry snatched it up and looked at the number before answering. "Henry Pets," he paused purposefully. "Private Detective."

Jackson waited as Henry spoke to the person on the other line, wondering off just far enough that Jackson couldn't hear the conversation. After a few minutes, he hung up and walked back.

"Who was that?"

"We have a case." He smiled and looked at Jackson. "You did bring more clothes than that, didn't you?"

"It was a beer tasting. Why would I bring a change of clothes?"

"Maybe I could say you're my bodyguard."

Jackson laughed and shook his head. "Where are we going?"

"It's on Rafaelin," Henry said.

"Which is?"

"North."

The brothers climbed into the car, and Jackson put the key in the ignition, then stopped. "You know, I don't think I should actually be driving."

Henry frowned. "Neither should I."

The two sat in silence a moment. Finally, Jackson spoke. "I could call Alicia?"

"That could be a good idea."

Jackson looked at Henry out of the corner of his eye. "By case you do mean an actual case, not a missing pet, right?"

"It's a murder," Henry said with a smile.

This time, Jackson didn't bother to tell him that was creepy.

ACKNOWLEDGEMENTS

This was not the first novel I started, but it is the first I've finished. It feels right. Henry Pets has been bouncing around in my mind for almost two decades since he first came into being in a short video I made with my brother Timothy and friends Lindsay and Julia. And our family dog. Just as time has changed me, it has morphed Henry into something new. The story we invented all those years ago is scattered through this new story.

I love murder mysteries and detective fiction. My parents introduced me to the genre through our local PBS station. Joan Hickson's Miss Marple, David Suchet's Hercule Poirot, and others brought to life the classic stories even before I could read. The beats and rhythms of Agatha Christie's storytelling are infused deep in my bones.

Without my teachers, I wouldn't be the writer I am today. Sandy Kafka (Mom), Toni Becker, Sharon Hall, and Laura Shamas. They taught me in elementary, jr. high, sr. high and college respectively. Each in their own way encouraged me in my passion and challenged me in my abilities. They made me push against the odds. Believe in myself. But much more importantly, they taught me to not use my weaknesses as an excuse but to work hard to overcome them. To be dedicated and diligent. To listen to critique. To never stop learning.

Speaking of weaknesses, I would never have pulled this off without help. I again want to recognize my parents, Tony and Sandy Kafka for braving the minefield of misspellings, typos and other affronts to the English language I committed in this process. Beyond that, their insights into ways to improve this story were invaluable. There is so much more I could say. Thanks for everything.

This book wouldn't be complete without thanking Amber Francis and Blake Beauchamp. I want to thank them for giving the text its final polish.

Amber's attention to detail is astounding. Her feedback was priceless. Her positivity is contagious. Blake's keen eye caught more than a few embarrassing errors and I never would have known pantsuit is one word without him. The work they put into those final edits will help me sleep better as people begin to read this book. I also want to recognize the input Blake and Michael Kingery gave me on the cover design. They helped me push it to the next level.

So many of my friends have put up with my incessant babbling about my books. The countless hours I spent poorly describing what I was trying to do were invaluable to this process. Specifically, I want to thank Joel Watters, Joe Widhelm and Mark Gerloff for their consistent encouragement.

I want to thank Joe B, Kyle N, Caleb M and Tim T for helping me bring Henry and Jackson to life for the cover design and a second thanks to Kyle for also buying me lunch.

Finally, I want to thank my brother, Tim Kafka. More than anyone else, it is safe to say this story wouldn't exist without him. All the way back to the roots of this story twenty years ago through the final page of this novel, he has been instrumental in shaping the character and story. His feedback on every version of this story has pushed it forward. Both large and small, his ideas sparked my own creativity in ways I never would have found on my own. Thanks for seeing what this story could be and pushing me to keep writing until it got there.

FURTHER ADVENTURES

A 1987 Oldsmobile Firenza is found at the bottom of a lake. More concerning, a body is found inside the trunk, a body belonging to a drummer for the metal band Skoll Fina Hati. In the media storm that follows, fellow bandmate, Piper Tiffany, is arrested for the murder. But did she do it or is the real killer still out there? As Piper's trial commences, it is up to private detective Henry Pets to find the drummer's true killer. Secrets, lies, surprises and a missing miniature pig add many twists and turns for Henry and Jackson to overcome before they can solve the case of the dead metalhead.

Want to read more about Henry Pets and Jackson? Sign up now for Micah Kafka's mailing list and not only will you have access to news and updates but also a downloadable excerpt from the next book in the Adventures of Henry Pets series. To sign up, go to micahkafka.com and click on contact.

27532104R00149

Made in the USA
San Bernardino, CA
01 March 2019